The Curse of Anuganga

HARINI SRINIVASAN

TreeShade Books

Published by TreeShade Books (VB Performance LLP) in 2019

The Curse of Anuganga

ISBN : 9788193642498

Published by
TreeShade Books (VB Performance LLP)
Ansal Corporate Park, Sector142, Noida, Uttar Pradesh - 201305, India
Email - publish@TreeShadeBooks.com
www.TreeShadeBooks.com

Printed and Bound in India by
Gopsons Papers Ltd., A-2 Sector 64, Noida - 201301, India

Cover Design: Munisha Nanda
Typesetting: Ruchika Khanna

The Curse of Anuganga

HARINI SRINIVASAN

TreeShade Books
www.treeshadebooks.com

This book sees the light of the day due to the blessings of my Guruji, Amma and Appa; a battered half, Vinod and an unrelenting 10-year-old, Nigamanth, who taught me many a thing!

Author's Note on the Historical Inspiration for the Backdrop

If one studies the history of the Indian subcontinent through the years, what does stand out is that there have been alternating eras of integration (by one strong ruler/ empire) and eras of disintegration, with a proliferation of numerous smaller local kingdoms. Even during the periods of integration, which have witnessed a semblance of unity under one strong empire, a time-honoured political philosophy, an unspoken diktat, of not sacrificing local powers for establishing a strong central state seems to have been followed.

This story is set in 403 CE and largely takes place in Nandivardhana (now known as Nagardhan near Ramtek in modern Nagpur district of Maharashtra).

Nandivardhana was the capital of the Vakataka dynastry. Founded by Vindhyashakti in the 3rd century CE, the Vakatakas extended from Malwa and Gujarat in the north and the Tungabhadra river in the south. It was during the reign of Pravarasena I (225 CE) Vindhyashakti's son, that the geographical area of the dynasty expanded. The dynasty was further divided into four branches, of which two are unknown and two are known. The known branches are the Pravarapura — Nandivardhana branch and the Vatsalagulma branch. It was the Pravarapura–

Nandivardhana branch that had relations with the Guptas, giving the name of the Vakataka–Gupta to the entire period. According to R.C. Majumdar and D.C. Altekar, this period (200 CE to circa 550 CE) was an important epoch in Indian history – 'a new political consciousness was created and national solidarity was restored after nearly 4 centuries of political disintegration and foreign domination.'

In the second century, just before the rise of the Vakatakas and the Guptas, the Kushanas and the Western Kshatrapas (Sakas) were leading political powers. Even though by now, they had become completely Hinduised, their ethnicity was different and the local powers had still not forgotten their domination. By the third century, the extent of the Kushana empire had shrunk and local kingdoms such as the Nagas, the Yaudheyas, Maghas had re-established their independence. By the end of the third century, the Kushanas had weakened considerably and been reduced to a minor power.

The decline of the Sakas (Kshatrapas) began likewise in this century. At one point in time, in the second century, the Kshatrapas ruled over northern Maharashtra, Gujarat, Kathiawar, Sindh and Rajputana. However, former local powers such as the Satavahanas, the Rajputanas re-asserted their independence and reclaimed their former territories.

In 225 CE, the rise of the Vakatakas as a strong local kingdom in the Deccan also added a further blow to the Kshatrapas. Even though there was a temporary revival under Rudrasena III in the 4th century, they were wiped out by the Guptas, led by Chandragupta II at the end of the 4th century CE.

The Gupta dynasty is said to have been founded by Sri Gupta in the late 3rd century CE. It was under Chandragupta I (319-335 CE) that Gupta empire expanded its territories and started rising to power. Under the great Samudragupta I and his son Chandragupta II, the dynasty reached its zenith — with political unity and solidarity being established in the country — Magadha once again became a leading power, this time after 500 years. It is said that the iron pillar near Qutub Minar in Delhi was erected as a dhwaja (banner) to Lord Vishnu by Chandragupta II.

Chandragupta II got his daughter Prabhavatigupta married to the Vakataka king, Rudrasena II, which helped him extend the Gupta empire's influence to the Deccan. When Rudrasena II died prematurely in 380 CE, his daughter Prabhavatigupta became the regent Queen and for all practical purposes, the administration of the Deccan remained under Chandragupta's guidance and supervision for nearly 25 years. During this phase, the height of the Vakataka–Gupta period, the Guptas were an all-India power. This Gupta dynasty's overlordship, however, did not last for more than a hundred years. What was interesting, and has been remarked by scholars too, is that despite the political unity and stability, there has been a cultural uniformity that existed throughout the country. Be it the administrative machinery, local self-government, the powers of the king and taxation laws; they have all been similar across kingdoms. Religions followed were also the same, be it in the east or west. Hinduism, Buddhism and Jainism were followed everywhere and the family structure, caste system and rituals were also the same and aided in fostering the all-pervading cultural unity.

In this Vakataka–Gupta period (3rd century CE) Sanskrit was the official language — used in government administration and by poets, scientists and philosophers. Common people across the country (including the South) spoke and understood Sanskrit. It was only in the 6th century that local Dravidian languages gained prominence.

This magnificent period in Indian history will forever be known for spreading Hinduism and Hindu culture in eastern Asia. Without any formal state policy, private citizens, merchants, monks, Brahmanas managed to spread the religion and culture across Java, Sumatra, Borneo, Cambodia and China (Buddhism). It was also an age of intellectual renaissance where organised educational institutions and Agrahara villages (which led to universities for higher education) were established.

This led to a period of inventions and discoveries in science, art, engineering, literature, philosophy, mathematics, logic, religion and astronomy — underpinning what we know today as Hindu culture. Sanskrit masterpieces such as the *Raghuvamsa*, *Mrichchhakatika* and *Abhijnana Sakuntalam* were composed. The Puranas were reworked and several new Smritis were composed. The six schools of Indian philosophy acquired their form and shape during this period. The decimal system of notation and the value of zero were discovered in this period. The progress of Hindu mathematicians in the fields of algebra and arithmetic was remarkable — as was the progress made in the field of astronomy. Aryabhata made the discovery that the earth rotates on its axis. The length of the solar year computed by this great scientist was nearer to its actual duration when compared to what was predicted by Ptolemy. The great Iron Pillar that still stands tall and erect behind the Qutub Minar is a testimony to the metallurgical skill of this age.

An age of peace, prosperity, cultural stability; an age where intellect was creative and notable achievements were recorded in various fields of literature, science, religion and philosophy; an age where *Dharma* (piety), *Artha* (economic prosperity), *Kama* (pursuit of pleasures) and *Moksha* (spiritual salvation) were balanced out; an era of harmony and prosperity — this era was truly a Golden Period of Indian history.

In 403 CE, the year the story takes place, Queen Prabhavatigupta (390 CE–410 CE) was the regent Queen, ruling over the kingdom on behalf of her two young sons. As mentioned above, the Queen is said to have consulted her illustrious father, King Chandragupta II of the Gupta dynasty, for advice.

There has been much study and debate about Kalidasa and his antecedents. Scholars of Sanskrit and history have placed him in the BCE era as well as the CE era. Being an amateur history buff, I am in no position to agree or disagree with any of these theories. For the purpose of this book, I went along with the theory that associates Kalidasa with the court of King Chandragupta II. One particular article I read about Kalidasa theorises that Kalidasa, as the state poet of Chandragupta II in Pataliputra, could have been a tutor and mentor for the two young Vakataka princes. It also surmises that Meghdutam was composed in Ramtek, a small town hardly 5 kms away from Nagardhan. Therein lies the idea of using Kalidasa as a major character in this story.

Another interesting point that came up during my study of this period is that Divakarasena, the elder of the sons of Queen Prabhavatigupta does not become the next king. Instead it is Damodara, the younger son, who takes over the reins of the Vakataka kingdom in 410 CE as Pravarasena II. I do remember reading that Divakara dies roughly in the 13th or 14th year of Queen Prabhavatigupta's rein, leaving her heartbroken, and forcing her to continue as Regent Queen for the next 5 years. The cause of death is unknown. The entire poisoning sub-plot — while here the Prince is much weakened and not really dead — came about from this factoid.

And then there is the case of Bana's Devi Chandraguptam, where King Ramagupta was mentioned. Did King Ramagupta really exist? Was he the elder son of Samudragupta? Did he trade his wife, Queen Dhruvadevi for peace with the Sakas/ Kshatrapas? This has not been proven yet but the whole story, whether or not it occurred, is fascinating and provides more matter. While writing this book and making this episode in history a key point in my story, I had two choices — dramatise the whole event and explore that in detail; and the other, to mention it in passing and build another tale around it. I chose to do the latter.

I have tried to be true to the period (whatever I have managed to assimilate through reading), as I can; however as someone from a much later time period, my own biases and views from a different lens may have come through in the book.

Prologue

376 CE

It was the end of a warm, humid day in Kotivarsha, a small village near the splendid city of Pataliputra. The sun was beginning to set, and darkness had begun to descend upon all the houses. Diyas were being lit in front of homesteads in a bid to keep the supernatural away by the grace of Lord Vasudeva and Maharajadhiraja Chandragupta. Prayers and piety were found here in plenty, as the pious, knowledgeable residents went about the business of life.

At the door of a small hut, facing the long road towards Pataliputra, stood an old lady and a young girl, not more than ten years old. They were looking out onto the road, onto the village gates, which had still not been shut. They were probably waiting for someone — a father, a son, engaged in muted conversation. Presumably, the conversation was about the day that had been or even about the person awaited, or just banal chatter.

Nightfall was soon to herald its arrival in a grand manner: one would not be able to see a thing – but for the dim light and the hovering fireflies and tiny insects.

For now, however, to an observer's eye, it was not so. Only remnants of a day, that was soon turning into night, remained.

It was then that the unnatural silence was broken. There was some movement on the road to Pataliputra — at a distance. All conversation came to a halt. The old lady and the little girl looked up alert, wondering what the chaos was about. At a distance rose some dust, or was it smoke? Unused to any commotion at dusk time, people from the other huts in that lane also stirred and came outside. This was an unusual occurrence and guessing from the expression on the old lady's face, it was clear that this was unexpected. This was not what they had been waiting for.

Two men on horseback were hurrying towards Pataliputra. Were they spies or soldiers? As they came closer to the observers, a collective gasp went up in the air. Was it him that was being dragged? But he is a good man! Why? A harried, helpless man was being dragged, his arms tied to the two riders astride. As they galloped at top speed, the man screamed and shouted; his voice, feeble and wracked with pain, rage and frustration.

"Lord Vasudeva will never forgive you! Anuganga will never forgive you! You shall pay for this grave injustice. Fear your karma; think of your children. You will pay. Some day. This is a dying, innocent man's curse on all of you..."

The curse, loud and clear, echoed in the air as nightfall descended upon the tiny hamlet, sending an eerie chill down the spine of the spectators.

The horseback riders and the protesting man were soon gone. The *Amavasya* night was to be remembered for a very long time.

CHAPTER 1

403 CE

Summer had been harsh and unrelenting in its spread and showed no remorse or even any signs of abating. Yes, there had been the rains in the month of *Ashadha*, pouring and sparking some life into the parched, hapless beings, providing a brief respite — but that was just that — a short break, fleeting and ephemeral.

As this particular morning of *Shukla Saptami* in the month of *Bhadra* dawned on the township of Nandivardhana, the heat was back — sticky, muggy, unpleasant and utterly insufferable. Ah! but this did not deter the natives of Nandivardhana; there was palpable excitement in the air, for Rani Prabhavatigupta, the queen, was to return from her journey to Pataliputra to visit her beloved father, Maharajadhiraja Chandragupta II that day.

There were many rumours about a major announcement that the Rani was to make — throwing open much speculation of impending celebrations. It was said that she would be accompanied by a large entourage. Why, even Kalidasa was said to be one among the retinue. The *Mahakavi* was visiting Nandivardhana after a decade, perhaps, or was it more than that? He had come once before with the great king Maharajadhiraja Chandragupta. What a heart-rending visit that was. Maharaja Rudrasena II had just passed away leaving the young Queen bereft and alone — to bring up the two boys and handle the kingdom. But for the Maharajadhiraja and his wise counsel and guidance, I wonder what would have become of Nandivardhana. It was during the visit that Queen Prabhavati requested the *Mahakavi* to stay back and teach young Divakara and Damodara till the time they could go to the gurukula. He had stayed back in Ramtek and Meghaduta was written then.

How things have changed. Years have gone by, seasons have changed – and the little boys are now strapping young men. The air of gloom from the *Mahakavi*'s previous visit has been replaced with frissons of excitement and pleasant anticipation. Maybe one of these boys, perhaps Divakara, is to be married! Maybe this is the announcement our Rani is to make.

The marketplaces and taverns were teeming with more people than usual — hungry for any new gossip. At mid-morning, some activity was reported at the town's southern gates. A royal messenger on horseback was said to have entered the city. He had been spotted by a grain merchant who had just come back from Ujjayini. The merchant was then accosted and plagued with more questions: whose royal messenger was he? The Queen's or some other kingdom's? Was the merchant able to see the messenger and observe his face? Was he bringing tidings of joy? Or did he look worried? Of course, he had no answers to these questions — the tired trader, back from his travels.

At that moment, the royal messenger was hurrying towards his destination in the jewellers' quarter at the other end of town. *Shukla Saptami* in *Bhadra* maasam was an auspicious day for this community and they typically started new assignments after invoking the blessings of Lord Vasudeva. It was into a busy locality that the messenger made his way, looking for the house of Vishnuveera.

Vishnuveera, Nandivardhana's most reputed goldsmith, was known for producing artistic masterpieces out of gold, like a magician creating magic out of thin air. His creations were in much demand through the year — with young nobles, royals and traders thronging his place to get new ornaments crafted. With steady work pouring in from Nandivardhana and elsewhere (why, it was rumoured he had just gotten back from Pratisthana after an especially lucrative assignment), Vishnuveera was indeed a much sought-after man.

This part of the town was clearly divided into two separate sections — the left reserved for goldsmiths and craftsmen dealing with precious stones; and the right for workers in other metals (bronze, silver, ivory).

At the extreme corner of the jeweller's section was a large, four-storeyed brick building with a vast façade opening onto the busy street. The signage on a stone signboard next to the building indicated that this was Vishnuveera's house and work area. The ground floor was where his artisans and craftsmen sat and worked. There was a languid atmosphere in the workshop in the absence of any customers or visitors, as the messenger entered. Two boys, barely in their late teens, were beating gold in a corner of the vast but sparse room and they were being supervised by a middle-aged man, rotund and pot-bellied, who did not seem very happy about the quality of their work. There were three–four experienced craftsmen who were engaged in some friendly chatter, careful not to get loud enough to irk the supervisor. A typical day's post-lunch scene or so it seemed to the royal messenger, whose entry had not been noticed.

One of the teenage boys soon took cognisance of this stranger and alerted the supervisor.

"Greetings! How may we assist you?"

"Greetings, Arya (Sir). Our great queen, Maharani Prabhavatigupta has sent me to convey a message to Arya Vishnuveera. Where can I meet him?"

"Arya Vishnuveera is in his chambers. I will inform him of your arrival. Please be seated."

As the messenger was seated and awaited the goldsmith, the workshop sprang into life. The friendly banter of the craftsmen stopped, and they resumed setting gems into ornaments. While the boys continued their gold-beating and getting their act right, they were clearly more distracted than before. A royal messenger in their workshop was definitely worth getting distracted about! Wonder what the queen wants their master for. But then their master's fame had spread far and wide. Even across the seas, or so they had been told!

Five minutes later, the renowned goldsmith made his way into the workshop and the royal messenger conveyed his message. Arya Vishnuveera was requested to pay his respects to Maharani Prabhavatigupta in her chambers at an auspicious hour the next day, preferably in the third quarter after sunrise. Of course, the goldsmith accepted the summons and confirmed that he would be present at the palace at the appointed time.

The summons left everyone present at the workshop in a tizzy. Despite Arya Vishnuveera's presence, work stopped for a while; the craftsmen were too excited and were discussing the meaning behind the royal summons. The rumours were possibly true and a royal wedding was indeed on the cards. There had not been a royal celebration in more than a decade. And what better than their master being summoned. Maybe he will be commissioned to craft some exquisite jewellery.

Only Arya Vishnuveera seemed unperturbed. Exhibiting a state of equanimity, he seemed lost in thought. The supervisor, clearly attuned to his master's moods and behaviour, stood quietly next to him. A few minutes later, Vishnuveera came out of his reverie and indicated to his supervisor,

"Somnath, when did we promise Arya Nandabhatta his jewels? How far have we progressed on that?"

"Arya, we need to give Arya Nandabhatta his *ratnanguliyas* - the finger rings encrusted with gems, before *Trayodashi.* We have five days left and Harihara and Deva are working on it. Sir, if you permit, there is another thing I would like to remind you about."

"Hmm, proceed."

"We are to visit Arya Vinayashura tomorrow at the auspicious hour. I met his servant near the chitrasala just yesterday. There is some celebration being planned at the house and he seemed rather keen that Arya should visit him and his Devi at the earliest so that they can let us know what designs of jewels they would like crafted. With your permission, should I convey our apologies at not being able to go tomorrow and maybe we can go on *Dashami?*

"No, Shaunaka should go, along with Kumaragiri and Ashwini. Go and call him," said the goldsmith then motioning to his servant who had accompanied him. He looked around the workshop, scanning the work area. "Ah, there you are, Ashwini. You go with Shaunaka and Kumaragiri tomorrow. Is Kumaragiri not here today? Is he well?

"Arya, Kumaragiri had to excuse himself today – his mother is slightly indisposed and he had to inform the Vaidya. Arya, if I may be excused for speaking out of turn. Would this not be a huge responsibility on young Shaunaka for such an assignment? Should we not start him independently on a smaller one?"

interjected Somnath politely, as the others strained to hear this conversation, with undisguised interest.

"Why not? At his age, I had taken up many such assignments. Have you not taught him what you know? He should be fine and this is the way he will learn. You should not protect him so much."

Shaunaka was Vishnuveera's eldest and only son — at present, an unwilling and a good-for-nothing apprentice. Back from the gurukula after completing his basic education in the Vedas and other sciences, Shaunaka had recently started his apprenticeship and training under Somnath. Vishnuveera was aware that Shaunaka did not have the experience or even interest to handle an independent charge but he was confident that his son would be able to deliver under pressure and with the help of two of the finest goldbeaters he knew. Like every other worker in the workshop, Vishnuveera was aware that Somnath was not too fond of the young lad. Indeed, Somnath did not have a high opinion of the master's son. This was largely due to what he perceived as a complete lack of attention and interest on the young man's part. Somnath had tried to impart all the training he could, based on his own extensive experience of twenty years, to the lad. But Shaunaka's mind was just not into learning the craft.

Somnath was too devoted to his master and his art form, to take the rejection of his suggestion personally. He was genuinely worried about how this boy with no interest in his work would manage!

At this moment, Shaunaka entered the workshop, looking a little hassled. As he stood in front of his father to pay his respects, this tall young man towered over most of the others present. There was something intellectual about this mild-mannered man of serious and quiet disposition; probably the mop of curly shoulder-length hair, the pair of dark eyes set in a round face, and the high forehead contributed to that impression. He was clad in a comfortable cotton kanchuka (tunic) with an antariya (lower garment); certainly not dressed to play the man of town, he had been resting, which explained his hassled expression. This was his favourite part of the day – when he would escape the drudgery of the profession that had been thrust upon him by virtue of his birth. This was also when he could spend time with his family, mainly his grandmother and mother, post a satiating meal. The summons was unsettling and certainly did not portend well.

"Arya, you called me? How may I be of service to you?" he asked, bowing his head respectfully in front of his father.

"Shaunaka, by the grace of Lord Vasudeva, you have been able to complete your education at the gurukula and have been learning our family trade. Somnath ji, as your guru here, has been teaching you all that he knows. With the blessings of Vakratunda, our *pitrus* (ancestors) and the entire family, I am now confident that you will be able to craft jewels beautifully and carry forth the tradition. The time has come for you to take on independent work.

"I want you to go to Arya Vinayashura's house tomorrow with Kumaragiri and Ashwini and understand what they require from us — what is the occasion and what kind of jewels they would like us to craft and by when."

The young man looked aghast, almost terrified at his father's suggestion but was quick to regain his composure. "Arya, as you suggest, I will go tomorrow to Arya Vinayashura's house," much to the surprise of the onlookers as they certainly expected him to oppose the decision.

"Good. You will go with Kumaragiri and Ashwini. They will give you good counsel. Pay heed to their advice, if need be."

"Yes, Arya. I will take your leave now."

Satisfied with his son's answer and conduct, Vishnuveera charted the next day's programme with Somnath with a rather extensive discussion on the designs they may have to craft.

The workshop was connected to the main building housing the living quarters by a long-winding path that took the visitor past a lush garden and the grand kitchen. After imbibing the instructions for the next day, Shaunaka left the workshop and walked past the kitchen, in a state of deep consternation. His mother, who was supervising the servants as they husked and ground the rice for the evening meal, noticed his state and called out to him:

"Shaunak, *putra*, what happened? Why do you look so worried? Come here."

"Maate, pranam, Pitashri has given me an independent assignment. I have to go to Arya

Vinayashura's residence tomorrow morning to understand what the occasion is and what kind of ornaments they would like made."

"Hmm, and you are worried that you will not be able to live up to your father's expectations? Shukla, clean that area and then place those utensils."

"Haan, ma, and that I am not yet ready for such an assignment."

"I think you are worrying unnecessarily. Believe in yourself. If your father thinks you are ready, you must be," said his mother, patting her son on his back.

This brief conversation with his mother, Gautami, left Shaunaka strangely uncomfortable and distinctly unconvinced. He loved his mother but lately, he felt sad at the thought that despite her efforts, she was not able to understand him. This feeling of discomfort and restlessness continued to envelop him as he walked back towards the main residence.

Gautami, on her part, had a pensive look on her face. It really bothered her to see the lack of communication between her son and her husband. Shaunaka's mind clearly was not in their family profession and she had brought it up with her husband many a times. While Shaunaka had not openly spoken about what he wished to do, she had gleaned his disinterest through conversations with him.

Just the previous evening, before they retired for the day, Gautami had brought it up. "Arya, Shaunaka does not seem too happy. Shouldn't we ask him why he is so unhappy these days? It has been three months since he came back from the gurukula. In comparison, look at Ashoka; he seems more settled and comfortable. I would like to check with him why he seems so despondent."

"I have noticed it too. It is evident that his mind is elsewhere; he hardly pays any attention to what Somnath tries to teach him. He probably wishes to engage himself in something else but he is in that foolish age. We should get him married. That will take care of his distraction."

"But should we not ask him what he really wishes to do? I do not like seeing him unhappy."

"Gautami, he is nearly 22 years old; I had taken over Pitashri's work by then. Do not be soft on him. Pressure and responsibility have never killed anyone. He should and will learn the craft and pursue this for a few years before he decides to do something else," countered Vishnuveera, turning the other side in bed, signalling the end of the conversation.

The next afternoon, Shaunaka found himself saddled with the burden of an independent jewellery assignment. Gautami wistfully recollected this conversation, as Shaunaka took his leave and made his way back to his first-floor room in the main residence, contemplating and ruminating the consequences of his father's orders. Pensive and reflective, Shaunaka was not impulsive by nature. Each of his actions was preceded by much thought.

"Ah! Shaunaka, there you are. I was about to retire for the afternoon. I thought you had abandoned this old woman and sought more interesting company," teased the old lady, Shaunaka's companion— his grandmother who had been waiting for him to return. Ahalyabai, Vishnuveera's widowed mother doted on her grandson and ever since Shaunaka had come back from the gurukula, they would spend an hour after the mid-day meal, playing a game of chaturanga.

Upon seeing his pensive and reflective expression, she became concerned and bade him to sit by her side:

"What happened, son? What urgent matter did Vishnu want you for? Could he not have waited? If only he would be less stubborn!"

"He wants me to take on an assignment all by myself. I do not feel confident enough, Pitamahi. I wished to tell him there at the workshop that I may not be able to acquit myself respectably but restrained myself. There were too many people and I was aware that my raising any objection would be viewed as disobedience and disrespect."

"You are a good child. You are smart and grasp things quickly; so do not worry about not knowing what to do. That you wish to be elsewhere and do something else is another matter altogether. Do not doubt your own abilities about handling this work. Will anyone accompany you?"

"Ah yes, that was reassuring. He has asked Kumaragiri and Ashwini to come along with me," smiled Shaunaka.

"Bah, you should have mentioned that! Of course you shall be fine. Kumaragiri has a wealth of experience and what can I say about Ashwini's skills?

Ashwini, a young man in his early twenties, had been adopted by Vishnuveera and his wife after he had been orphaned at a very early age. As a gratitude to the only family he had ever known, and the man who treated him as a son, Ashwini had focussed all his efforts on learning the art and techniques of the trade. To everyone's surprise, he soon became a skilled apprentice, displaying a special talent for this craft.

What also developed over the years was the bond and closeness between the two young men. Knowing Shaunaka's disinterest in the gold work, Ashwini would often cover for him and was his only ally in the workshop.

There was a knock on the door.

"Who is it? Come in."

"Shaunaka, there you are. Pranam Pitamahi! (Grandmother) May I join you?" It was Ashwini who had come looking for Shaunaka. It was wont for them to spend the evening together — either at home or at the town enjoying the entertainments on display!

"Of course you may! I was telling Pitamahi about our assignment tomorrow."

"Whose house are you expected to go to?" asked his grandmother, offering them some betel nuts, as she chewed.

"Arya Vinayashura. Who is he? Have you heard of him?"

"Arya Vinayashura? Is this the family that has a house in that locality where those rich Buddhist viharas had been constructed? Those Buddhist sanghas have too much money, I tell you, and they are wasting it. Arre, back in my day, they used to be bhikshus, going around asking for alms. Now see them, using the King's grants and leading degenerate lives. All of them — worse than the nagarakas, the fashionable city dwellers.

"Don't you both look at me like that. I speak the truth. Not for nothing is my hair so grey."

"Pitamahi, does this Arya Vinayashura also belong to a sangha?"

"Arre, no. This man and his family, from what I have heard, are from Pataliputra – nobility, they claimed when they came to Nandivardhana some thirty odd years ago. I forget when.

Known to be unfriendly and extremely proud, they have since kept to themselves. I heard that even the great poet Kalidasa visited their home last time he was here.

Have you heard anything about that rumour? Is there going to be an announcement soon? Is Kalidasa coming to visit too?"

"Pitamahi, I sincerely apologise. In my mental state, I forgot to share this with you. The reason Pitashri wants me to go to Arya Vinayashura tomorrow is because the Queen has summoned him to the palace."

"Oh! You should have told me this before. Ashwini, when will this boy stop worrying and start enjoying the experiences fate is throwing his way?

"There will be a royal wedding in our city soon. This city deserves some celebrations. It has been too long. When our Maharaja died ten-fifteen years ago, we wondered how the Maharani would cope. But look at her. What an amazing woman. Our Maharani has single-handedly ruled our country, protected all of us and has raised her two boys. We are indeed lucky people. Did I tell you, when I had moved to Nandivardhana from Mandhal…"

This was how the rest of the afternoon passed. Unlike most men his age, Shaunaka was pensive and reflective by nature — impulse and emotion did not rule his temperament. His responses were thought over and every action was preceded after contemplation. More than a hot-blooded reaction, he was often accused of failing to react or respond on time. Laconic and a loner, Shaunaka did not have many friends in Nandivardhana, barring Ashwini, who was more a brother! All of Shaunaka's friends from the gurukula were mainly in other towns and villages.

It was in Ahalyabai and Ashwini that this mild-mannered boy confided his ardent desires. He wished to travel, to visit Pataliputra and Ujjayini and other far-off places. Knowing that this may not be welcomed warmly by his father, he was biding his time to seek his parents' permission at the right time.

As he retired for the evening, Shaunaka wondered if the time to pursue his wishes would ever come. What did this independent jewellery assignment portend? Would it take him one step further away from his dreams, which anyway were just that — dreams?

CHAPTER 2

The next day, *Ashtami,* awakened to sudden rains pelting down the dry lands of Nandivardhana and its neighbouring towns. By the time the auspicious hour dawned, the rains had mercifully stopped and the sun God had taken his rightful place in the skies.

As was the practice, the craftsmen reached the workshop a little after sunrise. After paying obeisance to the Gods and partaking of a small meal at Vishnuveera's behest, work would begin in earnest. Shaunaka, who was accorded no special treatment on being the master's son, followed the same routine. Somnath, as Vishnuveera's second-in-command, had the keys of the workshop with him and it was his duty to open the doors every morning. By the time Shaunaka was about to enter, Somnath had settled down to commence work and was in conversation with Kumaragiri, apprising him of the task of the day.

"Arya wants you to go with Shaunaka and Ashwini to Arya Vinayashura's house. Arya Vinayashura had personally come here to request our time and presence at his home today. Arya had also agreed in-principle; we will be required to craft the jewels."

"Ji, I had heard that there is a wedding planned at Arya Vinayashura's home. It must be for that."

"A wedding? Oh Lord Vasudeva, this is worse than what I had anticipated. Many different types of ornaments would need to be crafted."

"Ji, but why are you and Arya not going to meet Arya Vinayashura today? Why are we being sent? Especially Shaunaka?

"Arya has been summoned to the palace by the Maharani. We will be there. Please manage to the best of your capabilities. Ashwini is a good boy."

The conversation was soon curtailed as Ashwini and some other young lads entered the workshop, slightly later than usual. Sensing this was an opportunity to enter the room without embarrassing the older gentlemen, Shaunaka made his appearance and presented himself to his guru, Somnath. With all the craftsmen piling in, the day had begun at the workshop.

Shortly before the auspicious hour, when the sun was shining brightly, three men were seen walking on a long road, paved with stones, in what looked like a prosperous area of the town. This was the Buddhist quarter, named so because it was home to the Buddhist *viharas* and also the new, prosperous merchants. Miscalculation of the distance between the workshop and the destination meant that the walk turned out to be longer than anticipated. There were no signs of the unexpected morning rain and the heat was intolerable. At one point, when they had walked for more than half-an-hour, Shaunaka stopped, clearly muttering a few curses under his breath. The two other men continued to drag their feet ahead. They seemed not to notice that Shaunaka had stopped walking behind them. Kumaragiri, a middle-aged man of average build, was walking slowly, stopping every now and then to grasp for breath. The heat was indeed unbearable. Ashwini was definitely faring a bit better, despite his tendency to slouch and a slightly rotund physique. The progress he was able to make on this long road could be attributed to his general state of being young.

What made the walk that much harder was the incline of the road. They had gone on quite a distance ahead when they realised that Shaunaka was not with them. Ashwini looked back and shouted out to Shaunaka. He finally stopped squinting at the sun and started walking hurriedly.

"Come on, Shaunaka. I know you are not too keen on this but we need to get there before the auspicious hour ends! We are already late and I am sure, Vinayashura must be wondering about our whereabouts," chided Kumaragiri.

"The corner house? You do not mean the one that had been much spoken about of late? Is that where Arya Vinayashura lives?" asked Ashwini with much curiosity as Shaunaka hurriedly caught up with them.

Kumaragiri, now unable to walk, glared at both the young men and trudged forward.

"Should we rest for a bit?" asked Ashwini thoughtlessly, only to be nudged by Shaunaka and glared at by Kumaragiri. "Oh I am tired, I would like to rest before we continue," he hastily tried to make up for his gaffe but to no avail.

"How many times do I need to tell you both that we are getting late?" bellowed Kumaragiri as he went forward. Shaunaka and Ashwini exchanged amused glances and followed him quietly.

"We are not far away now. I can almost see the building..." added Shaunaka softly.

The large corner house in the Buddhist quarter had become a known landmark rather quickly. It was a massive dwelling that had been recently constructed. Royal staff had been seen supervising the construction, or so the neighbours said. It was this that had gotten the other residents of this neighbourhood curious and had spread through the town like wildfire. Soon, almost everyone had heard about the large corner house of the Buddhist quarter and everyone wanted to know more about its occupants. The enigma and reputation of the house was further heightened by the inhabitants of the house. Arya Vinayashura and his family were known to keep to themselves. Not much was known about them and despite efforts made by the inquisitive neighbours, they did not interact much.

Interestingly, Vishnuveera, who usually knew most royals and noblemen from Nandivardhana and even Ramtek and Mandhal, did not recognise Arya Vinayashura when he visited the former's workshop the week before. Despite his regal demeanour and all its associated paraphernalia (he was accompanied by three servants and arrived in a palanquin), no one seemed to have a clue as to who he was when he stepped inside the workshop. All they could decipher was that this was an important personage who had made his way after their master's fame reached him. Upon hearing the introductions (glowing, of course), Somnath had been secretly thrilled. According to him, one of the perks of working closely with the finest goldsmith in town was that he could step into the inner households of rich, famous and chief people and gain insights into their lives and of course, some vital piece of gossip, which then could be shared with his friends at the local tavern! His friend Kumaragiri also felt the same way and as this was what was helping him retain focus despite the heat, he hobbled towards the corner house. Kumaragiri felt rather strongly that it always was useful to know more about people and their foibles. One never knew when information of any kind would prove useful.

After what seemed like an eternity, on an exceptionally muggy day, the *Ashtami* in the auspicious month of *Bhadra*, the three goldbeaters, novice and experts, found themselves standing in front of their destination — the corner house in the Buddhist quarter. When in front of the high and ornate gate, Shaunaka and Ashwini hesitated and looked to Kumaragiri for guidance. He was, after all, the most experienced among them. "What do we do now?" quipped Ashwini. This thoughtless question, very typical to the otherwise talented Ashwini provoked the tired and fed-up Kumaragiri. Barely disguising his irritation, Kumaragiri barked: "Whatever one does, when one encounters a gate, when on way to a certain place!" As Ashwini looked down rather shamefaced (he was actually amused and did not want to provoke the older man further by having him spot his laughter), Shaunaka realised that he was slightly nervous! Surprised at himself and shrugging off his nervousness, he moved forward to open the gate, looking to see Kumaragiri's reaction. Kumaragiri prodded him on, still visibly irritated and also hostile. The young man was fully aware of this simmering resentment amongst the senior goldbeaters and understood that his presence was unwelcome. As is, the older goldbeaters felt that it was unfair that Shaunaka, despite his lack of talent or interest, got so many chances because of him being the master's son. Any other goldbeater would have been asked to leave by now. There had been such cases earlier; why, Kumaragiri's nephew had barely lasted three months at Vishnuveera's workshop. Shaunaka remembered this when he saw Kumaragiri glare at him. He felt for the older man; the responsibility on Kumaragiri's shoulders had increased four-fold with this project, owing to his own lack of talent and experience. As he stood there, in front of the high gate, with such thoughts continuously blaring in his mind, Shaunaka decided that he would put in his best for this assignment and not let his father and all these men down.

"Look at this ornate gate. What a scene has been crafted on this. Wait, is that a *yaksha?* Aargh, it looks real and scary. Why, look at those trees; and those elephants. They seem real," said Ashwini, his voice piercing through the silence and minds of the other two. He had decided to intervene sensing the undercurrents of tension and seeing that Shaunaka had again lapsed into a state of reflection. Shaunaka's lapses into silence and inaction were well known.

To ensure that his two colleagues do not lapse into their own reflections — Shaunaka, because that was all what he seemed to know and Kumaragiri, because the exertion and tension had worn him out — Ashwini opened the gate and firmly stepped into the premises.

"Lord Vasudeva, I thought only kings and Gods lived in such magnificent palaces," exclaimed Ashwini, hit by the affluence of the dwelling. The other two, familiar with dwellings of the well-off and otherwise distracted, were not impressed. A dwelling in this part of Nandivardhana had to be expansive!

A stone path ran across the large garden leading to the spacious courtyard. The courtyard was flanked by the main house on one side and by a couple of large annexes on the other. Terracotta figurines of *yakshis* and goddesses adorned the lengthy stone path that was paved with bright-coloured tiles in a pleasing pattern. Ashwini, clearly dazzled by this opulence on show, paused to look more closely at the attractions on display.

"Now, now, we will never get to the main part of the house. Let us hurry; you can stare later," chided Kumaragiri, who had recovered his breath and spirit.

"There! Someone is there at the door of the house, probably waiting for us," remarked Shaunaka, who was now beginning to get irritated with both his colleagues.

Taking longer strides, the young lad walked more purposefully towards the door where a tall middle-aged man stood with a contemptuous look on his face. He was obviously waiting for these strangers to show up and introduce themselves.

"I think we should hurry. The man at the door is probably Arya Vinayashura and he certainly does not look happy." Ashwini and Kumaragiri walked faster to keep pace with Shaunaka.

Clad in a rich green tunic made of brocade and a white *antariya*, the man at the door exuded power and wealth. He was looking at the coming party with a hawk-like expression and condescension. There was impatience written all over his haughty face.

"Is he Vinayashura?" whispered Ashwini, as Kumaragiri nodded and glared at him.

"Pranam, my name is Shaunakaveera and I am Arya Vishnuveera's son. Here are my friends, Kumaragiriji and Ashwini. We are here to meet Arya Vinayashura; we have gotten delayed and are extremely apologetic for this."

"Ah, so the jeweller didn't come himself? I had heard of his repute; but did not know that his arrogance matched it. Where is that bald, obsequious man I met that day?" asked the haughty man derisively.

"Apologies, Arya, this was unplanned. My father had every intention of honouring this commitment; but a more pressing thing came up. He was summoned by the Maharani, which is why he sent me in his place. We will do our best to understand what we can do for you."

"Bah, I know your tribe. The same everywhere. My misfortune that I need your services now and your father came highly recommended. Come on then. You have wasted enough of my time."

He led them into one of the annexes next to the main building and motioned them to be seated. Without saying a word, the man then turned and left. The annexe was a huge, airy, well-lit room with two large windows; there were two locked cupboards to the right and a pot was kept in one of the corners. A small bench was placed just next to the window and the three men went and sat there uncomfortably.

"Is he going to come back? Lord Vasudeva knows I enjoy my work but I would not want to deal with this obnoxious man here," muttered Ashwini.

"Maybe he is not obnoxious and is just irritated because we are late," countered Shaunaka.

Just when Ashwini was about to counter this suggestion, Arya Vinayashura entered the room, this time, accompanied by a tall middle-aged lady who looked strikingly beautiful even at this age. And it was not just the royal blue *antariya* and the ivory and pearl ornaments that contributed to her radiance. Her husband's royal mien diminished considerably in front of her.

"Pranam, my husband tells me you have come from the jeweller. We have heard a lot about Arya

Vishnuveera's skills as a goldsmith and have seen some of his creations also. Our daughter is getting married in the coming fortnight, for which we want some exquisite creations handcrafted. I was hoping to meet Arya Vishnuveera so that I could explain the designs. But I suppose you will be able to convey these to him?" asked the lady in a soft voice.

"Pranam Devi, you need not worry. Arya Kumaragiri is one of the best goldbeaters in Nandivardhana; and Ashwini is equally skilled. While my experience may not be as varied as my father's, we will do our very best to match up to your high standards. You may please let us know the ornaments we are to craft and starting tomorrow, we will be here to finish making your order," replied Shaunaka politely, earning him a rare look of respect from Kumaragiri. He nodded to Ashwini, as if to say – "This boy may not know much of the work at hand, but his speech is sweet and he knows how to speak and keep these rich people satisfied."

Satisfied with his answer, the lady proceeded to explain what she wanted to the last detail — number of pieces, type, design and even jewels to be used. Ashwini and Kumaragiri who were both used to such fastidious clients made a note of each detail. Shaunaka, for whom this was a new experience, observed the room and surroundings and the entire scene, as if he were a part of an audience of a play. He was strangely fascinated by the demeanour of the man of the house, who was also observing this entire exchange with hawk eyes. Once convinced that her ideas about the design would be executed, she conveyed her wish that these be crafted as soon as possible.

"So since Devi is satisfied, I suppose, I will have to deal with you lot. Better not be late tomorrow. Be here right after *rahukalam* (the inauspicious time of the day) ends — not a minute ahead and not a minute behind."

"Tomorrow? Must we begin such an auspicious work on *Navami*, Arya? Should we not consult Varahaswamin?" asked Devi Tanirika haltingly, clutching the corner of the *antariya* tightly.

"No. This needs to get done; better these incompetent fools start their work as soon as possible," replied her husband, without paying any attention to the fact that the men he was insulting were standing right there.

The reactions of Vishnuveera's men were as different as their personalities; Kumaragiri whose outlook had already taken a beating thanks to a life of poverty and hardship, seemed overwhelmed at being meted such a treatment. Working in such an atmosphere was soul-sapping and he shrunk at the prospect, literally, bowing his head and moving a couple of steps behind the tall and strapping Shaunaka. The two young men, Shaunaka and Ashwini had similar reactions – infuriated and enraged enough to wish to do something. However, both of them, due to completely different circumstances, had the maturity not to react or show any emotion or do anything impulsively.

"Arya, as you command. We will be here tomorrow morning at the auspicious hour to start work on your most important assignment. *Pranam. Shubhamadhyanam.*" Using this as an opportunity to leave, Shaunaka bade farewell and gently led his senior colleague out of the corner house. At a level, he was relieved to have secured the commission, despite Vinayashura turning out to be such a difficult customer.

"Shaunaka, you spoke well. Now we need to work hard and make sure we deliver the ornaments well and in time. This Arya is difficult to please and I shudder to think how he would react if we fail on that count," said Kumaragiri appreciatively, as they made their way back to the jewellers' quarter.

"*Dhanyavadaha*, Arya. I do not know to craft anything other than a *ratnanguliya*. I do not think I will be any help. Maybe I should ask Pitashri if he can assign Suddhodhana as well. I do not want to become a liability," replied Shaunaka, now seriously apprehensive about the quality of his work.

"Pardon my interference, Arya. I think we will be able to craft most of the jewels between us. We will definitely need Shaunaka to tackle the obnoxious man. Are all rich *nagarakas* like this?" Ashwini added his two-bit to the conversation.

"Indeed, Shaunaka, we need you here to sweet-talk that arrogant man. Ashwini, no, not all rich men are like this. Vinayashura is uniquely obnoxious," Kumaragiri averred.

"Did you see the Devi? For all her beauty, she seemed reserved and caged?" commented Ashwini.

The residents of the large corner house were thus dissected and discussed through the journey back and a camaraderie was forged between the master's son and the two goldbeaters…

…A camaraderie, which was noticed by the others at the workshop. Even Vishnuveera commented on it when he saw his son and the two goldbeaters in an animated conversation, as they entered.

"Ah, so I am to understand that your time at Arya Vinayashura's house was spent productively?"

"*Pranam*, Arya, it was an interesting discussion. He was a bit upset that you and Somnath could not be present personally to offer your respects, but our young master, Shaunaka here, handled the situation impeccably," smiled Kumaragiri, as he then proceeded to give an account of what happened.

"Pitashri, Arya, would it be possible for you to send Suddhodhana with us tomorrow? His experience and knowledge would be of much help to all of us," requested Shaunaka. At this suggestion, Suddhodhana, a master craftsman and experienced hand, seemed rather pleased and accepted it instantly. Hailing from a poor Sudra family, he still had not come to terms with his good fortune of being recognised by the master goldsmith who had promptly taken him in his workshop. He had been rather overwhelmed earlier in the afternoon when Somnath had told him that he would be required to craft jewellery for the Maharani. Who would wish for such a huge responsibility? What if he made a mistake and lost his job? Working in a rich merchant's house sounded more convenient.

"Tomorrow? Arya wishes that we start work without consulting Purohitji for an auspicious time? This does not sound good. Hmm, I am not sure if I would like to spare Suddhodhana entirely. He can come with you just for tomorrow," asserted Vishnuveera. "We were called this morning to the palace, as you remember? The Maharani wants us to craft all the jewels for her, the princes and the royal family. The marriage of Prince Divakara has been fixed. Suddhodhana, as an experienced hand, and one of my best, is needed for that. I cannot see how this wedding at this Arya's place can take precedence over a royal wedding!"

"Shaunaka, your *gurubhai*, Kaushika is here. I met him in one of the courtyards of the palace. He is here as a part of the royal entourage from Pataliputra. Upon recognising me, he was eager to come and meet you. He is here now and is paying his regards to Pitamahi and your Matashri. You should not keep him waiting any longer and should go and meet him.

"Arya, as you say, your wisdom and experience in these matters is more than mine. It is my honour to observe Suddhodhanaji tomorrow and benefit from his experience at least for tomorrow, if not after. I submit to your judgment and would like to take your leave now. *Shubhasaayam*," said Shaunaka making his way to the inner chambers of his residence, where his childhood friend, Kaushika, who was now a Kumaramatya in Pataliputra, waited for him.

The day soon came to an end, with most of the workers leaving for their respective homes. Only Somnath and Kumaragiri stayed back to help

Vishnuveera put together a plan of action so that work could commence the next morning for two weddings at two different places — the palace and the corner house in the Buddhist quarter.

"I had been meaning to ask you the entire day. Did you see the Maharani? The princes? Are they as god-like in person? Is the palace as magnificent as it looks from the outside?" asked a curious Kumaragiri, the moment Vishnuveera retired for the day.

"Bhuk! So many questions! Words cannot describe what I was fortunate to see today. But I will try. We have a long way back home," said Somnath as they kept aside the tools and locked the workshop.

"Please go on. I am listening…"

"When Arya and I crossed the moat to the royal residences and the royal guards opened the main gateway — the one with the ivory and gold elephant and horse statues— I was overwhelmed. The palace is an entire city in itself – why it seemed to me like the kingdom of Kubera! Even Arya seemed a little dazzled. Even he had not stepped into these premises. As we entered, we were surprised to see a throng of people. A royal supervisor was shouting orders to his men who were filling the royal granaries. There are two large granaries as one enters, to the left and right of the main gateway. Next to that was the alms house. The queen had just finished distributing the alms in the alms house, we were told. Did you know that just like our dear Raja Rudrasena, who left us so soon, the Maharani also continues to offer her prayers to Lord Vasudeva and distribute alms twice a day?"

"What do I know of the dealings in the palace? All I heard was that the Maharani listens too much to her father and that Nandivardhana is turning into another Pataliputra."

"Yes, that is what I had heard too. But then with two small children and a kingdom to manage, that was the best she could have done. Get advice from her father — what an illustrious king her father is, blessed by the Gods with bravery, wisdom and good fortune! Now, now, we do not have all evening, do we?"

The conversation continued as the two goldbeaters walked past the temple and the Brahmins quarter on to the main road that took them towards where traders and merchants lived. Since the tale was of much interest to both the narrator and the listener, they decided to stop by at a local tavern, just past the *Chitrashala* – a departure from their regular schedule, an extravagance that they could ill-afford – but one that was worth the effort, especially on such a momentous day!

The local tavern was a noisy place – filled choc-a-bloc with people from all strata of society. There was an actors' troupe, drunk and loud as they flirted with a couple of women of disrepute. There were a group of merchants – of Yavana (Greek) origin, probably or maybe Romans, if one noticed their build and colouring – discussing business. Feeling a little bit like outcastes in this charged atmosphere, the two goldbeaters modestly walked up to a relatively free corner and seated themselves and Somnath continued his account of the day.

"As we were walking towards nowhere, even Arya did not know where we had to go, the royal emissary, the one who delivered the message met us. Suryadeva is his name, a good boy… He took us past all the grandeur into one of the inner structures – a private section, definitely. We were stopped by a huge man who had the meanest expression on his face at the gate and were let in after Suryadeva told him why we were there. The grandeur on display is to be seen to be believed. Polished, shining tiles with beautiful coloured paintings lined the entire courtyard. The beautiful, lush, green gardens, the massive Chitrashalas, the bridges, why even the massive balustrades seemed to be adorned with pearls and rubies. I thought my eyes were playing a trick. And you should have seen the treasury!

"Treasury? You walked past that? You were allowed to take a look?" Kumaragiri's mouth fell open.

"The treasury seemed like a town in itself; there were such huge rooms with craftsmen and artisans working in them. Silk and silk threads, pure cottons, gold, pearls, silver, rubies, corals and emeralds were everywhere. Jewellers like us, designers, weavers were intently producing new accessories and fineries. Why, I also spotted many well-known gold and jewel merchants in one of those rooms where the officials valuing and checking the jewels were seated. Why, Arya's close friend, Vibhishaka was there. He came over to convey his regards to Arya as we walked past. There was an indescribable air of grandeur, splendour and excitement in the inner quarters."

"Suryadeva confirmed that the Queen had indeed fixed the marriage of Prince Divakara to the Princess of Kamboja, upon the advice of her wise father. It was to take place within the next month — before the start of *Pitru Paksha.* The Rajapurohitji was yet to fix an auspicious time. He also mentioned that the royal party that had come in from Pataliputra the day before included several important officials who were here to help us all out. He opined that it was one of these officials who would be there presently to place the order with us. And while we waited for someone to come and tell us why we had been summoned, can you believe it? Maharaniji entered the room, in-person, accompanied by two of her advisors!"

"Ah the Maharaniji in person? How is she?"

"A combination of Ma Durga and Lakshmi, blessed with a beauty that goes beyond the physical appearance, with compassion and wisdom shining through her eyes. Why, her innate mental strength comes through – making her stand taller than her actual physical height. She made us feel welcome; was very polite as she explained to Arya the type of jewels she wished to get made. Imagine, we are going to craft jewels for the entire royal family! I feel blessed to have been there today and to have been in front of such an admirable Queen. You tell me, how was your meeting with Arya Vinayashura. Was he really as horrid as that Ashwini described him to be? He does tend to exaggerate quite a lot."

"Oh yes, that man was indeed despicable and for no reason, it seems. There are richer merchants in town — look at those Yavanas sitting there, they seem equally wealthy. Only Lord Vasudeva knows why Arya behaved that way. He seemed as if he had a problem with everyone. Shaunaka thinks that he is just a deeply unhappy man with too many resentments and that makes him be horrible to the rest of us. Probably Shaunaka is right. His wife, Devi Tanirika seemed scared and worried too – scared of her husband is what Ashwini thought. But Shaunaka was not too sure. I was too dazzled by her beauty so I did not look up to observe her," said Kumaragiri reflectively as he ran through the day's events.

"Strange man! Too much talk about that house though. Was it as impressive as has been rumoured?"

"Umm, I am not too good at describing it, but I felt awed by it. The house is large and beautiful but made dark by that horrible man. Aargh, I do not have any interest in working there tomorrow under his watchful eyes. Wonder what makes him so horrible. Is he not bothered about his next life? I think we should leave now, it is getting late and work will begin in earnest tomorrow morning."

As the two goldbeaters left, they did not observe the reaction of the middle-aged gentleman who was seated at the next table. Wearing a black shawl matching his dark complexion that covered his slight build and revealed only his sharp, observant eyes, he had a mop of curly, unruly hair tinged with silver on his round head. He sat there observing and watching the antics of his fellow tavern members – especially the noisy, rollicking theatre troupe. Had the two gold-beaters been more aware of the world they lived in, they would have recognised him as being the *Mahakavi* himself! Had they been less oblivious of their surroundings, they would have realised that the name Arya Vinayashura had taken the *Mahakavi* by surprise.

CHAPTER 3

A while after this conversation took place in a noisy tavern in the town centre, the gentleman being spoken about was living up to the reputation he had just acquired. As the second *prahar* of the evening commenced, two strangers, foreign traders of Romaka (Roman) origin, were seen by the residents of the quarter, asking for directions to the house of Arya Vinayashura. Neighbours then heard loud voices and there was a huge ruckus.

"Get out of my house! Don't you dare try to fleece me. I do not see why I should pay you rogues such an exorbitant amount. You want more money for cheating me?" Arya Vinayashura was standing at the main door and was yelling at the two men, who stood in the pathway, disbelief writ large on their faces.

The taller of the two, wearing a dark-red paenula, a cloak worn by the Romans, that looked almost black in the dim light, walked forward and attempted to clarify: "Arya, we are not trying to dupe you. This was agreed upon when we spoke the last time. Please return our goods if you are not willing to pay the full price for it."

"Deal? What deal? I have paid what I had to pay. Take it and leave. NOW. Else, I will have to have you thrown out."

"We have been civil. You have taken advantage of our foreign-ness and fie on us for having believed you. We shall take it to your authorities, your Queen, and get our dues," the shorter of the two traders yelled back, seething with rage, taking a step forward.

"Hah! You clearly do not know who I am, if you think they will believe you. Be happy, I was merciful to pay a little for your counterfeit, worthless goods. Just leave!" Arya Vinayashura turned and was about to enter the main residence, when he felt something hit his shoulder – with much force.

"Aaaaaaaaaargh. What was that? What did you curs throw at me?" yelped Vinayashura, as he bent down.

It was a sandal.

"Just a message for you, Arya. Have it your way today. We will leave now but I vow on your gods and mine, you shall pay before this month is over," sneered the shorter trader, now at the main gate, ready to leave the premises.

As the enraged and insulted Vinayashura yelled and hurled curses, the traders left the premises and bumped into a curious bystander (one among the many who had gathered to view the drama). Among them was the same dark person with curly hair and sharp-eyes, clad in a black shawl who had been observing customers at the tavern a short while ago. Kalidasa, the *Mahakavi*, the tutor to the Princes, was watching the altercation with an inscrutable expression on his face. As the traders left, so did he. Vinayashura's servants were now shooing people from the gate and soon normalcy returned to the large corner house.

Shaken by the altercation with the traders, Vinayashura also called it a day and preferred to retire in his large bedroom, the second one in a line of rooms, in the first floor of the main building.

"Such louts, I say. I should know better than to deal with those Yavanas or Romakas."

"Swami, forgive my saying so, you know that they were right. You had agreed to pay 1000 *panas* (gold coins) more for that ivory and other items the traders were selling. Whether the goods were counterfeit or original, that was the deal," Devi Tanirika quietly interjected when her husband was recollecting and going over the events of the evening.

"Bah! I will not get cheated by those stinking Romakas. Tomorrow those incompetent gold-beaters will be here. Do we have to get all those jewels crafted? What is the need? I do not see why I should spend so much on my insolent offspring. You have spoilt your daughter. I do not even want to see her face," yelled the haughty man riling now at his wife to somehow get over the humiliation of having a sandal thrown at his person!

"Shh, you should not say that. She is your daughter, Arya. Do not be heartless. She has had such a difficult life. You need to rest now. Please be calm and let us sleep," said his pained wife with a resigned tone rehashing a familiar conversation.

"Hmm, you are right. May the Lord Vasudeva bless her with happiness this time round. Madhav is a good man; so much better than that lout she got married to the previous time," grunted Arya Vinayashura and shut his eyes.

"The lout we got her married to, you mean... Arya," countered his wife softly as she watched her husband fall asleep.

As night fell and life came to a standstill in the busy town of Nandivardhana, Ahalyabai, Vishnuveera's widowed mother sat on a mat in a dimly-lit room on the first floor, chanting her daily prayers, when someone knocked on the door. It was Shaunaka.

"*Pranam, Pitamahi.*"

"Ah *putra*, Shaunaka. You have had a busy day. I was waiting for you when that dear boy, Kaushik, came to pay his respects. What a big man he has become!

"Hmm, *Pitamahi*, Kaushik is here for a few days to help with some arrangements at the palace. Ever since he has become a *Kumaramatya* (minister attached to the King) in the court of Maharajadhiraja Chandragupta, we have not had much chance to meet. He has asked me to visit him and see Pataliputra."

"Aha. Are you planning to? You could go with him when he leaves."

"Let us see, Pitamahi. I am not sure. There is this whole Vinayashura jewellery assignment. I do not wish to let Pitashri down and must do my best."

"Huh? I thought you were planning to apologise to Vishnu and excuse yourself. What prompted this change of mind?" asked Ahalyabai looking fondly at her favourite grandson.

"Um, I must confess, I went to that house reluctantly this morning. I did not want to take this on. But that man infuriated me; the disdain and contempt he showed Pitashri was enraging and then the way he spoke to old Kumaragiri and young Ashwini and insulted us got me riled up. While I still do not know the intricacies of gold smithy and can only craft a *ratnanguliya* just about the way it should be, I have decided that I will work at this. Maybe this is what Lord Vasudeva wants of me."

"I am proud of you, my child. Come, come, don't be disheartened and remember whatever happens is for the best. What you are doing is the right thing – one never knows what tomorrow will bring. Go and sleep."

Taking leave then of his grandmother, Shaunaka retired to his room for the night and slowly Nidradevi spread her gentle wings everywhere in the town of Nandivardhana, bringing *Bhadra Ashtami* to a close.

Bhadra Shukla Navami was a day of preparation at the goldsmith's workshop. Plans were being made and remade as designs were deliberated upon in trying to find the ones that would befit a regal betrothal and union. Stocks were checked – was there enough gold for two impending lavish weddings? Were there enough rubies, diamonds, emeralds, pearls and other gemstones in stock? Does sending someone to Kolar to get the gold need to be considered? Suddenly one of the goldbeaters remembered that there had been a buzz just the previous week about Romaka traders in town with gold and silver in tow, en route to Pataliputra. Known to be masters at driving hard bargains (a reputation that preceded them even before they reached Nandivardhana from Kalyan), they seemed to have gotten into several scrapes with the locals within a few days of getting there. As Vishnuveera mulled over whether he needed to go and procure more gold and silver, Somnath recalled that he and Kumaragiri had spotted a couple of them in the local tavern just the previous evening. While Vishnuveera and Somnath were estimating their gold and silver requirements and considering meeting the Romakas later in the day, Kumaragiri, Shaunaka, Suddhodhana and Ashwini reached their destination in the Buddhist quarter.

The group entered the premises and started walking towards the spacious courtyard along the stone path. Suddhodhana, who unlike Kumaragiri, till then had been keeping pace with the sprightly young men, stopped to take in the opulence on display. As he stood, open-mouthed, oblivious that his companions had gone on, "Such ornamental, elaborate statues and carvings on the gate; Is this an abode for human beings or the Devas?" he said, awestruck at the affluence. Seeing his expression upon sighting the colourful patterned tiles and realising that Suddhodhana would not budge an inch in his state of enthralment, Kumaragiri slowly started leading him on towards the courtyard. "Impressive, is it not? I know what you must be feeling. We have heard of such riches and wealth only in stories. Not for us, all this. Too much of *maya* and *mithya*; let us get going and finish what we have come here to do and go back to our reality."

Being of a practical, sensible nature, Suddhodhana snapped back to reality and they walked to where their two young companions were waiting for them. Just then, a middle-aged woman of medium height and a swarthy complexion came out. Going by her attire — an *antariya* and *choluka* (short blouse) made of cheap linen, it was clear that she was one of the servants employed in the household.

"Ah, are you from the goldsmith's place? Come on then. Devi has asked me to settle you down so that you can commence your work." Without any further ado or any kind of formal conversation, she led them towards the annexes flanking the courtyard.

"Is this how even the servants in rich households behave?" whispered Suddhodhana to Kumaragiri. The poor man had tried to offer her a slightly avuncular, shy smile, only to be snubbed with a look of utter disdain.

"Who knows. Stop looking around. Let us just focus on our work," advised Kumaragiri sternly. He was suddenly worried about the gauche Suddhodhana's conduct.

Shaunaka, who had quietly observed this entire exchange, was a bit concerned too. If the wealth and people at Arya Vinayashura's house could throw this man off, how would he react when he goes to the palace, he thought. As Shaunaka looked towards where the servant was leading them, he realised that they were now walking past the row of annexes.

The first annexe on the left resembled a huge store room housing provisions and grains. The servant stopped in front of the locked door to the second annexe and took out the key from her *choluka* to open the door. The entire action, while not intentional, embarrassed and unsettled the already uncomfortable Suddhodhana. She then walked across to a pavilion within this room and indicated that this would be their workplace for the days to come. Tucking the key back into her *choluka*, this time with an intentional provocative look towards Suddhodhana, the servant left the room.

"What a shameless woman. How am I supposed to work in such a place!", Suddhodhana protested, red-faced and flustered.

"This looks like a decent place for us to work. You must focus on the work – and not get provoked by this wench," demurred Kumaragiri, looking towards Ashwini and Shaunaka for help to diffuse the situation.

"It indeed is a good workplace – very thoughtfully constructed, I must say", agreed Shaunaka as he looked around the pavilion with satisfaction. A pavilion built exclusively for workmen, there were two low tables and an elaborate seating area. A shelf was conveniently placed for the workers to stack their tools. In addition to this setup, there were some crucibles also in the room.

"Lord Krishna has been kind to us. It is such a relief not to be sitting inside the main house with that arrogant creepy man breathing down our necks. This enclosure is far from the main house and too low-brow for the great man to come and check on us," quipped Ashwini who till now had been quiet because he had been busy opening the doors of the shelf and observing each of the crucibles. What he had not wanted to admit or show was that he had also been slightly flustered by the unexpected wanton behaviour of the servant. As far as his knowledge goes, servants in rich households are slatternly, not shameless!

"Why are we wasting time? Let us start," Suddhodhana remarked, finally regaining some amount of composure and interest.

Just when the men had settled down, saying a small prayer to the Goddess and making a special offering of fruits and flowers, Devi Tanirika came into the room, looking more statuesque, graceful and awe-inspiring than she did before. Her big kohl-rimmed eyes, high cheekbones, and pearly-white teeth, all beautiful features in themselves, were further accentuated by her attire and the jewellery she adorned. Dressed in a long red *antariya*, which was made of fine muslin, a black and red *choluka* which was knotted in the front; she used a long, golden-coloured *uttariya* (upper garment, shawl or a stole) to cover her bosom and present a modest appearance. Her long hair, tinged with a bit of grey, was tied up in a high bun over which she had worn a *muktajala*. Two big pearl *balis* and a long chain of pearls were further embellishments to her appearance, and it increased her splendour.

"Pranam, I apologise for having kept you waiting. I trust you have everything that you would require in this room." As Devi Tanirika welcomed them, the wanton help entered with some refreshments and laid them out in front of the workmen.

"This is Hemvati, my help. Please let her know in case you need anything. You must all be tired after the long walk from your homes. Please partake of these refreshments before commencing your work." Saying this, both the mistress of the house and the help left.

Suddhodhana, who was seeing her for the first time, was awe-struck. "She is like *sakshaat* Ma Lakshmi herself. She has such a regal countenance. If she is like this, I wonder how the Queen must be."

"She is a kind lady, freer with us than she had been when her husband was there," said Ashwini a bit too loudly.

"Ssshh, softly, the walls have ears too. Better not to speak about these people here," cautioned Shaunaka, as Kumaragiri agreed and motioned for the men to get going.

As per the discussed plans, each of these men had been allotted work, based on their capabilities. There was not much time before the wedding in the family and there were many exquisite pieces of jewellery to be made. Kumaragiri and Ashwini started beating the gold into thin sheets: their expert hands making it seem like child's play.

Suddhodhana had started making the *Vijayantika,* the exquisite gold necklace with pearls, rubies and emeralds.

"Do they really want us to make two of these? he asked Kumaragiri. While the glorious *Vijayantika* was indeed much sought after, he had not come across any instance when two pieces had to be crafted for the same person!

"Indeed. I also was surprised. The Devi clearly mentioned she wanted us to make two of these and two *nishkas* (a coin necklace). For the *Vijayantikas*, she specified the sequence in which pearls, rubies, blue sapphires, diamonds and emeralds need to be placed in both the necklaces."

"Well, what is it to us? Have any of you seen the bride-to-be? If the Devi is like a queen, she must be like a princess," chuckled Suddhodhana.

"Not necessarily, especially if she is Arya Vinayashura's daughter," quipped Ashwini causing the older men to break into laughter.

The laughter and good humour got Shaunaka's attention. He had been concentrating on the making of one of the two *ratnanguliyas*, the finger-rings studded with gems; Devi Tanirika wanted one ring with emerald and diamonds studded in gold and the other with little pearls and rubies set in concentric circles. Even though Shaunaka had learnt how to make craft *anguliyas* (finger rings) and *ratnanguliyas,* this was something he did not enjoy and hence focussed with extra attention.

"Do you need any help from us, Shaunaka?," asked Kumaragiri, almost in a paternal way.

"No, not yet. I will ask you if I do," replied Shaunaka warmly but with an apologetic expression.

"Don't worry, Shaunaka. Once I am done getting this beauty into some shape, I can help you with the *anguliyas*," Ashwini offered.

"Ashwini, I haven't brought you here to just beat gold. What about the *keyura*, *valaya*, *mekhala* and *nupura*? Who will make those?" chided Kumaragiri.

"All of them? Am I supposed to make all of them?" asked Ashwini, horrified at the thought of so much work being thrust upon him.

As the friendly banter continued in the pavilion, it struck Shaunaka that the previous two days had been a revelation. Through his apprenticeship, he had felt the hostility and resentment against him – the sniggers when he couldn't do even a simple thing right. All of this had vanished in one-go and now he was being included and treated like one of them. He was no longer just the master's useless son, the good-for-nothing outcaste.

Meanwhile, there was some sign of activity in the next room — the annexe housing the provisions and serving as a store room. Devi Tanirika's voice could be heard clearly, as she was instructing her help.

"Hemvati, Suvarna, do hurry up both of you. Will you stop giggling and measure the rice, barley and lentils."

"It promises to be another busy day," Devi Tanirika thought as she supervised the sorting of the daily provisions.

"That will not be enough. Add some more barley. Vishnuveera's men will also be eating here. And the *malakaras* are yet to come, are they not?" The giggling continued, unabated and Suvarna and Hemvati continued carrying out their assigned tasks at the same pace as before.

Devi Tanirika fought the urge to say something rude and yell at the two women and succeeded. The cool and calm veneer she had cultivated, through years of practice, of controlling one's temper, words, and action; a veneer that had become second skin, was increasingly fragile these days. She had had to double the efforts on her part to control her agitation and stop screaming. Why, even this current situation, when she was trying hard to stop herself from giving Suvarna and Hemvati an earful; where was the need, in the first place, to get irritated? All these women were doing was laughing and giggling in a silly way.

In a bid to focus her mind on other matters and control her irritation and not snap, Devi Tanirika looked out of the window. At that very moment, Shaunaka looked up from the rubies and emeralds he was setting. He shrugged trying to curb the nervousness and anxiety that filled him. This work was just not to his liking and noble intentions set aside, it was getting increasingly difficult for him to focus on it. Noticing this restlessness, Ashwini kindly suggested that they should stretch their arms and legs a bit. As they walked across to the window, a comely sight awaited them. A lithe, willowy woman with a shapely and an eye-catchingly attractive figure was walking into the bathhouse, situated opposite the row of annexes. The sight of a languorous woman swaying gracefully at a distance was indeed refreshing.

As Devi Tanirika spotted the two young men staring appreciatively at the receding figure, her irritation heightened turning into a familiar anxiety gnawing incessantly at her mind. The lady walking into the bathhouse was Tarika, her only daughter and the bride-to-be. Beauty can be such a curse – a truth learned from experience – first her own and then her daughter's. She felt a blinding headache — a companion all these sleepless nights, since the wedding had been fixed— return in full form. She needed to sleep. Maybe this wedding will get over and then the elusive sleep shall return. Devi Tanirika shuddered and stopped thinking about her head and heartache and forced herself to concentrate on the work at hand. The first group of guests from Pataliputra was due to arrive later that day.

"What a beautiful woman!" exclaimed Ashwini, with a low whistle. This prompted a whole session of ribbing and some ribald jokes, all at Ashwini's expense. "It would be easier to win the lady's approval, if you were to inlay these rubies well," Shaunaka also quipped joining in the fun. Kumaragiri laughed and added, "But she probably is the bride. What is the point of winning her approval?"

"So what if she is the bride? The bridegroom may never show up. Who knows!" replied Ashwini sassily.

The other goldbeaters frowned at this thoughtless, inconsiderate remark and chided him for taking the joke a bit too far. Ashwini was a bit shamefaced and he admitted that he got carried away in the moment. The little break over, and peace restored, the goldbeaters recommenced their work.

In the next room, Devi Tanirika was poring over the day's menu and giving instructions in a rather exasperated tone. "You know what to do. Better get on instead of giggling and gossiping about people with whom you have nothing to do. Why is Arya not out yet? There is so much to be done. I wonder why he is taking so long with his morning prayers today. Let me go and check on him.

Barely had Devi Tanirika spoken than they heard a loud thud coming from somewhere in the main house, followed instantly by a bloodcurdling scream. Simultaneously, parakeets started screeching, squawking and chirping noisily and noisy cats started running here and there. Upon hearing the sudden loud thud, Suvarna had scattered the barley everywhere on the floor and she looked shaken. "*Aho,* a bad omen again. Devi, you heard this one. These seem to be becoming more and more frequent. You should call the Purohitji; and offer something to the Gods to appease them as *pariharam* (astrological remedies to rid oneself of the ill-effects on one's karma from past lives.) I just pray Lord Vasudeva is looking after this house. I don't like this house!"

"Suvarna, someone dropped something, I suspect it is Arya, and he must have dropped it on his toes.

Bah! That is all. Stop blaming the house and get on with your work. I will now go and check on Arya. Vasudeva, now he will complain about this the whole day," said Devi Tanirika, shaking her head as she left the store room, walking determinedly towards the main building to see what the commotion had been about. As she left the room, Hemvati looked at Suvarna and said, "Poor Devi, what a tough way to live. Convincing herself and trying to see good all the time, when it is clear that the one thing wrong and bad in her life is the master. Suvarna, you are right. There is something not okay in the *vaastu* of the house. I myself heard Devi check with Purohitji some weeks back. They have built it so lavishly, but it lacks the things needed — good vibes, blessings and joy! Sad, very sad." The two maids went about their work, gossiping about people whom they knew but not giggling any more.

Devi Tanirika meanwhile had entered the central courtyard when her steps suddenly lost their determinedness. She was mulling over what Suvarna had said and was not that deluded yet to believe that everything was fine. Why, her bravado was for show, anyway. She started recounting the numerous bad omens that had occurred. When had these omens begun? It had been a few weeks, probably since the beginning of *ashadha*.

Lost in her thoughts, her pace had gone down when the squawking of the parakeets became louder. The clamour was unpleasant, almost ominous, as the shrieks and squawks got unbearably close and louder. Were the birds trying to tell her something?

"*Chhee*, I am spending too much with that nervous Suvarna." Chiding herself for such fanciful thoughts, she started hurrying.

In the second annexe, where the goldsmiths had been diligently focussing on the task at hand, there had been varied reactions to the loud thud and the scream.

"Aho baba, what was that? Not good at all. This house is inhabited by yakshas and yakshis. Vasudeva, protect us," gasped Suddhodhana, shaken.

"Someone has just dropped something in the main house. That is all," Kumaragiri tried to convince him, not so convinced himself. He looked to the younger men, who by now, had stood up and were debating whether they should go and check.

As the noise created by the birds and cats went up a notch or two, Kumaragiri's stance faltered and he told Shaunaka and Ashwini to go and check upon its source.

"What do you think, Shaunak? Do you believe these are bad omens?" asked Ashwini as they walked out towards the central courtyard.

"To tell you the truth, I do not. Poor Suddhodhanaji, blaming yakshas and yakshis. I don't think that something small has fallen also. What I am not sure is that whether we should be going to check on the source of that thud. We are workers; not friends of the family."

"Aho, that nasty man may take offence at our intervention and give us an earful. Maybe we should walk up to the main building and then go back after five minutes once this commotion dies down naturally. Look, isn't that Devi Tanirika running there?"

"*Haan* that is her. Is something really the matter? Should we go and ask her?"

As they pondered and hesitated about whether or not to follow Devi Tanirika and enter the main house, it seemed that peace had been restored. The parakeets had stopped screeching; the cats also seemed to have retired into some corner.

"Phew, some excitement that! Must be what Kumaragiriji said – someone dropping something heavy! Let us go; maybe we can catch a glimpse of that beauty coming out of the bathhouse wet and clean," chuckled Ashwini.

Shaunaka was looking at the main house. Thoughtful and serious, he did not seem convinced. "Something is wrong. You go, if you want to. I will wait here a while longer." As he said these words, the just restored silence of the morning was pierced yet again by another scream – this time, softer but filled with deep pain and anguish. The shrieking of the birds began again! This settled it.

The two men dashed in the direction towards the main house – following the steps of the lady of the house. The din and uproar was at its loudest in the central courtyard in front of the house.

"Ashwini, look up. What a racket these little creatures have been making," said Shaunaka pointing to a couple of parakeets and parrots above. Two bright, gilded cages were hanging from one of the windows in the first floor. The raucous birds, continuing to cause this din, were perched inside these cages.

"Should we go up, Shaunaka? I don't want to see that man's face."

"Hmm, we should. Something must be wrong. Come, come, that revolting man is not worth thinking about. Let us go and see what these birds are looking at and objecting to so vehemently. Look, the stairs."

To the left of the courtyard, there was a staircase that led to the inner rooms of the main house. As the birds continued to tell their tales, informing the world of what they had seen and heard, the two young men dashed up the stairs, the taller and athletic Shaunaka leading the way, followed by the slightly-out-of breath, rotund Ashwini trying to keep pace.

"Shaunaka, wait. I am stuck," Ashwini's *antariya*, made of a coarse linen, had gotten stuck to a protruding nail on one of the stairs. As Shaunaka waited for Ashwini to untangle his garment on the landing of the first floor, he got a good view of the building's layout. Two rooms seemed to be on both the right and left and could be accessed by a long passage. The carpeted passage was lined with colourful paintings and drawings, making the interiors glitter. Shaunaka was fascinated by the depiction of life on these paintings – no he was not a connoisseur of art; the scenes depicted in these was how he imagined life to be in Pataliputra, a city he was keen to travel to. As he stood admiring the paintings on the landing,

Ashwini came up from behind and said, "Narayana! What a beautifully decorated home. Shaunaka, is the palace also so glittery and shiny?"

"How would I know, Ashwini? Ha ha, I am a goldsmith's son; not a prince. I heard that Arya Vinayashura is from Pataliputra and is related to the King there. Perhaps that is true."

"Aho, but we did not come here to admire the paintings, did we? Left or right?" said Shaunaka, shaking his head, horrified at their lapse of judgment and inaction.

"Left. Sorry, we did get carried away."

As they started walking from the landing and turned left on to the passage, a shadowy figure emerged from the second floor and stealthily ran down the stairs, draped in a black shawl. He was of average height and slight build.

CHAPTER 4

The corner house was built in a fashion typical of the rich and the wealthy – with the first floor of the corner-house having four rooms – two to the left of the landing and two to the right. These rooms formed the inner quarters of the family and as with any abode, the décor and beautifications reflected the personalities of the residents. In the case of this house, there was much wealth and grandeur at display, which was what had sparked Ashwini's involuntary remark.

The entire passage was paved with colourful, patterned tiles and the walls had elaborate drawings and exquisite artwork. Shaunaka and Ashwini stopped by the first room on the left – the door of which was shut. Slowly but firmly, Shaunaka pushed open the door; to his surprise, the door was not locked from the inside and could easily be opened.

Signalling to Ashwini to not make any sound, Shaunaka peeped inside. There was a bed, all made and neat, near the door. On the wall, just next to the bed, there was a big round mirror, in front of which a small wooden shelf with perfumes and fragrances was placed. Keeping with the entire décor of the house, two colourful paintings adorned the wall: one depicting a sensuous dancer, ganika, in the process of dressing herself up for her performance. The other painting showed a beautiful dancing peacock in full glory as he welcomed the rains. The ambience of the room conveyed beauty and joy; it must be the bride's room thought Shaunaka.

"Definitely a woman's room and certainly not Arya Vinayashura's" whispered Ashwini, as he peeked in and took in the room.

"Sssshh, be quiet and look! There is someone," whispered Shaunaka, his attention caught by a crimson and yellow cotton curtain in the middle of the room. The curtain was acting as a partition in the room, on the other side of which was a sleeping figure.

"Should I go inside and check, Ashwini?"

"Yes, I think you should. Wait, I will go and stand by the door. Wonder if this was the sleeping person who shrieked."

Shaunaka tip-toed towards the centre of the room and slowly peered through the curtain. On a cot, there was a little child sleeping peacefully. Closing the curtain, Shaunaka came back to the door. "A sleeping child there, nothing amiss at all. Wonder who this is."
"Must be the bride's child," replied Ashwini.

"Child of the bride? What!"

aware of their status as being intruders in what was a very private moment for this family.

"Should we leave? Pack up and go back to the workshop?" asked Ashwini in a whisper.

"How? We cannot. A horrific crime has just been committed. We must be here. Besides, we could be suspects too," said Shaunaka as the various implications dawned upon him slowly. Ashwini looked much shaken and stirred. He liked a bit of adventure; just not this much. This was way too much!

"I will go and inform the others and fetch someone, anyone, a male servant, or a gatekeeper perhaps," said Ashwini who was longing to catch a breath of fresh air.

"Aho, do that. I will wait here." Shaunaka poured a glass of water from the *kumbha* and handed it over to Tarika, motioning that she give it to her mother. She was surprised at this unexpected thoughtfulness from a callow metal worker. Devi Tanirika seemed to be slowly recovering from the initial shock.

"What an unfortunate lady. Such beauty and so much sorrow!" thought Shaunaka as he took the glass from Tarika.

"My friend has gone to get some help and alert the police, Devi. I think we should wait for them outside."

Agreeing with this suggestion, Tarika helped her mother get on her feet and walk slowly. Shaunaka scanned the room with his sharp eyes, to spot anything

"Oh yes, I had heard that this is the second marriage. This was on that day, when Arya Vinayashura had come to our workshop. Imagine, how grand the first wedding would have been, if they are making such lavish arrangements for the second one of their daughter."

"Interesting. Let this poor child sleep peacefully. Who knows how her life will change in the next few days?" commented Shaunaka as they looked around the room again to spot something amiss.

"But if that shapely woman is the bride, not surprising why she is marrying again!" chuckled Ashwini.

Shaunaka shook his head and seemed a little lost. "Why is the jewellery so ornate for a second marriage? Two *Vijayantas?* Is that not a bit much? Will a second wedding not be a little subdued?

Finding nothing amiss, the two men left the room quietly and shut the door. "Shaunaka, the door to the next room is ajar. Should I peek?" Before Shaunaka could react, Ashwini had opened the door and walked inside.

"Narayana!"

"Ashwini, what happened?"

Shaunaka followed and looked around the room. There was a cluttered divan and a small sloping *peetha* (study desk) by the wall, as one entered. There also was a small shelf by the side of this table. A couple of long necked *kumbhas* were placed nearby. It clearly looked like a frequently used study.

As he looked to see what Ashwini clearly seemed transfixed with, a horrific sight, one he wouldn't forget, greeted his line of vision.

As with the other room, two bright, pretty curtains partitioned this room into two halves. There was another wooden cupboard next to the window. It was open. Devi Tanirika was sitting quietly, in a state of trance, clutching the end of one of the curtains. She was looking at her husband, Arya Vinayashura who was on the bed, with his eyes open, throat slit, utterly and completely dead.

"Vasudeva," it was now Shaunaka's turn to gasp.

"What do we do now?" asked Ashwini. Shaunaka was out of his depth now. They had come to help but this was not what they expected to find. "We need to go and get some help. Would you like to go?"

"Yes, please. *Dhanyavadah*, Shaunaka. I think I should go..."

"What is going on here? Who are you both? Where is Pitashri?" The beautiful woman, whom they had seen earlier through the window, the child's mother, the bride stood at the door of the room. Since the two young men were in her direct line of vision, she had been momentarily spared the shocking sight.

What were they supposed to answer? Shaunaka and Ashwini looked even more out of place and kept quiet.

"Are you both mute? Why are you standing like statues?" reprimanded the lady as she walked inside the room.

Regaining a bit of composure, Shaunaka wal towards her and said: "Devi, *pranam*. Our sin apologies. It is better if you do not go any fur There has been a slight problem. Please let explain."

"Listen, I do not know who you both are. Yo in my house and stopping me from looking int father's room. Step aside now," said Devi T looking at this stranger disbelievingly.

As she purposely walked towards the cen the room, Shaunaka and Ashwini moved t side, allowing her to get a complete view of happened!

"Pitashriiiii, Maate! Vasudeva!".

To the surprise of the young men, Tarika, the to-be, the deceased man's daughter proved made of sterner stuff than she looked. She s eyes for two minutes and then displaying an a amount of courage, started taking things i hands. She walked up to her mother and put on her shoulder.

"Maate."

Devi Tanirika looked up with a blank and stare. "Tarika, Look at this! Look at what he h He has torn my curtains. Why? Why my curtai all he wanted to do was to kill!" Devi Tanirik a wail of anguish and finally burst into inco tears in her daughter's arms.

Ashwini and Shaunaka looked at each othe of what needed to be done. Shaunaka wa

at all that would provide an insight into this heinous crime. Being innately curious, often interferingly so, his quick mind was plagued with one question – Who did it?

Meanwhile, once Ashwini had regained his composure, he ran quickly, almost like a mad man towards the annexes, shouting out for Suddhodhana and Kumaragiri. Of course, this did attract much attention and not only did they appear, so did a few others – the two maid servants for instance. As the portly man caught his breath and described the tragedy to the gathered audience in the central courtyard, a stocky, well-built young man walked up from the gate followed by two other men, who looked like his man-servants. The stocky man had spent much time on his appearance, perhaps to make up for the misfortune of his face. With a complexion that veered towards the darker side, small and deep-set shifty eyes, and protruding teeth, he was not classically good-looking. What nature had taken away, grooming and his toilette had more than made up for! His tunic and *antariya* were made of expensive cotton; the jewellery he adorned and the intricate head gear that accentuated his flowing locks clearly indicated that he was a man of town, a well-heeled *nagaraka*, and a pleasant-looking one at that.

"What happened? Why are you shouting? What is this commotion all about?" the swarthy man asked Ashwini condescendingly.

Showing an unexpected maturity, Hemvati intervened on behalf of a visibly irritated Ashwini.

"Pranam, Arya! There has been an unspeakable tragedy. The happiness of this house has been blighted by evil. This young, kind man was just alerting us about it. It seems that the master of this house has been killed. We must alert the police. The mistresses are all alone in that room. Would you please go and see if they require any help?"

"What?! Killed? What are you saying, woman? Come with me, you! Also, you go and alert the people in the monastery next door. The Dandaposika (Head of Police) needs to be informed." The man took charge and assigned specific tasks to his two servants and he started walking quickly towards the main house, leaving the motley group comprising three goldsmiths and two servants standing as they were. This young man, who had made such a grand entry, was Madhavasena – Tarika's fiancé and the bridegroom-to-be.

On the first floor, in the narrow passage, Devi Tanirika had recovered significantly by now. She was discussing matters of relevance with her daughter in a low whisper. Shaunaka, who had taken position as a guard and watchman, walking back and forth, had begun getting impatient. Every minute seemed like a lifetime. Where was that Ashwini? Did the dolt manage to alert anyone at all?

The sound of hurried footsteps in the stairwell was a welcome relief. Seeing Devi Tanirika and Tarika's reassured expressions upon seeing Madhavasena, Shaunaka finally exited this scene, heaving a sigh of relief.

It was, however, to be a long frustrating day for all those at the corner house. They knew that they could not leave until a semblance of order was restored. Shortly after, the Dandaposika and his two men also arrived and took stock of the situation. Bharavi, the Dandaposika of Nandivardhana was a well-known figure in the city, held in great esteem by most law-abiding citizens, and feared by the low-life — bandits, petty thieves, low-born criminals. In his mid-fifties, he had spent the past three decades, controlling the law and order situation and had become known for his largely ingenious and unconventional methods. The Mahadandanayaka (the Chief Judicial Officer) had given Arya Bharavi a free hand and it was largely to his credit that the town and its neighbouring villages were more or less crime free. The house sprang to life, yet again, when he made his appearance. Blessed with a tall and broad frame, with his kind, wise face framed with intelligent features, his presence was reassuring and commanding at the same time. He entered the corner house along with two of his men and asked to meet the deceased man's family.

Suvarna led the Dandaposika to the interiors of the main house, where Devi Tanirika and Tarika were seated. The room, used as a place to greet visitors, was appointed by two low *diwans* and a plush, expensive rug. Two full *kumbhas* and a couple of mud cups were kept by the door. Fresh flowers had been used to bedeck the room and incense had been lit earlier that morning to welcome guests from Pataliputra who were to arrive later in the day, perhaps towards evening. Devi Tanirika sat on the *diwan* by the window, forlorn and dejected, as she probably pondered upon the rest of her life. On the plush rug sat Tarika along with her little girl. They were playing dice. While the little girl had not been told what had actually happened, her subdued behaviour, and her quick, fearful glances at her grandmother and mother made it obvious that she was aware of some earth-shattering occurrence in their lives.

Seeing the Dandaposika, Devi Tanirika roused herself from her stupor. The Dandaposika was an old acquaintance of hers, from her Pataliputra days, and she was relieved to see him take charge.

"Pranam Devi! I would like to first convey my sincere apologies. This was not how I expected our next meeting to be. I was looking forward to attending Tarika's wedding. This is a sad moment and I assure you, we will find out who committed this unpardonable evil act."

"Dhanyavadah, Arya. Please let me know how I can help."

The Dandaposika requested permission to appoint themselves in one of the rooms on the first floor and to speak to everyone who had been in the house that morning. Arya Bharavi also made it clear that he did not want any of the people to leave the house until and unless they had been given explicit permission.

When Devi Tanirika mentioned that a group of people were to arrive for the wedding from Pataliputra, he requested that they be put up elsewhere in the town for a night. Offering to make all required arrangements for their stay, the Dandaposika deputed one of his men to stop the visitors near the north gate of the city and escort them to an inn nearby.

They got to work — checking the scene of the murder and the corpse for any evidence and interrogating the people around for possible clues or inputs.

The goldbeaters waited patiently for their turn to be questioned. They sat by the annexe, while rehashing the events of the day. Suddhodhana, being of a nervous temperament, did not participate much in the discussion. He was busy chanting some shlokas to ward off the evil in the house.

"Oh look, Rajpurohitji has come. He is accompanied by some other priests," said Shaunaka who had been staring out of the window. It was frustrating for him to be caged up in a pokey little annexe, when all the action was taking place elsewhere!

"Finally! They need to start the prayers for the soul of the departed. *Pretas* (ghosts) haunt the place where a death has taken place. Oh Vasudeva, what have I done that I am here?" remarked the nervous, superstitious Suddhodhana. Kumaragiri nodded in agreement. He was tired and also wished to leave. Besides, while he was not as superstitious as Suddhodhana, he did believe that a place where a death had taken place was impure and everyone associated with it also acquired certain degrees of impurity. He wished to go home and complete the purification rituals.

"Arya Vinayashura was such a horrible man. But did he have to die such a brutal death? Unable to get rid of the image of the dead man with his throat slit from his mind, Ashwini tried to think of other related aspects – why, how and who. He walked up to the window where Shaunaka was standing to discuss this in detail. Before they could have any kind of conversation, a policeman entered the annexe and ordered them to be present in the first floor for their interrogation.

By the time the *ghatika* (a type of clock based on water) in the town centre had been struck to indicate *sayankaal*, the news about the corner house murder had spread. The local tavern, the Chitrashalas, why even at the court, everyone was whispering about the gruesome murder. Vasudeva, what cruelty exists – no fear of Karma or next life, if this is the kind of hatred present in the minds of someone in their own town. It probably must be a foreigner, a stranger to the place, who committed this heinous act. Thus sprang many theories and rumours — probably the Romakas in town did it for money. Or was it the goldbeaters – there were five to six of them, all from Vishnuveera's workshop. Must be them, they have the tools, do they not? By evening, when the goldbeaters still had not come back, these rumours strengthened – they definitely must have been arrested.

The tension at Vishnuveera's workshop was palpable and increasing every passing minute. The master and his men sat in a huddle, sending out prayers above, for the safety of their loved ones.

"I think we should shut the main gate, Arya," suggested Somnath after he looked out. A crowd had gathered and was growing in number every minute. "Jobless people. Should I shoo them away?" asked Deva, a young apprentice looking at Vishnuveera who was deep in thought. He shook his head, indicating that Deva and Somnath do nothing.

"Have we sent word to Kumaragiri and Suddhodhana's families that we will inform them the moment we hear anything?"

"We have, Arya. I have asked two boys — Deepak and Ramakrishna — to hover near the intersection – the one crossed while exiting the Buddhist quarter. I have asked one of them to accompany the older men and the other will accompany Shaunaka and Ashwini back."

"Good, this is taking too long. If they do not come in the next *prahar*, I will request an audience with the Mahadandanayaka and ask for his interference. My men are not killers!"

At the corner house, meanwhile, after immense activity of an unexpected kind, *Bhadra Shukla Navami* finally came to an end.

"It was always supposed to be a busy day – just not this kind of busy," murmured Hemvati to Suvarna as they finally sat down to have a small meal.

"All those omens. Why did we ignore them? Oh Devi should have listened to me," moaned Suvarna.

"What could anyone have done? It is just karma – of one's last life, past misdeeds. Only Vasudeva knows what the master had done to deserve such a pitiful, brutal end. Om Shanti," reasoned Hemvati.

"Nothing, nothing at all. Has Devi eaten anything? What about Tarika?"

"No, Mahadandanayaka Yakshavatsa and Dandaposika Bharavi are still there with them. It looks like it will take a while. Devi has asked us to eat. She doesn't wish to eat.

"My poor Devi. She should eat. I will go and feed her … Mahadandanayaka Yakshavatsa?? He is also here? When did he come? Why? … I thought I saw some men leave when I had gone out to fill the *ghatika*. Who was that?"

"Aho, so many questions. The Mahadandanayaka came just a little while ago. I overheard Madhavasena's men talking – they say that Arya Vishnuveera requested his presence here to intervene for his only son who is caught up here!

"Arya Vishnuveera's son was here? Who?"

"That tall young man who was with Devi Tanirika when Arya Madhavasena came. One of the first to find the poor Arya's body."

"Narayana! He seemed like a nice, decent boy – and why would those poor goldsmiths kill Arya? Poor men. Did they finally get to leave?

"Oh yes, the men you would have seen leave, a while back would have been the four goldsmiths and probably Arya Vishnuveera."

"Narayana! What a day it has been! I do not want to think what would have happened had Madhavasena not been around."

Finally, after the intervention of Mahadandanayaka Yakshavatsa at the behest of Vishnuveera, when the interrogation of the four goldbeaters was completed, they were allowed to leave. The Mahadandanayaka was an old friend of Vishnuveera's, their friendship dating to the days in gurukula, long back when they were boys.

Hence Vishnuveera's request was promptly taken up and he went personally to the corner house and asked Vishnu to accompany him. His friend's son may not be a conformist and maybe slightly on the rebellious side; he certainly was not a murderer. He believed that but was also curious to see why the Dandaposika had not let them go. The Dandaposika was his protégé and having groomed him all these years, Yakshavatsa was sure that Bharavi would have a solid rcason behind each of his actions.

On the other hand, the Dandaposika had not even purposely detained these men. He was merely mulling over observation and interrogation and had lost track of time! This was an interesting matter – how can a man be killed, in plain daylight, with so sign of any struggle, theft, or anything amiss? And how can the perpetrator of such an act disappear from a busy house – where wedding preparations were on in full swing?

As the only outsiders, the goldbeaters were definitely both important witnesses and suspects at the same time. Even though the older ones did not have that much information to divulge, their experience of human nature and general observations counted. The younger men were important as they were among the first people to see the dead body. It was this that prompted Bharavi to interrogate and re-interrogate the four of them.

When Yakshavatsa arrived, the surprised Bharavi understood the larger concerns and let the goldbeaters leave, upon one stipulation — that Shaunaka and Ashwini would make themselves available for questioning, if required.

So, after thanking his childhood friend profusely, Vishnuveera left the corner house taking his four men with him. Yakshvatsa stayed back to discuss the corner house case. Now that he had come to the crime scene, his sense of duty became a higher priority.

"Haan Bharavi, what do you think? Were you able to glean any information? The whole town outside is agog, spinning stories about who has done it," asked Yakshavatsa, stretching his long legs as he stood up from his seated position. He had been seated in a small *moda* in the room on the second floor, where Bharavi had been interviewing people. Now that the two men were all alone, Yakshavatsa allowed himself to be less formal and more comfortable.

"Arya, it is clearly someone who hated him very much — the way his throat has been slit — pitilessly, and with so much fury, it is clearly an act of hate."

"Aho, so the goldbeaters may not have anything to do with it? They have no reason to hate this man – they barely knew him!"

"No, not at all. But they are an interesting bunch and important witnesses. Very useful. In particular, this one young man – Shaunaka? Arya, I believe you know him?

"Yes, I do. He is Vishnuveera's only son – not too interested in gold beating – but otherwise a good boy, I think. What has he done?"

"Oh, Arya, I think he is an extremely intelligent young man, blessed with superior observation and analytic skills. Pardon my interference, I believe he is wasting his talents beating gold. Arya, if I may so suggest, we should consider using his talents and skills to our kingdom's advantage and use. I see for him a bright future – other than making exquisite pieces of jewels."

"What do you have in mind? How do you wish to induct him?"

"For one, I would like to take his help in this case. As a key witness and having been present here, this case would be good for me to assess his strengths and weaknesses. Some kind of probation this. We can always review later."

Yakshavatsa listened to Bharavi with much interest. Just like he was known for his unconventional methods, Bharavi was also known for picking out talent and identifying the right young men for the job. This was indeed interesting – Vishnu had complained many times in the past about Shaunaka's lack of interest in his profession. How mysterious are the ways of working of *bhagya!* Of Vasudeva! Maybe this was Shaunaka's destiny. Who was he to thwart an opportunity fate seemed to be presenting a young man?

Yakshavatsa agreed with Bharavi's overall plan and told him that he would speak to Vishnuveera the very next day.

After what seemed like a never-ending confinement, the goldbeaters were relieved to be able to leave. Kumaragiri and Suddhodhana, in particular, had felt extremely harassed by the end of the interrogation. They could not fathom for the life of them, why the Dandaposika had asked them to stay. Their joy upon spotting Vishnuveera was, therefore, unmatched.

"Arya, thank you so very much. We will always be grateful for your intervention today," said Kumaragiri, as Suddhodhana also appeared extremely thankful.

"Na, that is the least I could have done. I sent you to craft jewels; not get detained for a crime that you did not even commit."

"Aho, that was so strange. Arya Bharavi kept talking to us – asking questions. At least in our case, there was not that much we could tell. We were cooped up in that annexe – waiting for some news, any news. It just seemed strange when these two boys who had gone looking for what caused that scream did not show up for so much time," continued Kumaragiri.

"My sincere thanks to you, Arya and to Lord Shiva and Krishna, for saving us today. The planets' movement must have been inauspicious this morning and we must have entered this place at a wrong time – which is why we went through so much tension. For no fault of ours. We did not step out of the annexe. Kumara tried to work, I started reciting some shlokas for my peace of mind and for the poor departed soul. But Arya Bharavi was adamant. He kept asking – what did you see? What did you not see? What did you do? Almost irritating," lamented Suddhodhana, for whom the entire experience had been very stressful.

"Now, now, calm down. You have not done anything. Everyone is assured. You do not have to worry. There, Gopala is standing there at the intersection. Good, I see that he has arranged for carts to take us back home. Go home, cleanse yourselves, have a meal and rest. It is okay if you come a little late tomorrow morning," consoled Vishnuveera.

Grateful and overwhelmed, Kumaragiri and Suddhodhana bade their respects to their master and colleagues and went home.

While the elder goldbeaters had been lamenting and sharing their experiences with the master, the two men who had been in the thick of the action were quiet. Now that they were alone and on the way home, conversation started flowing thick and fast. They dissected every moment starting from the time they found the body till the time they were allowed to leave. Vishnuveera looked at both the young men with much amusement. "One would think you had a good day!"

"It was interesting, Arya, though I would not wish to find any more dead bodies again in my life," said Ashwini, whose thirst for adventure seemed to be over.

"Ha ha, don't you want to find out who did it, Ashwini," asked Shaunaka. "Did you realise, Arya

Bharavi kept asking us what seemed like unrelated questions? But actually they were not?"

"What do you mean? Shaunaka, he was more bothered about the angle at which the window was open and whether it was open or not than the poor dead man."

"Hah, but that's the point. Om Shanti. Arya Vinayashura's current lifespan has been cut short – nothing can be done about it. However, the least he can do is nab the killers and get them punished in Mahadevi Prabhavati's court and bring the departed soul justice. Hence, he wanted to know if the killer had escaped through the window," countered Shaunaka, with an awe-struck expression. He clearly had been fascinated by the workings of Arya Bharavi and his men.

"Ha ha, maybe you should speak to Arya Bharavi and offer to help," whispered Ashwini as they reached the house where Ahalya devi and Gautami were waiting impatiently.

"Not a bad idea at all," smiled Shaunaka as soon as Arya Vishnuveera was out of earshot, and they walked to the family giving a low-down of their exciting day!

When the third *prahar* of the night commenced, the lights of the diya in the house were dimmed, a still quietness and complete silence descended upon the house and the town.

Bhadra Shukla Navami was finally over. What a day it had been!

CHAPTER 5

As the sun rose on Nandivardhana the following day, a particular house in the Buddhist quarter wore a mournful look. How lives can change in less than a day!

The sunrays lit up the corner house, but the house itself wore the look of a place that did not know whether to be sad or happy. Signs of an upcoming celebration thwarted suddenly by a sudden tragedy seemed to be everywhere. While the decorated gate; the colourful, patterned rangolis adorning the path up to the central courtyard, where a big lamp, decorated with blooming roses and jasmine flowers was placed; the bright *bandhanwar* and the *torana* of mango leaves and marigold flowers on the door to the main house, announced joy and happiness; one had to look past them to see the half-decorated annexes, flowers strewn and dumped in a corner and a ubiquitous forlorn look that had taken over. It was a confused, deserted and quiet house – unable to cope with what had come over it.

But it was morning again and another day beckoned. A day after her husband was killed brutally, Devi Tanirika woke up and stuck to doing what she knew best! Rousing herself from the sudden and unexpected grief fate had dealt her, Devi Tanirika quietly went about her morning rituals — ablutions, prayers and all— and slowly stepped out to the central courtyard. As she scanned the entire visage of the house, she shook her head. This certainly would not do. What a mess! One person is dead; life does not stop, does it?

"Suvarna, come over here. Look at this mess. Could you get this cleared? So many flowers about to wilt away. Call the *malakaras*, have them take the flowers away before they completely wilt and have to be thrown. Keep some, if you will, for the cremation later today. Where is Hemvati? Have you seen Tarika? Has she woken up? The guests will have to be called over. And ask Raghuveer to find out when the Rajapurohitji will be here."

There were to be guests indeed — ones who had come to attend a wedding but would be attending a cremation instead. The priest would also be there soon — to conduct the final rites and not officiate a marriage.

In a snap of a finger, the whole house woke up from stupor and regained semblance of its former self and started buzzing with some activity, except for one person – the deceased man's daughter, Tarika, who was inconsolable.

That morning, as she heard noises of the house coming back to life, thanks to her indomitable mother, she tried her best to get on with her daily activities – but found that she was unable to do so. Her guilt and grief were just unbearable. Memories of her father and their complicated relationship were way too overwhelming. Once the apple of her father's eye and close to her father, their relationship had deteriorated over the past ten years – to such an extent that they could not stay in a room without flaring up or yelling at each other. Hemvati found Tarika in bed, grief-stricken and gutted, when she came to look for her upon Tanirika's orders. The Rajapurohit had arrived for the final rites; so had Madhavasena and the other guests.

"Come come, now, my dear. You have to rouse yourself up and get on with the day. Mourn later – once the commotion dies down. You have a young girl to look after."

At the mention of her daughter, Tarika came to her senses and looked around her frantically. Her child was not in the room.

"Don't worry. Anagha has been up for a while; we have gotten her ready – clothed and fed her for the ceremony. Madhavasena is now playing with her. May Goddess Lakshmi shower her blessings on that boy! What a good boy he is. But now you get up," admonished Hemvati in a maternal tone. She had after all taken care of Tarika from the time she was a chit of a girl.

"Bhagini, I am so sorry, Had I known Pitashri would go so soon, I would have been nicer to him. I have been a horrible daughter — have been so angry with him all this while. I had just been ignoring him and replying to him disrespectfully. What have I done?"

"Oh Tarika! Stop torturing yourself. Nothing can be done now. One never knows when one's time will come. He had to go — so suddenly; he did. Yes, you could have been nicer to him. But it was not all your fault. He loved you, Tarika. His ego could just not take it when he realised, yes even before you accused him, that he had spoiled your life by marrying you to that brute! Devi had been unhappy as well. Your constant presence was then a reminder of his colossal mistake. Now what can be done? Nothing. By Mahalakshmi's grace, there is Madhavasena now in your life. I overheard Devi Tanirika ask Purohitji right now how soon the marriage will be permitted."

Tarika sat upright. "Marriage? So soon after Pitashri's death? Why is Maate in a hurry?"

"Not a hurry, she is concerned about you, my dear. Come now."

Hemvati's gentle coaxing and maternal love paid rewards and Tarika managed to come down to the main hall, where preparations for the cremation were on. Arya Vinayashura's body, cleansed and decorated, was ready at the further end. Devi Tanirika, clad now in white, was sitting beside him with an inscrutable expression on her regal face. As Tarika entered the hall, Devi Tanirika looked up and gave Hemvati a look of gratitude and a small smile. Acknowledging that, Hemvati nudged Tarika to go and sit next to her mother. She looked around to see what could be done. The guests from Pataliputra were seated in mats on the opposite side of the hall. Dressed in clothes that were clearly meant for a more joyous occasion, they looked sombre and unhappy. Most of these were close friends and relatives of Arya Vinayashura and Devi Tanirika. The Rajapurohit, Arya Varahaswamin, was seated near the body. He was inspecting the herbs and other *samagri* required for the final rites.

Arrangements for the cart and the funeral procession up to the cremations ground were being supervised by Madhavasena. A group of drummers had also assembled in the central courtyard and started beating their drums.

"Why does the Rajapurohit (Royal priest) look so displeased?" whispered Hemvati as she joined Suvarna in arranging the required ingredients. Cleverly leading her to a distance from where they couldn't be heard, Suvarna replied:

"Oh he is appalled that the cremation did not take place within four hours of the death yesterday. It is not done — this — keeping the body for one whole day! Thank Lord Vasudeva, you showed up with Tarika. He was beginning to get irritated about that as well."

The cremation of Arya Vinayashura had not taken place the previous day due to Arya Bharavi's prolonged presence at their house — talking to everyone and asking them improbable, unrelated questions. A couple of times, Devi Tanirika had tried to intervene to inform him that arrangements needed to be made. But Arya Bharavi did not pay heed.

Soon the arrangements were complete; Arya Varahaswamin started reciting his prayers and mantras, a group of mourners started howling and the cortege left the corner house making its way towards the cremation grounds. A large group of people had gathered near the gate since morning. The corner house had always invoked much curiosity. Its grandeur, the rumoured royal origins of the residents and the fact that royal workers and guards were reportedly spotted during its construction made it the talk of the town and people wanted to know more about the residents of this place. The news of the murder of Arya Vinayashura was received with mixed emotions by most people in town. Malicious thrill at the downfall of a fellow human being and shock were the immediate reactions and their curiosity had taken over. Now that Arya Vinayashura was not there to defend himself, discussions about the failings of his character — his arrogance, pride, pomposity abounded. People from different parts of Nandivardhana had assembled since morning to get a glimpse of this rich arrogant patron and to follow the cortege. The motley crowd included children, vagrants, sadhus, jobless actors and drunkards — people who had nothing better to do. And also hopeful of getting a chance to partake of a feast at the royal house! Had someone noticed and observed this group closely, they would have spotted some familiar faces — the two traders who had fought with Arya Vinayashura and a man with a black shawl who just seemed to be everywhere.

The goings-on in the corner house indeed had become a topic of fervent discussion in Nandivardhana. From the crowds in front of the house to the monks in the Buddhist monasteries next door, from the drinking houses to the street markets, this was the constant topic in town. Why, even the royal guards, chamberlains, mahouts and the various officials in the palace estate were discussing this brutal murder. Such evil and violence in their midst. Who could have done it? Why? Was the town under any threat?

In his death, Arya Vinayashura had overtaken Maharani Prabhavatigupta and Yuvaraja Divakarasena to become the most debated person in Nandivardhana.

At the moment, the cortege left the house gates and started moving towards the cremation grounds, in one of the halls in the interior of the palace estate, this very topic was being discussed with much fervour and interest.

The hall — used often as a meeting place for councils and other officials, was also used by the Queen to receive and meet with well-known residents of the city— was an airy room, sparsely decorated but well-appointed with just the right furnishings. Whether or not the Queen was inside, two sentries — mean-looking men of a particular physical build— guarded the room at all times.

The Maharani was expected to attend this meeting, which had been called to discuss the law and order situation. Arya Yakshavatsa and Arya Bharavi had been summoned to attend this meeting by the esteemed Kulaputra (nobleman), Arya Agnisvamin. As the esteemed officials inside the hall were awaiting the Maharani's arrival, Arya Agnisvamin, the esteemed Kulaputra asked the Mahadandanayaka, "Arya, what is this about Arya Vinayashura's death? Do you have any more information than what my *guptacharas* have told me?"

The Mahadandanayaka replied thoughtfully, "It is with extreme sadness that I have to report that we have, so far, made no headway. We have no more information than what your *guptacharas* (spies) have already given you. Arya Vinayashura was someone respected and known to most of us here. It is a strange business – evil and worrying. Someone with a deep hate for the Arya killed him — brutally, without any remorse. And that too in a full house. Preparations were on for his daughter's wedding, and the goldsmiths and the *malakara*s were there – and yet it is not them. Arya was killed in daylight and amidst all these people."

"It is worrying. Mahadevi was extremely upset upon hearing the news and had to retire to her chambers to recuperate. We are concerned, Arya. This may just be a case of personal enmity; however, Arya Vinayashura was too important a person in his days. I am worried that it may just be a bigger matter. I thought you had posted someone in Vinayashura's house to keep an eye."

Arya Bharavi intervened at this juncture, even though the question had been addressed to the Mahadandanayaka. "Arya, pardon my interference. Your worry is indeed justified. I have been extremely concerned too. We have had reports about some activities within Nandivardhana that have been provoked by our enemies. We are tracking these elements and suspicious people to uncover what the actual plot is. However, based on whatever little knowledge I have gained through my years, this murder does not seem related. The method employed was so violent – reflective of the intense hate the murderer had for Vinayashura. It seemed to me that the motives were personal. Siddeshwara, our man, had been working at the house for over a few months now. He did not report anything amiss."

"Bah! And yet a murder took place … Do something about it."

"Yes Arya, I had a request…" said Arya Bharavi, only to be interrupted by the announcement of the arrival of the Maharani.

In her late-30s, Mahadevi Prabhavatigupta exuded maturity and strength far beyond her years. Her quiet and stern demeanour, acquired since the time the responsibilities of the kingdom were thrust upon her, kept people at a distance. She was a person definitely not to be messed with. Of medium height and a wheatish complexion, she had sharp features that gave her a pleasant appearance, which was further accentuated by her fondness for bright silks and fine jewels. As the royal guards announced her entry, she walked in, with a determined stance and a fast pace. Surveying the room with a quick look, she seated herself in the richly furnished *diwan* in the centre of the hall and nodded at the Kulaputra indicating that he should start the proceedings.

Kulaputra Agniswamin greeted the Queen and took her permission to discuss the matters at hand.

"Pranam, Your Majesty! The law and order situation, as such, has been under control and no untoward incident in public places has been reported. We have placed our men in taverns, drinking halls, markets and brothels, almost everywhere. They have been given orders to pick up any suspicious looking person."

"Yet, we have had an unfortunate incident at the Buddhist quarter yesterday. Arya Vinayashura's family was dear to me and my father. And he was killed, butchered in his own house, in my city? This worries me, Kulaputraji. It has just been a few years since Pitashri defeated Rudrasena and took over his country in the West. Also I have been informed by someone close to me — he should be here any moment — that Rudrasena's close men are still hoping to stir more trouble and have sent their spies into our city. Are you sure that this is not related to the murder?" asked the Queen, looking rather forlorn and affected.

At that very moment, a middle-aged man with a black shawl entered the hall, confident and composed. "Pranam, Mahadevi. Pranam, Arya!"

"Pranam, *Mahakavi*. Please be seated. I was waiting for your arrival," said the Queen to the man who was known to the world as Kalidasa, the great poet and playwright!

Arya Bharavi shot a surprised look to Arya Yakshavatsa, as if asking a question, 'What is an artist doing here?' Arya Yakshavatsa averted his glance and looked down; it was not a question he could answer.

"Arya, you all must be wondering why I have called the *Mahakavi* to a meeting where we are discussing matters other than art and poetry. The truth is that the *Mahakavi* has been so much more — he has been a counsellor, a spy, and an ambassador for Magadha. I invited him here under the pretext of the wedding of Yuvaraj Divakarasena, to offer us his wise counsel."

"Dhanyavadah, Mahadevi! Your kind words are most encouraging. Arya, I am a mere poet and an artist, looking to the world around me for inspiration. If my mere observations of people can help keep my country safe and secure, of course, I will help. This is what I have been doing. Guptachara, Dutaka, Spy, these are words that sound too big for me. I am a Brahmin, dedicated to my *vidya*," said Kalidasa, humbly.

"Arya, please proceed with the arrangements that have been made in the city," said the Queen to Kulaputra, who in turn looked at Bharavi and indicated to him to answer.

The Dandaposika gave a quick update about the arrangements in the town. He confirmed having received reports about suspicious elements, who may cause trouble and had increased the number of spies in certain parts of the town. Bharavi also spoke about the corner house murder and the state of the interrogation and investigation in detail, mainly because it seemed to be such a high-profile one. Using this opportunity, he politely requested permission to hire more people into his force and in particular, raised the topic of Shaunaka.

"Shaunaka? Who is he? Where did you spot him now, Bharavi?" asked the Kulaputra, aware of Bharavi's rather unconventional strategies.

"He is the son of Arya Vishnuveera, the jeweller–goldsmith."

"Is he a tall young man who was at the house on the day of Vinayashura's death? The same one who found the body first?" interjected Kalidasa, much to the other gentlemen's surprise.

"Yes, Arya, that is he. I found him to be rather sharp and observant and I have heard, from my sources, that he is not too happy being a goldsmith." Bharavi's reply seemed to satisfy Kalidasa as he said no more.

"Why, *Mahakavi*, do you know the boy Bharavi is talking about?" asked the Queen.

"Mahadevi, I have been spending a lot of time outside the palace the past few days. Arya Vinayashura's house had also been under my surveillance. I have seen this boy there – and I agree with Arya Bharavi's observation. The boy is definitely intelligent and observant and may prove to be indeed useful. We could pursue what Arya Bharavi has in mind."

"Arya Yakshavatsa, you have been quiet. I believe you know Vishnuveera well. What do you say? Would he be happy to see his son pursue another path?"

"Mahadevi, it will be good for the boy. I do know that his mind is just not into gold smithy and Vishnuveera has been concerned about this. If your majesty permits, may I speak to Vishnu?"

"*Tathastu.* You can proceed to speak with Vishnuveera and then induct the boy into the force."

"Mahadevi, it is not my wish to interrupt Arya Bharavi's plans. I would be grateful if he could spare this boy to help me with my work," requested Kalidasa.

"Work in the theatre?" asked a surprised Bharavi. He was yet to get over the fact that the *Mahakavi*, worshipped and revered for his literary genius, was also a spy!

"Na, I am currently on a secret mission. I had been keeping a watch on Vinayashura as well. I would request if the boys are allowed to help me."

"Boys?"

"Ah, I have been informed by my source in the house that on the day of the murder, there was another boy with Shaunaka when the body was discovered. He was interesting – can be of some use too." Kalidasa's serious face had a crinkle of a smile as he said that.

"Ashwini, I think his name is that. He is the adopted son of Arya Vishnuveera and Devi Gautami. Mahadevi, should I then speak to Arya Vishnuveera, requesting permission for both his sons to be released from their duties?" asked Yakshavatsa, wondering how his childhood friend would react.

"Aho, do that. You can tell me if Arya Vishnuveera is not too happy about this suggestion. I will speak to him, if need be," said the Queen, with a finality to her tone, indicating the end of this conversation.

Vishnuveera's workshop was bristling with a constant stream of visitors — friends, relatives, acquaintances — curious to gather more information about the gruesome murder since morning. Word had spread that Shaunaka, Ashwini and two other goldbeaters happened to be at the corner house when the murder took place. Keen to know more and to commiserate with the affected eyewitnesses, people made a beeline for the workshop.

"Aho, do these people have no work, Bhagini? Swarming this place like bees, since morning," complained Charukeshi, Vishnuveera's widowed sister who lived with her brother and her sister-in-law. The women were in the kitchen preparing the dishes for the mid-morning meal and had no headcount of the number of mouths they had to feed. Not that food was in shortage. There was always more food in Vishnuveera's home than the number of people who lived there. But that day was different — there were just too many people walking in to either meet Vishnuveera or his wife — with no obvious work.

Gautami nodded at her loquacious sister-in-law. She had too many things on her mind and too much to do. She did not wish to engage in any meaningless conversation, be it with her sister-in-law or anyone else. The past two days had been full of excessive anxiety —first because both her sons — natural and adopted — were not back still and also because they had gotten embroiled in a murder scene. She had chided them when they had told her that they were the ones to find the dead body. She could not understand why they exceeded their brief and ventured into the main house. Could they not have stayed put like the older gold beaters and restrained their curiosity? Her apprehensions had worsened since morning, with this stream of people who came looking for news. Charukeshi was right – they had nothing better to do.

Raghuveer entered the kitchen with, an empty pail of water to refill in his hand. An old help of the household, he did not seem too happy either. His limp, a result of an injury some years ago, seemed aggravated by the to-and-fro he had done today.

"Ah, Raghuveer, some more guests?" asked Charukeshi, with the hope of getting some juicy gossip herself. Gautami showed no interest at this question; she, in fact, had a tinge of disapproval on her otherwise calm face.

"Bhagini, too many people since morning. Two important men, very big people, I think are visiting. Arya has welcomed them personally in the private hall. I have been sent to get the *madhuparka.*"

"Private hall?" Gautami's attention had been caught.

"There you go. This silver cup has the *madhuparka* in it. Who are these people, do you know?", asked a curious Charukeshi, handing him two bowls filled with the sweet concoction made of curd, ghee, and bananas that was always offered to special and important guests.

"Aho, one of them was the Mahadandanayaka, Arya's old friend. The other man with him looked equally important — going by his clothes and the way he entered and surveyed the place. Kumaragiri and Suddhodhana recognised him. I overheard them whisper that the second man was the Dandaposika," said the man as he hobbled his way back to where the guests were seated.

Gautami was clearly distressed upon hearing this news. What did these men want? Were her sons in trouble? Unable to cope with these fast-flowing, terrifying thoughts, she just sat down. Even Charukeshi was flustered. Harmless gossip aside, what were these important people doing in their house? The boys, including her own, Kaushika, who was away at the gurukula, were good boys. It was just bad luck and *grahagati* that poor Shaunaka and Ashwini found themselves in that ill-fated house. Arre, Shaunaka had not even wished to go. Seeing how Gautami had crumbled and sat on the floor, Charukeshi walked up to her and placed her hands on her shoulders. That was the least she could do. The women found themselves at a loss.

The important visitors were indeed Arya Yakshavatsa and Arya Bharavi. Arya Vishnuveera had been equally surprised to find these esteemed, well-respected gentlemen at his doorstep. Yakshavatsa may have been his childhood friend but he never made such public, unannounced visits to his workshop in the middle of the day.

Welcoming them as warmly as he could, he led them into the private hall where he received special guests and requested them to make themselves comfortable. While curious about the purpose of the visit, he was careful not to come across as nervous or over-eager.

Questions were flying fast and furious, the same ones that were now being discussed in whispers, in the main workshop. Why were these men here? What did they want from him? Were they here to question the goldbeaters?

"Arya, Namonamah. We are here on the behest of Mahadevi, the Maharani," started Bharavi, causing Vishnuveera's heart to lurch. Did the Queen no longer want his services?

"No, no, please do not look concerned," interjected Yakshavatsa, seeing his friend's face. "There is nothing at all to worry."

"Yes, Arya, please permit me to get straight to the point and ease your worries. Yesterday, I had the pleasure of interacting with your son, Shaunaka and his friend, Ashwini."

"Ashwini is my son, Arya," said Vishnuveera calmly.

"Aho, I met both of them when I questioned them about their presence in the house of that cursed, ill-fated man. I must admit I was struck by Shaunaka's intelligence and observation skills in particular. Following a discussion about Shaunaka with the Arya here, and then Mahadevi and some key officials whose names I cannot divulge, we have come here with a request."

"Request? What can I do for you? For the Queen? What do you wish from Shaunaka?" asked Vishnuveera visibly more surprised than before.

"We would like Shaunaka to work with us, for the kingdom, as a *guptachara* and a *dutaka* to begin with.

Ashwini has other skills that would be of use to Nandivardhana. We would like you to release both your sons from your profession and permit them to join the police force, albeit discreetly," said Bharavi in a quiet, firm tone.

This unexpected, unanticipated request from Bharavi astounded Vishnuveera. He had not seen this coming. He clearly was in a fix. The royal wedding commission meant that he needed every pair of hands working on crafting the jewels. How could he then release both Ashwini and Shaunaka? To become a *dutaka*? A *guptachara*? He could imagine Shaunaka enjoy doing this and excelling in it as well. His son had always been too adventurous, curious and observant. But Ashwini, who was developing into one of the most talented gold workers in the entire city? Would he be happy becoming a *dutaka*, a *guptachara*, running around lanes, visiting strange places ferreting for information?

As he seemed lost in thought, processing the sudden request and its implications on his work, home and family, Bharavi said, "Arya, please take your time. I know this would have come as a major surprise and you would require time to think over it calmly. Also, please be discreet about this. We would request you to let us know your decision."

"Yes, Vishnu, please intimate us by tomorrow. Take your time now and do not fret over it. If you wish to discuss it further with me, please come by this evening to my place. Now we will take your leave," Yakshavatsa added.

Jolted out of his reverie, Vishnuveera rose to his feet and replied, with folded hands: "Thank you, Arya. What you are suggesting will have major repercussions on my work and family. I do require some time to think over it and also discuss with my mother and my wife, besides my sons."

The two men then left the workshop, which by now had attracted a huge group of onlookers standing outside it. Many more visitors were seen trickling in after this, curious to know the purpose of the officials' visit.

The renewed stream of visitors was to be a major irritant to the two women in the kitchen, who, after the initial anxiety and fear had recommenced their work.

"Really, Bhagini, one would think this house is a palace – and Jyeshtha a king! This is too much," Charukeshi was now visibly agitated – the concerned sister and aunt in her had trumped the gossip-loving lady!

"Well, we can't do much. Till Aryasuta leaves the workshop and retires to the interiors, these guests will need to be tolerated. It looks like Arya Yakshavatsa and the Dandaposika left, which may explain these new guests."

"And to think we need to be the ones who should know what that particular visit was all about."

"What is all this commotion about? I have not been able to concentrate on my prayers since morning.

Who visited?" asked Ahalya Devi imperiously, as she entered the kitchen and seated herself on a stool that had been placed for her in the corner. It was time for the mid-morning meal which she would have with her son.

As she waited for her son to come and eat, her daughter and daughter-in-law apprised her of the recent visit. Arya Vishnuveera soon came in to eat and Siddeshwara brought word that the people at the workshop would now have to be fed. Taking stock of how many people were there that morning for food, Charukeshi, along with Raghuveer and another help, started making arrangements to serve the food in the lunch hall.

Lunch over, the family withdrew for a short afternoon break to the common hall on the ground floor after Vishnuveera indicated that he had news of some import that he wished to convey.

Taking his time, and thinking it over, he broke the news to his wife, sister and mother, albeit discreetly. He informed them that the Mahadandanayaka was looking for some additional help and wished to recruit Shaunaka and Ashwini into the forces for a short period of time. They may also be required to go on a trip away from Nandivardhana for a period.

"We could always tell people that we have sent them away to one of the *agraharas* so that they are away from all this noise," concluded Vishnuveera, aware of the adverse reactions that would soon be hurled at him.

The reactions were varied. Charukeshi, who was known to speak first and think later, quipped, "Aho Bhraata, this sounds absurd to me. They are goldsmiths. How can they help in the forces? Why would they even pick on these boys?"

Ahalya Devi, who had been observing her son closely, quietly said: "I understand, you may not wish to tell us the entire conversation. Are the boys in trouble? Do we need to send them away?"

"No, Matashri, they are not in any kind of trouble, from what I can make out. I am telling you what I understood. They are being recruited into the forces – for what and where – I was not informed. I was asked to permit them to proceed on those duties."

"Bhraata, what did you say? Bhagini, why are you so quiet?"

Gautami, known for picking the right time to raise topics, was keeping quiet. She was in the throes of too many conflicting emotions. "Aryasuta, are they telling you this because they have their suspicion pinned on my sons and want to keep an eye on them? Well, whatever it is, if the Mahadandanayaka and the Dandaposika were here, requesting your permission, I suppose you must grant it."

"Yes, Gautami, I do not have much of a choice. It may just be an opportunity for Shaunaka – his mind was not in the gold work. But Ashwini, he is such a talented and skilled gold worker. Moreover, he is a simple boy, not like Shaunaka, restless and pensive.

"Anyhow, if that's what the Queen wishes, so be it. I will meet Yakshavatsa later in the evening and indicate my assent. We will tell the boys once they are back. To keep them away from prying eyes and the incessant stream of nosy guests, Shaunaka and Ashwini had been sent out to the market area to run errands – errands that would keep them out for a major part of the day."

CHAPTER 6

This was how lives changed in a matter of a day. One man had his life snatched from him and two men got brand new lives!

As the seasons changed and by the time Ashvin, the propitious month of festivals and celebrations had commenced, Shaunaka was now firmly employed with the police force under Arya Bharavi, the feared and respected Dandaposika of Nandivardhana and Ashwini found himself an actor with a theatre troupe that was busy preparing for a grand performance to be staged as part of the royal wedding! But we will delve into this later.

The goings-on at the corner house had lost their place as the most discussed topic over the past month. Several other happenings, all centred around the Buddhist quarter and the neighbouring districts that housed most of the guilds, had gained prominence. A spate of robberies at the Buddhist monastery next to the corner house and then a violent robbery attempt at the Sreshthi's residence, which unfortunately led to the demise of a servant, who valiantly put up a struggle and foiled it in the process ensured that the murder of Vinayashura soon faded into the background and speculation was now at its peak. Had their peaceful town of Nandivardhana come under siege – from a group of armed robbers, bandits, who had stepped into the city limits and expanded their territorial boundaries? Or was there an ulterior motive to these robberies? Who were these robbers? Was it the dreaded Angulimala and his gang?

Be it the markets, or the taverns or even the palace premises, these incidents had taken precedence over Vinayashura's murder. In fact, this unknown, unnamed gang was being credited with that heinous act!

The police force had been kept on its toes. For Arya Bharavi and his men, the neighbourhood, the Buddhist quarter and the guilds quarter, had become like a second home. With each passing incident, real or imagined, they had received frantic summons to show up and start their investigations, which unfortunately was proceeding nowhere. No inroads had been made towards either unmasking the identity of these armed robbers or even the murderer of the now-forgotten Vinayashura. The Mahadandanayaka and the Dandaposika were now under constant pressure, from the Queen and the populace. And for the men working under them, these were equally trying times.

More men had been deployed in the Buddhist quarter — for a period up until the upcoming royal wedding in the month of Kartik — to deal with the public outcry and calm the frightened populace. Lined with massive, fully-grown *vatavriksha* trees, the long road in the Buddhist quarter was a haven for travellers during the day and summer months. However, in the absence of the rows of lamps lit outside the big houses or the monasteries or illumination of any kind, the road acquired an eerie, haunted feel, worsened due to the constant hooting of owls, during evenings and nights. An old man who had been employed by the late Vinayashura for security would go on his beat through the night — his cry, often the only reassuring voice for those awake.

After the murder in the corner house, Arya Bharavi had posted three men to watch over the street at night, but what was confounding was the fact that a couple of the robberies took place at midday.

One of the men who had been assigned to watch over the Buddhist quarter at night was Shaunaka, for whom this was an initiation into the police, albeit under such trying times. Relieved to be freed from the drudgery of the gold and metal work, Shaunaka put his heart and soul into his assignment – which was definitely more suited to his keen, observant nature. From night to dawn, he waited behind a banyan tree, keeping an eye for any suspicious activity – be it on the street or the houses. Then he would go back home, rest for a while and shortly before dusk, he would go and report what he had seen and observed to his superior in the administrative office complex of the town.

And so it had been.

The beautiful city of Nandivardhana, decorated for the many forthcoming celebrations, was gleaming in the twilight hour when the sky was lit up in hues of pink and orange. The Deepavali festival, symbolising the slaying of Narakasura by Lord Krishna and the subsequent *pooja* of Goddess Lakshmi, celebrated with much fervour and piety was just round the corner. A frenzy of activity had gripped the city of Nandivardhana; the goldsmith's quarter had gotten busier. Vishnuveera's workshop, in particular, was teeming with activity – a royal wedding in tow and fresh orders for the festival, while being four hands less, meant more work days and nights. Moreover, to their surprise, a messenger from the corner house had arrived, informing Vishnuveera that the order placed by the late Vinayashura was still binding. The wedding at their place had merely seen a postponement and not a cancellation, so would the kind goldsmith continue preparing the jewels! Not a happy news to receive when one is four hands short, but since every order was seen by Vishnuveera as a blessing of the Goddess, it was welcomed and worked upon!

Shaunaka did his bit by completing the *ratnanguliya* he had been crafting and offered his help when he could, for which Vishnuveera was both grateful and pleased. While Vishnuveera was aware that Shaunaka had been assigned a watch, he did not know the exact location, and hence, was making plans to visit the corner house in the next few days to hand over some of the crafted jewels for inspection and approval. As Shaunaka sat in the workshop, putting some final touches, and fixing the rubies and emeralds in place, he overheard Vishnuveera speak with Somnath.

"Do you think we will be able to deliver at least some of these to Arya Vinayashura's house by tomorrow?"

"Oh yes, Arya, definitely. Are you planning to go over there?

"Probably, on my way to the palace or maybe later in the afternoon," replied Vishnuveera.

"Pitashri, if you will permit, I could go on the way to the administrative block later this afternoon and hand these over," interjected Shaunaka. He had been looking for an opportunity to re-enter the corner house. A couple of foreign-looking traders had been seen lurking around the house the past few days and he had been asked to keep an eye on them. What better than this opportunity to enter the house and gather information.

Both Vishnuveera and Somnath looked surprised; as did the majority of the workers seated in the working hall. Knowing the sensitive nature of Shaunaka's assignment, Vishnuveera said nothing but agreed to him bringing the jewels to the corner house. As a consequence, Shaunaka set forth from his home, earlier than usual. The ready jewels, a couple of small pieces, rings and earrings had been kept in a small *potalaka*, which had been firmly tied to his *uttariya* and hidden by his long *kancuka*.

More than a month after the catastrophic incident, the corner house had changed. The elaborate cremation and Shraddha rites had been completed; the visitors who had come to celebrate a wedding but had to attend a cremation, had left. The corner house was bereft and standing all alone, making the absence of its lord and master, however obnoxious, extremely conspicuous. The sense of desolation that the house now conveyed hit Shaunaka as he stood in front of the imposing gate — composing and preparing a story in his head. He needed to look and sound plausible to gain the confidence of the women. As he opened the gate, and started walking towards the house, Suvarna spotted him. It took her a while to recognise him. "*Swagatam*! Ah you are the goldsmith's son? Please come this way." Leading him to the same annexe, the one next to the granary and store room, she requested him to wait till her mistress was free to receive him. Saying this, she left him to his own devices. Mildly disappointed at his own inability to engage anyone in small conversation, he started looking out of the window. The window looked out on to the passage to the right of the main house. A line of trees lined the passage on the opposite side, behind which lay a couple of other annexes, slightly hidden, probably used as additional store rooms or rooms for the staff.

The Kartik afternoon sun was beginning to dim and the sky was lit with the hues of pink and orange. A mild wind was blowing towards the east. Shaunaka was admiring the estate, especially the thoughtful way in which it had all been laid out. The imperious façade of the main house and its intricate architecture had him completely captivated. Just then, he thought he saw some sudden movement in the far-end corner of the passage from the corner of his eye.

Dismissing it as rustling of leaves in the wind, he continued to admire the impressive house, but found it difficult to concentrate. There was a niggling sense of him missing something. Taking liberties with the mistress's hospitality, he decided to walk down the passage. As he casually strolled towards the far end, there was a sudden movement behind the trees. A young man, of average height and build, dressed in a shiny red *antariya*, with a blue silk shawl covering his upper body was hurriedly coming out of the corner-most annexe. Upon seeing Shaunaka at a distance, he started running towards the gate. Without thinking much and checking instinctively to see whether the jewels were in place, Shaunaka, whose suspicions were now fully roused, gave him a chase. Despite Shaunaka being in top form, when it came to agility and physical stamina, he found it difficult to catch up with the intruder who was running as if Lord Yama was following him! It looked like Shaunaka had almost caught up with him as he reached the gate of the Buddhist Vihara near the intersection of the Buddhist quarter, with the traditional merchant and tradesman's quarter. However, just at that moment, as luck would have it, the gate opened and a procession of young monks from the Buddhist Vihara set forth, bringing with it, hordes of people. Shaunaka's path was obstructed. In a bid to stop the intruder from running away, Shaunaka stretched his hand and managed to catch hold of the shawl and tug it. Using this opportunity of being surrounded by *bhikshus*, the intruder let go of the shawl and disappeared among the crowd. Dismayed and annoyed at having let the stranger escape, Shaunaka held on to the shawl and then checked whether his jewels were intact. They were! Thanking his stars and the Lord Vasudeva, he walked back to the corner house.

At the corner house, Devi Tanirika and Tarika were still recovering from the shock of seeing a stranger running out of the main gate, only to be followed by another relatively less-familiar person, the goldsmith's son! Only the little girl was nonplussed. They had chosen the moment to step out of the main house, to see their guest off, the Rajapurohita, when they were presented with such a sight!

"Suvarna, Hemvati, what is going on? Was that not the goldsmith's son? Who was the other man? Where is Siddheshwara?" For Suvarna, this was as much of a shock. "Aho, Devi, I don't know. What is all this? Yes, that is the goldsmith's son. I had left him in the annexe. Siddheshwara had gone to the market to bring some fresh produce of barley and rice."

Advising the women to consult the Dandaposika, the Rajapurohita then took his leave. The main courtyard was lined with a couple of benches. Perching themselves on one of these benches, as the little child played nearby, the mother and daughter decided to wait for Siddheshwara. A few minutes later, they saw him enter the gate in deep conversation with the goldsmith's son who was holding a *potalaka* in his hand. Siddheshwara went directly towards the store room to deposit the sacks on his back, while Shaunaka walked up to where the two women were sitting watching the child play.

"Pranam! I am not sure if you remember me. My name is Shaunaka, and I am Vishnuveera's son. My father bade me to deliver these jewels to you."

"Pranam, thank you for these jewels. But what was all that? Who was the man you were running after?" asked Devi Tanirika, much to his surprise.

Shaunaka recounted the entire incident with as much detail as he could remember and showed them the *uttariya* he had managed to latch on to.

"The corner-most annexe? Oh, that is where Madhav's things are kept. Hema, Bhagini, can you please go and check if everything is in its place?" said Tarika to her mother.

Devi Tanirika was examining the shawl with much interest. "This is expensive silk, you know. If this man was wearing this, he must surely be from a wealthy background. Arya Yashasvi, who was a friend of my late husband's, would know whether his guild has made this."

"Devi, I suppose we could always check with the Sresthin. With your permission, may I take this to my father, who is well-acquainted with Arya Yashasvi so that he may find out more?"

"Oh yes, please. That would be of much help," said Devi Tanirika, feeling grateful towards this man.

"Matashri, we should go inside. Arya, *dhanyavadah*. We will also inform the Dandaposika. I think we have taken up your time for too long," intervened Tarika, rather dismissively, irritated with this young man for his unnecessary interest in their matters, and asked him to leave. A primary reason for her irritation was also that it was a kind stranger helping out instead of her fiancé who should have taken care of matters. What made matters worse was that her normally effusive fiancé had cooled off the past two days and was being rather secretive.

Not that Shaunaka minded the dismissal. He wanted to leave as it was anyway time for him to take his place at the vantage point behind the big banyan tree in front of the house. The sun was about to set and darkness was to cast its blanket. So, he wanted to carefully examine the shawl, which he was happy to have in his possession. Eventually he would, of course, show it to both his father— so that he can check with the Sresthin— and to Arya Bharavi. But for now it was with him. He folded it and tucked it in his *kamarbandh* and pulled his *kanchuka* over it. Taking his place atop one of the lower branches, he took out the *uttariya* and inspected it. Made of a fine silk that was soft to touch, it had a woody smell, indicative of the perfume worn by its wearer – a typical *nagaraka* from the looks of it. As Shaunaka peered at it closely, he noticed a strange pattern and that too one that displayed no regularity. Small circles, squares, dots and other characters were strewn all over the place. While it did not strike him at that point in time, much later, during the night, a thought dawned upon him. What if the pattern were characters or alphabets from a script, one that he could not decipher? And if they were letters, what were they trying to convey? Who wore clothes with words splashed on them? Was that a fashion from where this piece of garment came? Or had it become a fashion here— to wear *uttariyas* and *antariyas* with strange characters?

As thoughts, such as these flashed through his mind, he decided to go to the administrative quarters first thing the next morning and show this garment to the Dandaposika. Just then, some commotion at the gate of the Buddhist Vihara next to the corner house, diverted his attention for a while. A drunk man, bereaved lately, was standing at the gate, crying and shouting. A couple of monks, barely out of their teens, clad in their garnet-red robes, came out of the Vihara and handled the man expertly, offering him solace and consolation and finally calming him down. As Shaunaka marvelled at the monks, their handling of the situation and the serenity and composure they displayed despite their young age, he saw a rather distressed and agitated looking Madhavasena opening the gate of the corner house quietly. The manner in which he did so, carefully, without making a single sound, and the furtive way in which he looked to his right and left alerted Shaunaka. He climbed up three branches and positioned himself such that he could get a view inside the courtyard. To his surprise, instead of going to the main house, Madhavasena walked through the courtyard and turned right into the passage that led to the annexes. Of course, it would be to check whether his possessions were intact, thought Shaunaka but what did not make sense was the stealthy manner in which he was doing that. Strange! After what seemed like quite a while, Madhavasena reappeared, looking somewhat relieved. His prized possessions were probably intact, thought Shaunaka as he saw Madhavasena enter the main house, where he did not stay for long. After having paid his respects to his fiancé and his mother-in-law to-be, Madhavasena left the house and started walking, with a relaxed gait, in the direction of the residential quarters of the city, where his luxurious abode was said to be located. And then it was all quiet in the corner house.

The rest of the night passed without any incident at all. Shimmering with gold and orange, the Nandivardhana sky at dawn brought in another beautiful morning in the cool month of Kartik. The seasons were definitely changing and signs of the change were visible as reflected in *prakriti* (nature). As he walked towards the administrative offices to give a report immediately to his superior, Shaunaka got to soak in the sights, smells and sounds of the city that morning. The chants from the line of the Buddhist viharas on the street, the chiming bells from the nearby Vishnu temple combined with the constant chirruping of the birds perched on the trees greeted him as he made his way to the centre of the town. On the way, he passed the taverns, which were now shooing away the last of the drunk revellers and merrymakers from them. More than seven or eight such gaming and drinking establishments existed on this road, and Shaunaka wondered how all of these remained profitable. Clearly, they were doing brisk business going by the number of drunk men being shooed away at dawn!

Shaunaka was witness to one such ignominious shooing away of a group of six to seven howling, drunk men, mainly actors and acrobats, looking at the way they were dressed. As they staggered out, holding each other for support, cursing the owner of the tavern, Shaunaka's attention was drawn to two of them in particular. A stout man dressed up supposedly as a King or some person of royal lineage, albeit in a farcical manner, was supporting a taller man, dressed in an equally ludicrous costume as they stumbled out. The taller man was clearly of foreign origin – there was nothing that cried local about him. But what about the stout, short man? Using an *uttariya* that looked more flimsy than royal, this man had covered his head and most of his face. Who was he and why was he so familiar, thought Shaunaka, as he walked towards the group to take a close look! To his utter astonishment, the short man looked up and shot him a piercing glance – as if to warn him not to go any closer. A look that went unobserved by the rest of the men around them, who were completely sozzled and unable to register where they were headed.

The look did it. Shaunaka recognised the man – it was Ashwini. Taking Ashwini's cue, Shaunaka nodded and started walking, slower than before. The tiredness of the previous day had begun to settle in his bones and Nidradevi (Goddess of Sleep) seemed to be beckoning him into her sweet lap. A quandary arose in his mind — should he go home first or head towards the administrative quarters of Nandivardhana, where he hoped to seek an audience with Arya Bharavi? Noting the shawl and its script as being important, Shaunaka decided in favour of the latter and set about resolutely.

On his way to the administrative block, Shaunaka passed by the residential quarter of the city that was now slowly coming to life. It was a part of the city he was very familiar with. Most of the educational establishments were located here. In fact, the tall building on the side road next to the large public hospital was where his *Acharya,* the revered Swamideva lived these days. At the cross-section of two main roads, one of which led directly to the administrative quarter, right behind the palace estate, Shaunaka felt slightly uneasy. It was a feeling of being observed and watched. He looked around to see whether he was being followed but could not spot anyone. He was now next to an ornate building with large, decorated, airy windows — a much-visited haunt for most young men his age. This was the magnificent Chitrashala, a palatial picture gallery owned by the renowned courtesan, Vasantasena, said to be the mistress of the chief of the royal armoury and prisons, and a favourite of the nobles and young men.

Alert and taut at the possibility of being followed or spied upon, Shaunaka looked around him and increased the pace of his footsteps. Call it sixth sense or a very keen ear, a whirring sound from somewhere nearby forewarned him. He was about to start running when a middle-aged man, whose face and upper body were covered with a black shawl, emerged from nowhere and pulled him down, and in time too. A knife from the opposite side of the road missed Shaunaka by a whisker, scraping the door of the Chitrashala instead. Numbed by at this sudden, unexpected assault, Shaunaka looked up to spot the wielder of the knife — a tall, hefty acrobat who had started running after missing his aim.

"Get up now. You are fine," urged the middle-aged man, his saviour, who was now standing and looking down at him rather amusedly. Shaunaka pulled himself up and thanked him profusely.

"Don't thank me, Shaunaka. Remember rule no. 1—Keep your eyes and ears open. While you did sense someone was following you and while you did get alerted to the attack, you would still have been hit, had I not saved you," said the stranger as Shaunaka stared at him in wonder. How on earth did this man know his name?

"Who are you?"

"Doesn't matter who I am. Now, let's hurry along. You are on your way to seek an audience with the Dandaposika, I presume. I need to meet him too."

Dismissing all possibility of any kind of small talk or conversation, saying thus, the middle-aged man started walking at a pace that a younger and supposedly agile Shaunaka found hard to keep up with. As the man walked in front of him, Shaunaka observed him closely, memorising the physical and other traits he could gather. Of average height, thin and slight in build, the man seemed to be in his late 30s or early 40s. What could not be missed was his darkish complexion, bordering on swarthy, curly, messy hair atop his head and those eyes — sharp and alert taking in every detail they saw. He was indeed impressive, in an understated way.

The administrative headquarters of Nandivardhana was a prestigious complex that comprised a series of buildings housing the offices of the commissioner, royal scribe, and royal treasurer among others. No matter what time in the day, the complex was always heavily guarded and entry into it was usually a cumbersome process. Therefore, it was to Shaunaka's wonderment that the guards recognised his companion and let him in also without any extensive interrogation upon the middle-aged man's word.

Shaunaka had not been sure whether he would get an audience with the Dandaposika and had been mentally prepared for a long wait outside his office. However, wonders were never to cease. His present companion wielded that much influence and power that a mere sight of his walking towards the Dandaposika's chamber and office had people scurrying to their feet and welcoming him (and Shaunaka because he seemed to be with him). They were led directly into the sparse room that passed off as the Dandaposika's workplace.

Upon seeing them enter, the Dandaposika, who was seated till then on a comfortable *diwan*, stood up and greeted them.

"*Swagatam*, *Mahakavi*! Arya, Shaunaka, *pranam*! Please be seated."

"*Pranam*, Arya. While on my way here to meet you, I met with your young man under some interesting circumstances," Kalidasa said, proceeding to take a seat on a plush, low *diwan*, next to where Bharavi was sitting.

Mahakavi? Shaunaka couldn't believe his ears. Who had not heard of *Mahakavi* Kalidasa, one of the nine gems of the court of the great King of Pataliputra, their beloved Queen's father, and perhaps the greatest playwright and poet of their times! Shaunaka had heard that Kalidasa, who was also tutor to the princes, was in town; but who would have thought he would be scouring the streets of the town, early in the morning, and saving men half his age! It simply did not make any sense.

"Now, Shaunaka, stop standing and staring with your mouth wide open. You are here to see me for a reason? Did you witness any suspicious activity during your watch last night?" boomed the voice of Arya Bharavi, waking Shaunaka out of his reverie.

"*Pranam*, Arya. *Pranam*, *Mahakavi*. My sincere apologies at not having recognised you," said Shaunaka, as Kalidasa just shook his head with a smile.

Addressing the Dandaposika, Shaunaka detailed his experiences from the previous day, trying to capture everything that had occurred, after which he handed over the *uttariya* that he had tucked under his tunic. Both Bharavi and Kalidasa listened to Shaunaka's story attentively and as they examined the *uttariya* silently, they looked at each other, engaged in a silent conversation of which Shaunaka was not a part. After what seemed an eternity, Kalidasa spoke, once Bharavi nodded, as if in assent. "Well done, Shaunaka. This is an important find. We will keep it with us."

"Arya, umm, actually I had promised Devi Tanirika that I would request my father for his assistance and get this piece of cloth examined by the Sresthin. Should I then inform her that you now have this in your possession," asked Shaunaka, hesitant and unsure, as he looked at both the older men in front of him.

Kalidasa looked at him and asked, "Do you know these people very well? This dead man, Vinayashura, his wife and daughter?"

To this question, Shaunaka replied in the negative that he did not know them at all. The first time he met them was on the day of Vinayashura's murder.

"Can you come up with any reason as to why you can get to know them better? Prolong some discussion, talk to both the wife, daughter and maybe even that son-in-law to be?"

Shaunaka thought hard at this question and then said that since his father and his workmen were still working on the jewels that Devi Tanirika had wanted made, he could definitely sneak in and try making some conversation about that. But besides this excuse, he couldn't think of any way of furthering this acquaintance.

Hearing this, Kalidasa picked up the *uttariya* and quickly tore him a small piece. "This should be enough for your father to hand over to the Sresthin."

Shaunaka tucked this small piece of cloth into his *kamarbandh* and assured the two men that he would use any opportunity to know more about the inhabitants of the corner house. Saying which, Shaunaka took his leave and left for home as the older men indicated that they wished to be left alone.

Over the past month that the two older men had started working together, they had developed a healthy respect for each other. It took Bharavi a while to digest that the man celebrated and renowned for his creative genius was much more than just that. As he spent time with the great poet/ playwright, he was exposed to other aspects of this multi-talented genius. What was of great surprise was the many roles that he played for his dear King – on and off stage. Citizens of Nandivardhana, for whom the *Mahakavi* was a famous name from another kingdom, had heard that he was wont to taking off from the court for periods to express his creative outpourings as a poem or a play. But now it seemed to be more of a perception and image that had been specially cultivated. He was in reality a spy, who put to much use his expert skills of observation, astute perception, and disguise for the sake of statecraft.

This prolonged stay in Nandivardhana was one such trip. People had heard that the *Mahakavi* had accompanied Queen Prabhavati to their town to help make arrangements for the wedding of his beloved student, Divakara. However, barring a few officials, not many knew that this was a ruse and the real reason he was there was to unearth a devious plot that was being apparently hatched by the enemies of King Chandragupta. Since the exact details of what was being planned had not been deciphered, the King had dispatched Kalidasa to stay in Nandivardhana and figure out what was going on.

And what the *Mahakavi* had figured out so far was alarming. Under the thin veneer of peace and stability that existed, there definitely was some unrest being stirred. The intelligence received was spot on. Rudrasimha's people could not stomach the thorough defeat at the hands of the great Chandragupta. What they could not achieve through fair means, the cowards seem to be marching towards, through deceit and underhand tactics. Ujjayin, which was now the great King's capital, had once been theirs; they would dare not enter there. Hence, they were trying through Nandivardhana. Something big was being planned and probably in the very near future. It was to figure this out and get some more information that Kalidasa had requested Bharavi for more men, among whom Ashwini was one. Their tasks were well defined. Play a particular character, an actor (in the case of Ashwini) and pass on a daily report on what has transpired. In addition to this band of men, Kalidasa himself (in some form of disguise) spent a lot of time on the streets through the day. A major plot was definitely in the offing.

Arya Bharavi, on his part, was grappling with the same sense of foreboding — something evil was definitely about to occur. Unable to pin-point what it exactly was, he did what he knew best. Handpicked young, eligible men and posted them at watches across the city so that they could report any untoward behaviour. Together, by joining their forces, the two older men realised they may be able to stop whatever was happening. And for this purpose, they had been meeting every morning, just after dawn.

"Arya, did you take a closer look at this *uttariya*? The boy was right. There is a pattern here. Look. These are certainly some kind of letters and characters," pointed Kalidasa to Bharavi as he peered at the *uttariya* closely.

Touching the cloth, Bharavi looked at it and said "Hmm, this silk is an expensive one – one brought here by those traders. Do you know what this pattern could mean?"

"I have a few ideas. If you permit, I will take this with me to show it to Upendra, a dear friend of mine."

"Aho, that is fine. While there may be a pattern, I wonder if this cloth has any significance. From Shaunaka's account, it seems that the intruder was happy to let go of this while trying to escape," commented Bharavi as he leaned on the *diwan*.

"Umm, maybe, maybe not. I would not dismiss this off-hand right away. He may have thought that it is better to get rid of this rather than get caught," said Kalidasa pondering a bit more on the cloth.

Another quarter of an hour was spent discussing the overall situation in the city and passing on any information that may be relevant.

"Those two men — the ones we have not been able to locate — they worry me, Arya," said Bharavi thoughtfully.

"No news from Pataliputra, either, is it not? Did they never set out for Pataliputra as they had been claiming they would?"

"How did you get that bit of information? My sources heard exactly the opposite. That they would resume the journey back home."

"Ah, I had followed them for a few days – but this was before Vinaya was killed. I heard them boasting about a high-value order they seemed to have bagged which would require them to travel to Pataliputra."

A couple of traders, Yavana or Romaka by origin in all probability, had arrived from Kalyan a week before the murder of Vinayashura. They had been spotted in some taverns near the palace quarters where they had informed people about their next halt — Pataliputra. However, spies of both Kalidasa and Bharavi were unable to trace any evidences of them having travelled to the great city or obtain any information about them on route to the city. This disappearance then weighed heavily on their minds.

"Two men in their prime do not vanish into thin air just like that. Either they are victims of some kind of foul play or they are committing or have committed a foul act!" said Bharavi assertively, to which Kalidasa nodded and added, "Or maybe they have gone into hiding. I do not trust these Yavanas – Lord Vasudeva knows. They are as much our enemies as the Kshatrapas."

A gong went off in the distance. The *nadika* in the city centre had been struck to indicate the passing of another hour.

"Ah, it is time. I need to take your leave, Arya. The Queen has summoned me just before the *Abhijit muhurtha* this day."

"As you wish, Arya. I hope all is well at the Palace. The reports I have received from my sources are slightly worrying."

"Umm, it is worrisome, to say the least. I pray daily and hope that the situation gets better. May the Ascetic-Lord, the all-knowing one with the three eyes, dispel the darkness hovering over our heads," said Kalidasa plaintively as he rose from the *divan*, indicating that the meeting was over.

Chapter 7

An air of festivity had enveloped the entire city of Nandivardhana. The wedding of their Yuvaraja, Divakarasena, to Princess Avantika of Kamboja would be the first happy occasion in their kingdom in a long time — the first since the death of King Rudrasena, more than a decade back. Prince Divakara was then a wee child of 5; and now, in his 18th year, had become a young, strapping lad gearing up to meet with his destiny as the King.

With the wedding now hardly a week away, the gateways to Nandivardhana and the palace had been adorned with a variety of flowers and garlands.

The preparations at the palace had commenced in full force. Not just the palace premises, the entire city was being decorated. *Bandhanwars* had been put up in front of the houses, temples and other state buildings. Sweepers and other cleaners were scrubbing the entire city in anticipation. The police force (both the formal and informal network) was more active and the overall surveillance in the city had gone up.

Inside the palace premises, there was a hustle-bustle matched only by the commotion that a consecration of a new King would accompany. The public area of the palace premises was bustling with people. *Malakara*s were putting up massive floral arches and decorating the numerous halls, pathways and gardens with flower patterns. The royal granaries were being checked and stock was taken as mounds of grains, pulses, milk and ghee were readied, and offerings to the people, guests and priests were piled up.

The private sections of the palace were no less busy. In the section reserved for the treasury, jewellers and the royal designers were busy getting the trousseau ready. Buyers and merchants were entering with their wares which were then valued and apprised by official valuers. In the inner sections, past the well-laid out gardens and the royal temple, near the entrance to the royal quarters, Agniswamin, the revered Kulaputra was in deep conversation with the royal architects, discussing the construction of a special pavilion, wherein the Vedic marriage rites would take place. Piles of sandalwood and other wood to be used for the sacrificial fire were being lined up next to the pavilion.

Courtiers and officials were moving around busily, an important air enveloping their heated discussions — with each one assigned a task that needed to be completed before the date. Spies and informers were also watching the place like hawks ready to swoop down on any suspicious and unwanted element. It is strange then that a young man of nondescript appearance, completely covered in a plain shawl, escaped their notice. He stood stealthily, behind a pillar near one of the halls, where the Queen held her councils, observing the hullaballoo around him. As he cautiously walked past the halls and gardens, it looked like he was making his way out of the private sections into the more public arena. At the massive gates that separated the two portions of the palace, the fierce-looking porter — a huge, towering man named Harsha — stopped this young man, bidding him to uncover his face. Signalling Harsha to be quiet, the young man produced a royal insignia and showed it to him. Harsha, now bereft of his fierceness, was stunned into silence. Here was the man of the moment, the Prince, the Yuvaraja, wishing to go out without any security. Bowing quietly, Harsha excused himself and told the Prince that he could not possibly let him go. However, the Prince had made up his mind. It was an order, and besides, he was not going to leave the palace unaccompanied. And thus it was that Prince Divakara sneaked out of the inner palace!

What was he up to and why? It so happened that an afternoon, not so long back, as Divakara was in his palatial quarters, painting a scene from a play he had seen before, he overheard an interesting conversation. The voices were coming from outside the window. Two maids, enjoying an afternoon's rest, were discussing a new group of actors — a theatre troupe that had come from somewhere up in the north, maybe Kasi or Kosala. Hearing the maids describe the acting and oratory of these actors, Divakara had an urge to see them perform. It was not widely known, in fact it had been suppressed, that during his growing years, acting had been a passion for the young prince. Growing up under the tutelage of the great poet and dramatist, Kalidasa, meant that both Divakara and Damodara had been exposed to many plays — of contemporary and ancient renown. Both the boys had been enamoured. If Divakara wanted to act, Damodara wished to write plays! The Queen did not mind this interest nor did she actively discourage it till the time the 15-year-old Divakara wished to become an actor and an acrobat. Of course, a youthful indiscretion with a girl of dubious repute was partly responsible for this sudden ambition. The Queen intervened and put an end to both his indiscretion and his dreams of becoming an actor. Now, three years later, while the indiscretion had largely been forgotten, the embers of buried ambition still lingered. Upon hearing this conversation one afternoon, the prince, who had been feeling more and more like a caged bird, wanted to break free. Just for an afternoon. Just to see the actors rehearse.

This was how Divakara sneaked out of the inner palace courtyards and managed to sneak into the main public section. Once out, he made his way towards the Chitrashala. Actors, acrobats and other performing artists usually had their rehearsals in one of the big, empty, decorated halls, which were located near the Chitrashala. The actual performance would take place either near the specially-erected royal pavilion, closer to the main gate, or in front of the large public halls, where the Queen and the Prince would go out to greet the public.

As he walked on, appreciating the mammoth efforts that were in progress for the wedding, a niggling pain that he had been trying to dismiss emerged once again in the pit of his stomach. Divakara had dismissed these pains as symptoms of the usual nerves and anxiety before such a life- changing event. He realised that he was soon to abandon his boyhood and take on responsibilities as the King and a husband. Aches and pains resulting from nerves were probably common. Aware that this was his one afternoon of freedom, he hobbled on towards the main hall where these actors were said to be practising. There they were. A group of actors and several acrobats stood and sat in the main hall, opposite the Chitrashala. A group of onlookers, mainly citizens who had wandered into the palace estate out of sheer curiosity, had assembled in front of the hall. Divakara found it easy to remain incognito in this crowd to watch the rehearsal. The pain, which he had been ignoring had assumed gigantic proportions and he looked around to see if he could rest anywhere without drawing any attention to himself. Next to the hall was a huge banyan tree under which several onlookers were either standing or sitting. Divakara walked slowly up to the tree and leaned against it.

The actors were rehearsing Malavikagnimitra, one of the *Mahakavi's* most celebrated compositions, a favourite of both the actors and the audiences. Just like the onlookers, Divakara was also familiar with it and he could immediately identify the scene that was being rehearsed. As the rehearsal progressed, amidst cat calls and hoots and many goof-ups, Divakara felt his pain take a turn for the worse and felt faint. As he leaned further against the tree, clutching a branch tightly, a tall, young man standing next to him asked him if he needed any assistance. "Yes, please, help me towards the inner courts," Divakara somehow managed to whisper as he clutched the branch harder. The young man quietly shifted the weight of the ailing prince on to his able shoulders and then said, "Arya, please try and walk. I will take you to the inner courts." "Please do not attract any attention," whispered Divakara, now for the first time, ruing the foolhardy idea of stepping out without any protection.

Slowly, the young man led Divakara towards the interiors of the palace, through the laid-out royal gardens. Unfortunately, it seemed that their movements were being observed and they were being followed. The young man may not have known that he was helping the Yuvaraja. However, a couple of spies had identified the Prince and had been keeping an eye on him. Just when they reached the main gate of the private section, the interiors, the Prince doubled up in pain and collapsed. Upon recognising the Prince, the porter, now terrified at the role he played, and several other officials who were hovering about, alerted the Vaidya. They lifted the prince and took him to his quarters. The young man, however, found himself in dire straits. The spies apprehended him and pinned him down to the ground as they waited for the royal guards to appear.

"Help! What have I done?"

"Shut up. You tried to kill Yuvaraja Divakara!"

"Yuvaraja? That was him? I only helped him— he seemed to be in pain."

"Shut up. Save your excuses for the courts, you scoundrel. Guards! Take this rascal away. He tried to kill the king."

"Call the Mahadandanayaka or Arya Bharavi. I have done nothing wrong."

As he protested his innocence rather loudly, the guards pulled him away. At that moment, the *Mahakavi* and some other officials from one of the council halls nearby came to the gate.

"Guards, stop! Leave him. Shaunaka? What is all this?"

"Arya, pranam! These *dutakas* here are mistakenly accusing me of trying to kill the Yuvaraja. I did not even know he was the Prince." Shaunaka explained his side of the story. Satisfied with the answer, Kalidasa ordered the *dutakas* and the guards to leave and summoned Shaunaka to meet him in his chamber. A tired Shaunaka, obviously affected by the recent turn of events, grumpily followed him inside the gate, walking silently behind him. Dazzled by the magnificence around him, Shaunaka noted the towering balustrades of the various council and meeting rooms. As they walked past the bustling, massive treasury section, where scores of artisans, designers and craftsmen were working on the wedding finery and jewel merchants were having their precious stones valued, it struck Shaunaka that his absence since the previous afternoon would soon be conspicuous. Feeling guilty at having disappeared like this, he walked a bit faster, keeping pace with Kalidasa. Walking past the ornate gardens lined with shady trees, colourful flowering plants and the temple for Lord Vishnu, towards the palaces of the Queen and the Princes, they finally reached the administrative block, which housed the working chambers of the royal officials such as the Kulaputra, the Rajapurohit and the Rajavaidya (Royal healer).

"Shaunaka, now spill — what are you doing here?"

"Arya, when I took your leave at Arya Bharavi's chambers, I was headed home. I got out of the administrative block and was walking past the markets in the city centre, wherein the action for the day had begun. The traders from Nandivardhana and elsewhere — tailors, weavers, clothes merchants, garland makers, vegetable and fruit sellers, bangle sellers — had all set up their line of stalls and were exhibiting their crafts and wares, energetically calling out to each and every passer-by. It was in one of the stalls where two foreign traders, probably Romakas, were selling fine garments of expensive silk that I noticed something strange. A woman carrying a child on her hip was arguing with one of the traders. Probably haggling over the cost of one of the shawls is what I thought at first. And then I noticed that she was pointing to a shawl in one of the men's hand and yelling about that. The two men were shaking their heads and trying to reason with her. It did not make sense to me. Why would a woman insist on just that one piece of fine silk when there were so many more attractive, colourful ones on display? To understand what the fuss was all about, I went to the stall and pretended to look around. The woman with the child left, irritated and angry, after a futile attempt to buy the same piece. As the man attempted to fold and pack it away, I managed to get a closer look at the shawl. An exquisite red piece of expensive silk, it glittered in the morning light – or so it seemed to my novice eyes. It was just when he was about to put it away that I noticed the dull pattern etched on the cloth. It was the exact same pattern as the one on the *uttariya* I had handed over to you. To my surprise, when I politely asked to see the beautiful cloth, the younger man of the two rudely asked me to leave. "It is not for sale. Don't you people understand this? Just leave now."

Not wishing to create any scene, I left that particular stall and stood in front of another one, pretending to be interested in the other items that were on sale. The Romakas had calmed down once they saw me leave without any protest and had again assumed the role of sellers, enthusiastically peddling their goods. Some time passed and just when I was about to leave the market, a young neat looking man, clad in an ostentatious attire – a rich regal *kanchuka*, a crisp *antariya* and an elaborate headgear, with a bottle of perfumed wine in his hand came to the stall. The two men at the stall started their sales pitch, showing him their fine silks, muslins and expensive clothes. Dismissing these efforts, the young man took out a note from his *kamarbandh* and handed it over to them. Upon reading it, the two men quietly picked up the bag (in which they had tucked the piece of red silk with that confounding pattern) and gave it to him for free. It was definitely not a transaction as the young man mouthed a thank-you and left. It was when he turned in my direction that I recognised him. He was the intruder at the corner house. I followed him and to my surprise, he entered the palace estate. I managed to keep track of him up until the hall where the rehearsal was on. Unaware that he was being followed, he seemed comfortable standing among the onlookers. It was to keep an eye on him that I went and stood behind the banyan tree, which is where I found the prince in pain. Krishna knows that I had no clue that this was our dear Yuvaraja and my only intention was to help and save a fellow human being. I do hope and pray you believe me."

Listening to this long account, Kalidasa shook his head, "I believe you, Shaunaka. I do. Things seem graver than what I had imagined."

"Do you know who this man is?"

"No, but what do you think of him?"

"Arya, he seems of a noble origin, a *nagaraka*, an affluent young man who is well-versed in the fine art of *shringara*. I am also convinced that the pattern on this *uttariya* and the other one has more meaning. It is not a pattern. Perhaps it is some sort of a code," said Shaunaka thoughtfully, as he took out that small piece of the first *uttariya* he had managed to confiscate earlier that morning.

Kalidasa merely nodded, without lending any credence or acceptance to Shaunaka's theory. "You should leave now. Go home. I am sure your family would be wondering where you are."

Just then, two guards entered and informed the men that the Prince had summoned Shaunaka to his palace. Shaunaka took leave of Kalidasa and followed the guards into Prince Divakara's palace. As he entered the palace, he found himself in a large veranda appointed with plush *diwans* and seating spaces. A *kumbha* filled with water and several glasses were kept in a corner. Bright curtains made of rich silk hung on the windows and also in front of the door that acted as a partition to the inner chambers of the palace. This was where Shaunaka was asked to wait for the prince, who appeared in a while.

"May the God Vishnu protect you from all harm and bless you with good health always, Yuvaraja. I am sorry if I showed you any disrespect when we met. My sincere apologies for failing to recognise you."

Weakened after bearing much pain, Prince Divakara said with a faint smile, "I should be the one thanking you. Had it not been for you, I would have collapsed in front of the tree itself. What is your name?"

"Arya, I am Shaunaka, the son of Arya Vishnuveera, the goldsmith and jeweller."

"Ah, I have heard of your father. He is making the jewellery for my wedding, is he not? I would like to thank you once again and here, take this. This is a token of my appreciation," said Divakara handing him a pouch filled with gold coins and some jewels.

"Thank you, Yuvaraja. May I now take your leave?" asked Shaunaka.

It was with a sense of worry that he left the Prince's quarters and instead of going straight back home, he took the liberty of walking into Kalidasa's chambers without any prior permission.

"Apologies, Arya, for disturbing you. May I have a word with you?"

"You are back, Shaunaka? What is it now? Sighted your favourite intruder again?"

"No, Arya. I had just been to meet the Prince who thanked me for my help and gave this to me in return. The sight of the Prince was even more disturbing. He looks so ill and pale; almost fragile. What is wrong with him?"

"Hmm, the Prince indeed has not been well. The Rajavaidya has not yet been able to diagnose the cause. His *nadi* seems to be fine most of the time and the *marmasthanas* also show no particular disease. This is indeed a matter of major worry because the wedding is hardly a week away and dignitaries from other kingdoms are expected to start arriving soon. Yes, Shaunaka, we do have a problem at hand – unfortunately one that can be solved only by the blessings of the gods and *pitrus!* Do pray for the Prince and for Nandivardhana," said Kalidasa pensively, indicating that he wished to be left alone.

Vishnuveera was a worried man. It was past afternoon and there was no sign of his elder son. Moreover, efforts to track down his younger son, Ashwini, who was now an actor with a roaming troupe of artists (of all the career choices) had proved to be vastly unsuccessful. Shortly after noon, Ashwini, slightly inebriated walked into the house.

"This is appalling and totally unacceptable! Arya, I understand that we have given him permission to become a *dutaka* or whatever that is Arya Yakshavatsa has turned him into; but coming home at this hour and that too intoxicated, is not done," said an anguished Gautami to her husband, as he sat down for lunch in the kitchen. She was particularly incensed as she was fed up of the comments that were being passed by relatives and neighbours, about both her sons.

"Umm, yes, Gautami, but what say do we have in this matter? Ashwini has agreed to be a *dutaka*, while pretending to be a rebel son who has run away from home to become an actor. To play the role convincingly and fit in with the members of that particular *saartha* (caravan), I suppose he will need to look intoxicated," said Vishnuveera torn between his wife's anguish and understanding his son's point of view.

"Arya, I am trying to understand. I know my sons have not gone astray but then what do I tell all the ladies who come in to commiserate with us. I pray to Krishna all the time for our sons and for patience. And now where is Shaunaka?"

"Gautami, do not worry. Shaunaka will be back soon. Something must have come up. He is mature and sensible. Have faith in Lord Vasudeva. The next time, when the ladies show up, call me. I will handle them," said Ahalyabai, to her worried daughter-in-law.

Truth be told, the entire family was worried. Ashwini joined the family shortly in the kitchen.

"Pranam, pitamahe, pitashri, maathey, please forgive me. I came back to the house completely intoxicated. I will try that it does not happen again, but unfortunately, cannot commit to that," said Ashwini.

"Now, come and eat. Sit," admonished Gautami, her heart melting at the sight of her younger adopted son. She knew that her boys were good and rued the day when they stepped foot in the cursed corner house! All a consequence of that one day!

"Where is Shaunaka? Has he already eaten?" asked Ashwini, about to sit down to eat.

"We do not know. He is not back yet," replied a worried Vishnuveera.

"Should I go and look for him, Pitashri?"

As Vishnuveera was pondering over the answer, there were some sounds at the main door. Shaunaka was back. Paying his respects, without entering the kitchen, he indicated he was well and that he would join the family after washing up. The rest of the family ate in silence, peacefully, waiting for Shaunaka to update them with what had kept him for so long!

Over the next hour, Shaunaka narrated his adventures a couple of times – once to his parents — a sanitised version, omitting certain facts; and the second – a more truthful account to Ashwini and their grandmother.

Sitting on a mat on the floor in Ahalyabai's spacious room at the rear of the main building, Shaunaka and

Ashwini shared their experiences with each other, a weekly, if not a daily routine being followed for ages. Their grandmother, a fixture in this routine, was present now also. She was lying down on her cot with her eyes shut and catching a quick afternoon nap.

"This was why I got so late, Pitamahi. Ashwini, when I saw you in front of the tavern, this morning, who were those men with you?"

"Oh, those men? They are my fellow men; we all belong to Budhashresthi's *saartha* – and are on our way to Kasi and Kosala. I am an actor; I have fought with my father and have run away from home. Once our performances here are over, we will move on from here to Ujjayini and from there to Sanchi and Kasi and finally Kosala."

"Ah, Budhashresthi's *saartha*. Is that not one of the *saarthas* under surveillance?"

"Aho, it is. My role is clear – maintain a low profile, be unobtrusive, be friendly and try to get information from everyone. It helps that I am essaying the role of Vidushaka – they think I am a buffoon who knows nothing," chuckled Ashwini, adding that he did get a bit concerned when he spotted Shaunaka in front of the tavern early that morning.

"Oh, I had to meet Bharavi to update him about that intruder at the corner house. Let me show you this. This is that *uttariya* – those traders at the market had some more of such shawls with them. Can you make something of this?"

"Ah, this is so soft to touch. Fine silk, I must say. We actors hardly use such finery. Our clothes do glitter but they are not so fine. What is that? A pattern," observed Ashwini holding that small piece of uttariya that Shaunaka had brought back.

"Actors!? Ashwini, dare you forget your roots!" Ahalyabai sat up on the cot, knotting her messy white hair. "Bring it to me. This piece of cloth." Ashwini handed the piece of cloth to her and sat down by her side.

Ahalyabai looked at the piece, with much interest, running her fingers on the pattern of strange characters. Suddenly, without any preamble, she stood up and walked over to a large wooden trunk, placed in the far-corner of the room, and pulled out an old parchment. Bringing the parchment over to where the two young men were sitting, she sat down on the mat and placed it on the floor. "Look! Of course this is a pattern – look at these characters. They are definitely letters. Brahmi script. Who has the *uttariya* now? Bharavi? Get that to me. I will tell you what it says. Close your mouth, Ashwini. Shaunaka, no one has died here. Stop staring and do not touch it."

"Pitamahi, how do you know? What is this? You never went to a *gurukula,*" Ashwini muttered, stunned beyond his wits. "If you think a *gurukula* is the only place where people can learn – you are a fool," chided an irritated Ahalyabai. "Did you not mention that *saarthas* are under surveillance? Do you know specifically why?"

"Oh *saarthas* coming from the west are being watched closely; that is what I have gathered. Why? A specific reason, I know not. But logically, *pitamahi*, there is a huge wedding in a few weeks; obviously miscreants and enemies of Nandivardhana will be on the lookout to create some trouble."

"I know that the security at the palace has been increased substantially. Why, I was at the receiving end of their hospitality this morning. At the market, some of the traders were also mentioning that the western gate is heavily guarded. The threat seems to be from the west," added Shaunaka, as Ahalyabai sat looking rather thoughtful.

"Such idiots both of you are! Bharavi should have made me a *dutaka* instead of the two of you. Are you still unable to get a clearer picture, based on what you have been babbling just now? Unable to deduce anything?" Ahalyabai asked as her grandsons who looked at her blankly. "You said that you are aware that the threat is from the west. I just told you that the pattern and characters on this *uttariya* are nothing but the Brahmi script. Now will you put two and two together?"

"Arre, you are such a genius, Pitamahi. Ashwini, looks like Rudrasena's men are up to some mischief. Isn't the great King Chandragupta also expected to attend the wedding?" asked Shaunaka, with bright eyes, as if several answers to many unanswered questions had been revealed.

"You mean, the Kshatrapa king, the one that King Chandragupta defeated? Hmm, maybe! Could there be a threat to the King's life?"

"Vasudeva! Now you get it – be careful, both of you. Only the Lord knows what is being planned and what destruction we may have to witness. Have any of you noticed anything suspicious lately?"

This question threw Shaunaka into a thoughtful silence; it evoked a sense of unease and a disconcerting feeling that something was wrong at the palace. Despite speaking to Kalidasa and the Prince himself, he had been unable to shake it off. While Shaunaka was making up his mind, whether to disclose anything and how much, Ashwini replied, "Pitamahi, there was this intoxicated foreigner I helped this morning. You saw us, didn't you, Shaunaka? This man told me that he was from Pratisthana and that his name was Amaruka but I think that he is a *mleccha* (of foreign origin), probably a Romaka or Yavana, who is lying about his antecedents. But why?"

"That man you were supporting? Pratisthana? He seemed too pale, too fair. I thought him to be a Yavana too. What do you plan to do?"

"Nothing much, just speak with him. We have a rehearsal in that Chitrashala, the decorative building that has been painted with red and blue lacquer, the one owned by that *ganika*, when the sun goes down. I plan to be around him and see what I can find out. Do you have your evening watch today?"

"Oh yes, I do. Let's go together. Pitamahi, I told you that I got into trouble at the palace, right, trying to save a man who had collapsed? Actually, that was the Prince himself. Apparently he has been ill for a while now."

"The Prince? Since when?"

"I could not get details — naturally. He had summoned me to his palace, to thank me for helping him; as I sat, waiting in that opulent room, I felt very uneasy and am unable to understand why."

"Could just be sleepiness, Shaunak. I cannot function if I do not sleep properly. Your schedule anyway is skewed nowadays!" chimed Ashwini, only to be responded to with glares!

Reflecting upon Shaunaka's account, Ahalyabai started pacing up and down the room. "Can you describe the room to me? Do you remember?"

"It was a spacious rectangular room; there were two *diwan*s, one on each of the longer walls, besides which a *kumbha* was kept. On the left side, there were two windows with flowing curtains. The door to the inside also had flowing, colourful curtains. There was a sweet smell, sickeningly sweet I thought, of some flowers which were placed near the window. That was what I remember."

"Hmm, aho, that sounds like a normal waiting chamber to me. Maybe Ashwini is right after all. Go and get some rest. You both will need to leave in a couple of hours, anyway," said Ahalyabai, as she opened her wooden trunk and started looking for something and indicating she wanted to be left alone.

CHAPTER 8

The sudden long and continued absence of Shaunaka and Ashwini from the workshop invoked curiosity and sparked off rumours among the close-knit community. What were these sons of Vishnuveera up to? With Ashwini being sighted, intoxicated, near the taverns with certain actors of low repute, the rumours had taken an even more vicious turn. Being privy to something close to the truth, the goldsmiths at Vishnuveera's workshop tried to deflect these nasty rumours, but to no avail. Kumaragiri and Suddhodhana put up a passionate defence, in particular, as they had an inkling that this had to do with that corner house incident.

So, shortly before dusk, when the two brothers left the workshop for their respective workplaces, they were careful not to be seen together. Leaving the workshop from the back door of the house, Shaunaka made sure that he was, at all times, several steps behind Ashwini. Though their paths were different, one going straight into the heart of the city, near the palaces; and the other, closer home, towards the affluent Buddhist quarter, that day was different. The discussion with Ashwini and his grandmother had activated his curiosity and he wished to go beyond his given brief and just explore. When Ashwini mentioned casually that he would, perhaps, meet the same Yavana or Romaka actor again that evening before their rehearsal at the stipulated agreed location, Shaunaka decided to take a longer detour, via the taverns, markets, and public outhouses in the city centre, keeping an open eye and ear!

The twilight hour lent the well-laid out city of Nandivardhana a magical appearance. Hues of pink, orange and gold lit up the evening sky, casting their pristine glow on the ground below. As he set out for his night-watch, most of the passers-by were on their way back home, exhausted from a day's living, readying themselves for the comfort of home. While these were the common scenes he witnessed, every evening, they were in stark contrast with what he encountered towards the city centre. The heart of the city seemed to have sprung to life; a life of its own! Fashionable city dwellers, shoppers, well-heeled *nagarakas* out on their nightly assignation with their mistresses, beggars, vagrants, and thugs thronged the market. Fascinated by what he saw, Shaunaka slowed down his pace, pausing at each and every stall, and admiring whatever was on offer. From the corner of his eye, he could see Ashwini flirting with some passing women of easy virtue, while waiting for his actor friends in front of one of the shady taverns. Shaking his head at his brother's put-on antics, Shaunaka turned to the next stall, a florist's stand, lined with pretty, blooming flowers of all varieties. Arranged in attractive decorative combinations, the flowers and stalks seemed to have an innate hierarchy, reflecting in the way the strands of coral jasmines, gerberas, blue-water lilies, *ketakis*, *champakas*, *madhavis*, roses and lotuses were lined. Shaunaka lingered on in this stand, appreciating and admiring the handiwork of the Gods in the riot of colours; and also because he saw the same foreign actor walking in his direction. The actor was soon at the flower stand, appraising the flowers and picking the best, definitely for his would-be companion for the night. As the florist handed the stalks, he included a couple of stalks of a strange flower, not local to these parts, much to Shaunaka's surprise. Straining further, on the pretext of observing the flowers, Shaunaka shrewdly asked the florist to give him a few stalks of the flowers that he named. The florist went about his business of taking the stalks, as Shaunaka got just enough time to observe the strange violet and lavender flower, before the actor put them away. As the actor took out some coins from the *kamarbandh*, a cloth piece, tucked away, fell to the ground right at Shaunaka's feet.

"Aho, what is this? You seemed to have dropped it," said Shaunaka as he bent to pick it up.

"*Dhanyavadah*, my sincere apologies. Could you please hold it for me for a moment requested the flustered actor as he balanced the flowers, a bottle of perfumed wine and coins in his hands.

Shaunaka waited for the actor to finish paying the flower seller and as he was biding his time, he looked at the cloth in detail. It was the exact same pattern that had been there on that *uttariya* he had confiscated from that perfumed stranger. Stunned, he took a closer look and noted both the fabric and the characters. There definitely was a connection between this pattern, the intruder at the corner-house and these foreigners – traders, actors, whoever they are pretending to be and wherever they were from. Had he not heard about a sudden increase in the foreigners, merchants mainly? Where had he heard this bit of information? Curious to know more, Shaunaka pretended to admire the fabric, and innocently asked, "This is such a soft, fine piece of cloth. I would like to procure an uttariya for myself. Could you please tell me where I can buy this from?"

"I am glad you liked this. But this is not from here. This is from Pratisthana, where I come from," replied the actor with a smooth smile as he quickly took the cloth from Shaunaka's hands. "Such a pity, this is indeed a very fine piece. *Shubhratri*," Shaunaka moved on to the next stand, to avoid eliciting any further suspicion.

Satisfied with his purchase, the actor then proceeded towards the tavern, where Ashwini was playing the role of an idle man about town, flirting and eve teasing passing ladies. "Aho, *bhrata*, you are here? Do we not have to go to the Chitrashala for the rehearsal?

"Arre, Arya, Pranaam. We do. But there is time still for some *soma*. Please join me."

Shaunaka watched them enter the tavern. Biding his time, Shaunaka looked around the rest of the stalls, putting up an act of haggling over prices, complaining about the quality of the goods. To a random observer, he looked like a bored young man, dissatisfied with everything around him, probably as a result of being rebuffed in love. Had he known this was how he appeared, he would have been highly satisfied. Rather than ruminating on the fickle nature of love and its vagaries, his mind was preoccupied with the tumultuous events of the past month, right from the day of the murder. As he thought more, he was convinced that there was a connection between that intruder who had not been seen since and the two traders from the morning market and now this actor. But what was the connection? If, as Pitamahi says, that indeed is the Brahmi script, what do the letters mean? A message? A code? Or was it just a new pattern made of characters that mean nothing? That does not make any sense; why would the traders not sell the *uttariya* in every store as a novelty? Was something nefarious being planned? Was Nandivardhana in some major trouble as Pitamahi and the *Mahakavi* had indicated?

After he was convinced a reasonable time had passed, Shaunaka made his way into the tavern. Barely past dusk, the tavern was buzzing with life. The period after the *Pitru paksha* is definitely a good time – when the *nagarakas*, after propitiating and fasting for their *pitrus* look forward to the upcoming festivities in the next month.

The tavern owner, pleased with the crowds so far, was standing in a corner. A couple of tables right at the back were free. Who was that? At the far-end of the room, a now-familiar man, who had his upper body completely covered in a black shawl bent over the table, writing on a birch-bark. Ashwini and his actor companion were also standing towards the other corner; Shaunaka took his cup of soma and seated himself in an empty table close to them and started eavesdropping on their conversation, which was bordering on raucous and raunchy.

After a while, when the conversation turned raunchier and he was certain that nothing of note could be gleaned from it, Shaunaka got up, on the pretext of refilling his cup and signalled discreetly to Ashwini to meet him at the other end. When Ashwini joined him in front of the kitchen where an attractive lady was refilling cups with *soma*, Shaunaka whispered, "I have to leave now. That man, your friend has an *uttariya* with the exact same pattern in his kamarbandh. See if you can flick it from him before the night is over and if you do, hand it over to Pitamahi at home."

"Aha, the same one with the pattern? That should be no problem. Shubhratri," Ashwini replied as he staggered back, with a full cup, to his table.

It was pitch dark by the time Shaunaka took his place on one of the branches of the big Bodhi tree in front of the corner house. The long road was quiet; barring the fellow spies on the watch further down the road, his other companions, and a pair of hooting white barn owls, there was not a person in sight.

The drum in the vast Buddhist *vihara* neighbouring the corner house had been struck thrice to indicate the completion of the evening prayers at the Buddhist vihara next door. The laymen believers had long left for their homes and the senior monks were readying to start their teaching sessions for the night. A stillness had descended upon the road, and as Shaunaka observed them, tired from the hectic activities of the past days, he dozed off. But not for long. The hooting of one of the owls woke him up. It was a much-needed wake-up call, as the many lamps lit on the walls of the massive vihara revealed two familiar-looking men walking on the street past the *vihara.* Adjusting his position, and seating himself such that he could get a clearer view, Shaunaka waited and looked. Upon reaching the massive gate of the corner house, the men stopped, hesitating to enter. As the light from the lamps on the gate fell on their faces, Shaunaka recognised them as the two Roman traders he had encountered earlier in the day. A few minutes passed, before their hesitation disappeared and they entered the house.

Shaunaka climbed up a branch or two higher to see what happened next. While he could see clearly, he was not sure if he would be able to listen to any ensuing conversation. He strained his ears and waited with bated breath for the scene to unfold.

Hearing the sounds at the gate, a maid (whom Shaunaka could not recognise) walked out from one of the annexes. She stopped upon seeing the two men, unable to recognise them and unsure as to what to do next. Holding the lantern high, close to their faces, she tried to recognise them but when she still could not, she panicked and hurriedly asked, taking two steps back. "Who is this? Whom do you want to meet?" The older of the two men stepped forward and said: "Pranam, can we meet the mistress of the house, please?"

The maid, now slightly scared, nodded and started walking back towards the door of the main house. The older man walked up to one of the benches in the central courtyard and placed the bag he had been carrying. He then sat down on the bench. The younger of the two men, also the shorter and stouter one, walked around the courtyard rather menacingly. Clad in a simple tunic and a paenula and foreign-looking sandals, both the men were carrying a bag on their shoulders – they seemed to be prepared to set out on a journey.

Before the maid could walk up to the door of the main house, it opened and Devi Tanirika came out, elegant and in repose. Bidding her maid to wait there, she walked towards the men, hands folded, "Pranam, Arya. How may I help you? I do not believe we have met before." Seeing the mistress of the house come out, the older man of the two stood up from the bench and bowing to her respectfully, said a few words in a low tone. The younger of the two men seemed to be getting more impatient and he walked a few steps ahead and interjected in a louder tone, "Your late husband has cheated us, kind lady!" Glaring at his impetuous colleague, the older man continued to speak to Devi Tanirika, for whom this entire exchange was a major shock. She was obviously taken aback at what she had heard. Seeing her mistress in shock, the maid quickly came to her side and helped her sit down on one of the benches.

After a few minutes, she regained her composure and whispered something to her maid, following which she went back inside the main house.

The younger man, for whom patience was certainly not a virtue, began pacing inside the courtyard and started a conversation with the older man. Clearly angry, he seemed to be complaining to his colleague. The older man's replies were calmer and much more measured. Unable to follow the gist of the conversation, as it was in a foreign tongue, the wise lady understood that this was directly related to what she had been told a few minutes back.

Gathering herself and standing up to her full height, the lady then addressed the two unexpected visitors, in a clear voice, "I apologise on behalf of my late husband. I was unaware of his business transactions and relations as that was something he never involved me in. I had no inkling that he owed you both such a large amount or that he had refused to pay you the last time you had come by to collect that. He is now no more. Please forgive him if you can. You will get your money now." The two men did not say anything but just bowed their heads.

It was clear to Shaunaka, who had been observing the nuances of the conversation, while being unable to listen to what was spoken, that the men seemed to have been pacified by what had been conveyed to them. Curious as to what exactly had transpired, he strained further on the branch, careful not to break it and land with a thud on the ground! In a few minutes time, the maid reappeared from the house. She had with her, a small pouch, which she promptly handed over to her mistress. After checking the pouch to ensure that it is the right one, Devi Tanirika handed it over to the men, who then left the house.

What surprised Shaunaka as he continued to observe the scene being enacted in front of him was that the mistress of the house just did not move. Sitting on the bench, she in fact looked years older suddenly, with worry enveloping her entire being. Concerned, her maid tried to ask her if she required anything, any help, but Devi Tanirika dismissed her queries with a shake of her head. It was evident to Shaunaka that she was crying and having a private moment of grief. After what seemed like an eternity, the lady finally recovered her composure and walked back, albeit with a slow gait.

The whole scene left Shaunaka with a sense of discomfort and unease. At one level, this probably had been a normal exchange. Vinayashura may have been involved in a business dealing with these foreign traders and may have been killed before he had cleared his dues. These men could have then come to claim what had been owed to them and the lady of the house, reminded yet again of her husband, may just have been grieving his untimely and brutal death. While this explanation would have sufficed, Shaunaka tried to read between the lines. He just could not fathom why the lady looked years older and extremely worried as if the weight of the world lay on her shoulders. Recollecting the younger man's agitated reactions and expressions however, Shaunaka wondered whether the truth was not what it appeared to be. Had the woman just been blackmailed by these men? Having met Vinayashura before, it was conceivable to Shaunaka that he may have been involved in shady deals and matters with strange foreign traders. And again were these not the traders who had been handed a similar *uttariya* (with the strange pattern) by that shopkeeper at the market? As Shaunaka reflected upon his day and evening, remembering and storing each and every little detail, these and several other questions bogged his mind. He made up his mind to report all to Bharavi early next morning. He also decided to go and meet his old teacher, the revered Acharya Swamideva before going home. While he trusted his grandmother's intelligence and wisdom, like Ashwini, he was not sure whether she would be able to decipher the script as she had claimed. He decided to visit the Acharya to see whether he would be able to decipher the script, if it were one at all, or give him a view on the pattern!

As he made his plans for the morning, the entire palace puzzle came to his mind. Shaunaka finally could lay a finger on that uneasy feeling that had been troubling him all day. It was that cloying, sweet smell in the waiting chamber of the Prince's palace that had become unbearable by the time he had left. Just as he recalled the sickeningly sweet smell, the visibly ill face of the Prince came forth, almost juxtaposed with this smell. Had he also not smelled the same scent at the florist? Shaunaka thought back, trying to remember the flowers placed in the waiting chamber – and to his surprise, the same lavender-coloured flower, the single stalk of which the florist had quietly slipped in, popped up. It was there – right there – by the window in the waiting chamber. Was it the flower with the cloyingly sweet scent? He had never seen a flower like that before. What was it? Where was it from? Was it poisonous? Was the Prince being poisoned? Was this the dastardly plot that was being hatched against Nandivardhana? Was there then a connection between the sick smell and the Prince's condition? These chilling thoughts kept him company that night.

Bharavi started pacing the room after he listened to Shaunaka recount his adventures of the past two days. Shaunaka had approached him at the turn of dawn and had sought to apprise him of all that happened and also his suspicions and fears. Bharavi had acquiesced immediately to grant him an audience. Remembering each and every detail, Shaunaka gave him a thorough report – part of which he had even written on a birch-bark which he then handed over. Bharavi listened to this young man, without uttering a single word and remained thoughtful and pensive long after Shaunaka had stopped speaking.

Standing in one corner of Bharavi's workplace near the door, Shaunaka waited patiently. As he looked around the room, he spotted the *uttariya* kept beside some parchment leaves. Startled to see those parchment leaves, he wondered whether it was proven that the pattern was indeed a script, as Pitamahi had surmised. He was also curious to know how much Bharavi had found out.

Coming out of his reverie, Bharavi stopped pacing and sat on the *diwan* and indicated that Shaunaka sit too. "You are a smart boy and going on the right track, Shaunaka. Continue keeping your eyes and ears open. About the Prince, hmm, the *Mahakavi* did tell me about your episode at the palace. I must say that your surmise is right. The Prince is indeed being poisoned. The Rajavaidya and the Queen have been extremely worried about his safety and life. Shaunaka, this conversation should stay between just the two of us. I do not want it to get out – no, not even to your brother or someone else."

"Yes, Arya. Definitely. Please permit me to ask a question. If this is already known, why hasn't it been stopped?"

"Ah, the problem we are facing is that every time we are able to single out and identify the cause of poisoning, a new strain of poison makes its way into the palace. Certainly the work of an insider."

"That is rather alarming. Especially if the insider has still not been found," said a rather shocked Shaunaka, who couldn't believe his ears.

"But you have provided us a major clue. One of the things baffling the Rajavaidya was that none of the poisons being used were from here – nowhere in Bharatkhanda have they been found. We had been trying to ascertain the origins of these poisons for a while now. Your investigation will help point us now in the right direction. These foreign traders, Romakas you said? And that *mleccha* actor – they will help decipher the truth. "

"Arya, do you mean this *uttariya?*"

"No, the uttariya may lead to something vital, but I am talking about the flower you mentioned seeing at the palace and later at the florist."

"That flower?! It is not from our parts, right? I do not recall seeing it anywhere. Is it a flower from the dreaded *visha* plant? The one from which the *vatsanabha* (aconite) is prepared?

"No, that would have been too simple, no? That flower is alien to our parts and comes from the far west – the land from where the Romakas hail. Similar to *Kashmirajanman* (saffron), the flower we get up north from the mountains, this flower is said to be poisonous. I did not make the connection till you pointed it out. The palace guards had mentioned seeing lavender-coloured flowers at the palace," explained Bharavi.

"What remains then to be found is who is supplying these varied poisons and to whom?" murmured Shaunaka, utterly stumped at the ingenious plan that had yet to unfold.

The Dandaposika smiled, a heavy sad smile, agreeing to the weighty task that lay ahead. He was consciously aware that every minute that he was unable to crack this puzzle and find out who the conspirators to this dastardly plot are, meant that the life of the Prince of Nandivardhana was in trouble; and so was his job!

Just the previous evening, he had been summoned to the Palace by the Queen, who had seemed extremely anguished and vexed. Unable to see her son suffering, the mother in her took precedence over the Queen, as she planned to postpone the wedding and clamp down on the festivities. She wanted her son to recover. The latest episode of poisoning, suspected to be due to those strange flowers, had thrown her completely off. The orders to her officials were clear. Nothing was more important than the life of the crown Prince. They could do whatever it took but the message was clear — she wanted results in a day else she would postpone the wedding. Queen Prabhavati had already sent an express messenger to Pataliputra, to her father, intimating him of the gravity of the situation at hand and her decision to postpone the wedding and clamp down on the festivities. What was left unsaid in the message but heavily hinted was request for additional help. This was something the Mahaamatya (Chief Minister) and the Kulaputra were unhappy about – this was a direct statement on their inefficiency. An insider was clearly involved and at least three attempts had been made, using different poisons each time – each poison more alien than the other. What was also concerning was that the Queen had decided to change the entire inside staff at the Palace in case this was not solved soon. The Mahaamatya and Kulaputra were worried about the number of innocent people who may soon not only lose their livelihood but also live with a blot on their reputations for the rest of their lives. The Dandaposika who had been privy to both these discussions was thus grave and apprehensive. Coming at the right time then, he acknowledged to himself that Shaunaka's observations could prove useful and could throw some light on this puzzle.

The reverie was broken with the announcement by the *dvarapalaka* (gatekeeper) of the *Mahakavi*'s arrival. Looking a little dishevelled, Kalidasa entered, a little harried and eager to meet with Bharavi. He looked startled to see Shaunaka there and nodded brusquely. Addressing the Dandaposika, Kalidasa said, "Pranam, Arya Bharavi, I was not informed that you were with Shaunaka here. May I request some time in private? This is of prime importance and requires your urgent attention?"

"I believe, this has to do with the situation in the palace regarding the Prince's well-being? I trust, by Lord Krishna's benign grace, our Prince is in good health?" replied Bharavi.

"Yes, indeed. This has very much to do with the sensitive matter at hand. Shaunaka, may I please request you to wait outside?"

Shaunaka bowed to Kalidasa and Bharavi and was about to head out when Bharavi stopped him saying, "No, Shaunaka, stay here. *Mahakavi*, apologies, I understand you have something urgent to apprise me of; however, please listen to what Shaunaka has unearthed. I have a feeling they may be interconnected. Please take a seat and give us five minutes of your time and patience. Shaunaka, please narrate what happened."

Kalidasa sat beside Bharavi as Shaunaka narrated the events of the past day and evening. Midway through his narration, Kalidasa got up, agitated and much affected by what was being told. He asked Shaunaka a barrage of questions — "Oh, so the traders came back? Did you take a close look at their appearance? Were they aggressive with the lady of the house?"

Bharavi and Shaunaka both were visibly surprised at this uncharacteristic reaction of the *Mahakavi*. "Do you know of these traders, *Mahakavi*?" asked Bharavi as Kalidasa now started pacing up and down, a strange light gleaming in his bright eyes!

"Ah! yes, I know of them, indeed I do. I had sent some *dutakas* to look for these men – but they had been unable to trace them. Shaunaka, well done." Kalidasa paused, and after possibly rephrasing his words continued, "This goes back to the time when Vinayashura was alive and well. We had received information that traders coming from the west, and in particular, along with one *saartha* originating from Kalyan, could be either spies or here to cause any trouble. I had instructed my men to keep a low profile and watch these traders closely. A few days before the murder, one of my men reported witnessing an altercation, an argument between two foreign merchants and Arya Vinayashura. Apparently, it was late at night and my man was on his way back home when he heard an intriguing conversation between two foreign traders at one of the taverns. The men were complaining about an Arya who, according to them was a rogue, as he had cheated them of their dues. They were also planning to make another attempt to extract their dues from him again. So they did. Intrigued by the conversation, especially because the traders here were the aggrieved party and we get complaints that they are the ones who cheat and wishing to know the identity of this nobleman, my man followed them. To his surprise, the gentleman was Vinayashura. What followed was an ugly altercation. It seemed to the observer that the two traders were definitely aggrieved and were cruelly dismissed by Vinayashura. The observer also commented on their outfits – the men were wearing cloaks similar to what the Romakas wear and on their way back were conversing in a foreign language. Also, from a distance, the older of the two men, seemed to the observer to be calmer and milder; the younger was the more aggressive one and he may have uttered some threats."

"Arya, do you think these men could have then murdered Vinayashura? They definitely had a reason – though I know, for a fact, that they were nowhere near the house that morning." commented Shaunaka hesitantly, as he mulled over what he had heard.

"I don't think so – that would be too simple. But they are not innocent either, as they disappeared just about the time of the murder and have only resurfaced now – more than a month later," averred Kalidasa.

"Arya, this definitely is vital – both what Shaunaka saw last evening and the additional background details you supplied do have some bearing on this murder," murmured Bharavi.

"Yes, I am glad that you insisted on Shaunaka staying back. Arya, I bring bad tidings from the palace. The Prince, who has taken to his chamber since yesterday, is said to be faring poorly. The Queen is with him now and I met the Mahadandanayaka who is personally supervising the security at the palace. Mahadevi Prabhavati is distraught; she is considering postponing the wedding and clamping down on all the celebrations. With so many people moving in and out of the palace premises on the pretext of the preparations, it is becoming quite a nightmare."

Listening to Kalidasa's update from the palace, Bharavi grew more thoughtful. "Doubtless our great Maharani, with blessings of her ancestors and Lord Krishna, will make the right decision, one that is best for all of us; however, I am still concerned about the postponing of the wedding. That could trigger several types of rumours and give fillip to rumourmongers and troublemakers in the city. May the Lord Vasudeva protect our city and people from such turbulent times."

"This is what the Kulaputra fears. The Kulaputra, Mahaamatya and the Mahadandanayaka have been in constant consultation with the Queen and they are monitoring the situation at hand. I just pray that the people of Nandivardhana are blessed with enough strength to bear whatever has been decided. May the blessings of Lord Vasudeva be with us," said Kalidasa rather dejectedly.

Shaunaka was aware that there were many nuances and internal matters in the court that he was not privy to; however this conversation had brought many more questions in his mind than before. Mustering some courage, he then asked, "Arya, I am an ordinary person and just like every common citizen of Nandivardhana, I pray to Lord Vasudeva for the good health and long life of Yuvaraja Divakarasena. If I may enquire on his well-being, what has the Rajavaidya said?"

"Shaunaka, I did speak with the Rajavaidya who is extremely concerned. The different poisons in the Prince's body have weakened him so much that the antidotes are not working and an overall quick recovery has become difficult. It is an alarming situation. The Rajavaidya is afraid that another such attempt may be fatal."

This pronouncement by the *Mahakavi* underlining the gravity of the situation dampened the already-tense atmosphere in Bharavi's chamber. Breaking the uneasy silence that enveloped the room, Kalidasa, after a few minutes said, "I pray to God for bestowing upon us peace. May Lord Krishna protect the city of Nandivardhana. However, we must do what we can. Shaunaka, did that intruder episode not take place the last time you entered the corner house on the pretext of giving some jewellery? Find some reason and go and gain their confidence. There is something amiss there and you will help us find that out."

"Arya, definitely. In fact, pardon my incessant questioning. That *uttariya* out there..." Shaunaka replied, turning and pointing towards the parchment leaves and *uttariya* kept on the low *diwan*. "May I please take it back to the lady of the house? I could use that as an excuse to enter the house. I apologise for my extreme curiosity. Is the pattern indeed made of letters, characters from a script – perhaps the one on the parchment leaves here? Is this a recognised script perhaps of a foreign land?"

"Umm, this is indeed a recognised script, Brahmi, from the West – where the Kshatrapas used to rule. The sentence is most definitely a code. The letters and the words they form, by themselves, do not make any sense. Yes, do take it. If this can get you an entry into the house and an opportunity to find out more, please do," replied Bharavi, also signalling the meeting to a close.

Chapter 9

In the month that had passed by since the death of Vinayashura, many changes had come to the corner house. Now wearing a desolate look, the house stood, telling a tale of helplessness and disarray in each and every corner. The once-shining, impressive gate showed signs of rusting and not having been scrubbed enough to gleam anymore. The path to the central courtyard, once strewn with many flowering plants, now stood bereft as if lacking any purpose. The grass in the courtyard also seemed to have grown wild, not having been trimmed and brought to shape.

Even though Shaunaka had been unfailingly keeping a watch on the house almost every night, the disarray in which he found the house in took him by surprise. As he walked towards the central courtyard, the door of an annexe that lay on the right opened. One of the two maids that he recognised and knew from the day of the murder walked out to check who it was. Ah, this was the one named Hemvati, the one who made poor Suddhodhana extremely uncomfortable, thought Shaunaka. Seeing her slow and unenthusiastic gait and her messy and shabby attire, it occurred to him that the death of the master of the house was some sort of a death knell – taking away happiness and even signs of life from this place. Considering his own brief acquaintance with the deceased man, in which he had not really acquitted himself too well, Shaunaka wondered about the other facets of the dead man's personality. He remembered Vinayashura as supercilious and downright obnoxious and going by the *Mahakavi's* account, that was how he behaved with a pair of traders. But yet, his loss was being felt – not just by his family, but also by the house and even the maidservants!

As he thought harder, he recalled a recent particular conversation at the workshop between his father and Somnath. They were commenting about how unenthusiastic Devi Tanirika had been about the delivery of the jewellery. Gone was the precision, the perfection she had once demanded. She had made no mention of the payment even though the order had been completed – in time. Vishnuveera and Somnath had decided not to pursue the matter further, especially since she had just recently been bereaved. Shaunaka wondered whether the family had hit upon severe financial times? Had Devi Tanirika paid all she had then to the traders? Was she being blackmailed? Was there something underfoot? Whatever the reason - this certainly was not the ostentatious palatial abode that had been much talked about.

The maidservant had by now recognised Shaunaka as being the jeweller's son. She politely enquired the reason for his visit – her voice laden with a little fear and worry. Was he here on behalf of his father? Shaunaka shook his head in the negative and assured her that it was not on behalf of his father but his own promise to Devi Tanirika that brought him here. His cryptic reply seemed to confuse her, but she let it pass. She bade him to wait on one of the benches in the vast central courtyard. Devi Tanirika came out of the main house, composed and elegant. Upon recognising Shaunaka, she beamed a warm smile and welcomed him. "Namaste, please be seated. Has your father sent you to collect the payment we owe him? You are the jeweller's son, are you not?"

"Namaste Devi. I have not been sent by my father for collecting any payment. I have come here to return this to you. I am not sure whether you remember but some days back when I was here to hand over some jewels, I came upon a stranger trying to get away from one of the annexes in your residence. This was the stole that I managed to grab during my futile chase. I am here to return this to you."

Devi Tanirika seemed not to have any recollection of such an incident. The maidservant who was serving the guest *madhuparka* and other refreshments, whispered something to her mistress. Following a brief pause, Devi Tanirika said, "Aho, yes yes, now I do remember. I have some kind of a recollection. You must think it strange – how come this old lady does not remember an intruder barging into her house, hardly a month after her husband's demise, but the truth is that we have had so many strange incidents in the past few months. Is it not, Suvarna?"

Suvarna nodded and waited for further instructions, if any at all from her mistress.

Surprised at this sudden disclosure and wanting to know more, Shaunaka tried probing," Oh really, Devi? What type of strange incidents do you recall? And a few months, you said? Does this mean it started even when Arya Vinayashura was fine? Pardon my excessive curiosity. I hope you have informed Arya Bharavi and his men."

It was Devi Tanirika's turn to be surprised now. This was the first time she had thought about these strange incidents as having a pattern and it was also the first time she had spoken to this normally quiet and self-effacing person. As she struggled to recall all the incidents she considered strange, her beautiful daughter walked out of the main house towards the store room. Gone was the glowing bride-to-be; in her place was a young lady, worn down by the burden of life and whom sleep and hunger seemed to evade. Though still pretty, she looked emaciated and exhausted as she went about some chores. Shaunaka was struck by this marked change in her appearance and looked astonished. He looked around the house and its surroundings to assess how it had changed —altered it definitely had — his earlier concerns about the financial state of Devi Tanirika and Tarika now deepened and he pondered whether to make a mention of it or not. Noticing his evident shock, Devi Tanirika said, "I know, the changed circumstances can be shocking, young man. But such is fate. What has to happen will. My daughter is very unhappy.

She is yet to recover from her father's death and now this. Actually Madhavasena called off the wedding this morning. We are still trying to understand why."

"This morning? But did he mention why?"

"He said something about having to go to Pataliputra and not come back for another year or so. Since it is not wise to keep a betrothal open for so long, he begged to be released from this verbal contract. We did not ask him many questions. As I said, strange things have been happening in this cursed house. I am sure the Gods and our *pitrus* are displeased with us. It is but natural that Madhava does not want to associate himself with us then."

"Devi, I apologise for asking again. What do you mean strange things?"

"It all started with the death of our dog a few days before Arya himself passed away! He had been with us for so many years, our old friend, we used to call him. What a day that was. Tarika and I had gone to the temple in the palace estate. When we returned Arya mentioned that the poor dog had died. Just like that – he was running to get some meat and he dropped down dead. I did not think much about it then but the watchkeeper's dog died just yesterday and this came back to my mind. Suvarna, do you remember at all what happened?"

Suvarna, who had been standing still, now answered, "God forgive me for my impudence, Devi. I have been with you all these years but such things never took place in the past. Why, I remember the day our Yoshaka died. What a loving kind soul that was. I just hope that Chitragupta is kind to him and he gets a better life the next time. Where was I? Ah the day he died. You and Tarika had gone to the temple. I was feeding the little princess and playing with her in her room when we heard a bloodcurdling shriek. What a shriek that was. We had to shut our ears for nearly five minutes. When I went down, I found Arya and Hemvati and a couple of other people all gathered near our gate. The poor mutt had fallen dead, a piece of meat in his mouth."

"A shriek you said? Did we not hear one yesterday also?", interjected Devi Tanirika now looking more serious than before.

"Aree, Devi, of course we did. *Bhootas* and *pretas* live in this house, we should not have come here. Forgive me, but I again would like to make a suggestion. Let us leave and go back to the quarters where we resided before. Next to the venerable Acharya Swamideva."

"Acharya Swamideva? He was my guru," said Shaunaka, upon hearing his name.

Devi Tanirika smiled at the reference of her old neighbour and the revered Guru. "Aho, you are a good man then. A reflection of your wise teacher!"

"Suvarna, get this nonsense out of your head. No *bhootas* and *pretas* are here. We have had three *yagnas* here to clear your head of this irrational fear but you still seem hung up on the same thought. A simple explanation could just be that both dogs were ill and old and their time was up. They probably were in pain when Yama's *dutas* came to take them away.

And that's the shriek we heard." Devi Tanirika's firm rebuke closed this matter and Shaunaka figured that maybe it was time for him to leave. He had gotten enough information.

Just when he tried to take his leave, Devi Tanirika asked him about the *uttariya*. "So were you able to ascertain anything from this piece of cloth? Whom did you take it to, you say?"

"Oh Devi, yes it was useful. I took it to my father's close friend, Arya Yashasvi to check about the origins of this expensive silk. He confirmed that it is definitely not from Bharatakhanda and has foreign origins – maybe from the far west, Gandhara or even maybe Romakapura."

"Oh, Vasudeva, what days are you making me see? There were two Romakas who came to my house just yesterday; Arya had to pay them for some work they did and now you tell me that the silk *uttariya* you confiscated from that thief could be from Romakapura."

"Devi, please do not fear. They may not be related at all. There have been many *saarthas* from the west in the past few months and Nandivardhana has seen an influx of products and goods from Romakapura and there are many Romaka traders selling their wares now. This *uttariya* may itself be a stolen good! And Arya may have bought something from those traders and unfortunately not have paid them before his death. Please do not worry and trouble yourself," said Shaunaka as he tried to reassure the anxious lady in front of him.

"You are probably right. These may not be related at all. But I wonder what the purpose of the intrusion was. Nothing was stolen that day from the annexe. Madhavasena checked his stuff and he mentioned everything was intact. So barring the jewels stolen from Arya's cupboard that terrible day last month, we have not lost anything?"

"Something was stolen that day?" this was news to Shaunaka. He wondered whether Arya Bharavi and his men were aware.

"Oh yes, we did not realise it then. Else we would have mentioned it to Arya Bharavi. But when Tarika was clearing and putting away her father's things, some days back, it came to her notice that a couple of family heirlooms have gone missing. We remembered that the cupboard door was open when we found Arya in that heinous state. I know, there is so much that has happened in this accursed house. All our own wrongdoings – from a past life! Don't look so concerned, boy. It is our karma – and what has to happen will always happen. I just pray to Lord Vasudeva to give me the strength to bear what has to happen. "

"Devi, your stoicism is admirable. Not many people would bear the kind of adversities you have been through with such strength and equanimity," said Shaunaka with admiration, giving the old lady a chance to speak more. Being a good listener, this was something he liked to do.

"You are a good boy. Life is long and sometimes very tough, child. What would you know about the kind of adversities I have undergone? I think you should go now and leave this old woman to her troubled thoughts. Do tell your father that I will send Siddeshwara with the payment in a day or two. Also, may I request you to hand this over to Arya Bharavi on my behalf? I do not think I would like another meeting with that intimidating gentleman," said Devi Tanirika smilingly.

Happy to have the *uttariya* in his possession, Shaunaka then left, walking along the road, assimilating all the information he had gathered during his long conversation.

The city of Nandivardhana woke up to a shocking announcement the next morning. The royal messengers were up and about, announcing the postponement of the Prince's wedding, due to unavoidable circumstances. But obviously, within a few minutes the entire city was abuzz. Speculation about why this decision was taken was intense — a section opined that the Queen was unwell; the other opined that the Prince probably was unhappy with his mother's choice of a bride. Another section concluded that the city was cursed – first a respected gentleman gets killed and then the Prince's wedding gets stalled. This viewpoint found many takers in the jeweller's quarter, where it was felt that it was Vishnuveera who was possibly cursed and not the entire town. After all, it was already known that he and his men had been working on crafting jewels for both the weddings — the one of Prince Divakarasena and that of the ill-fated Vinayashura's daughter. And both the weddings were now stalled. Was it not reflective of Vishnuveera going through a particularly bad patch of luck? That and how his two sons have stopped helping their father was also an indication. It was not a surprise then that well-wishers and curious onlookers also stopped by to check on the state of the workshop that morning. The interiors of the palace were inaccessible but Vishnuveera's workshop was not.

When Shaunaka came down from his room that afternoon, after having rested a bit, he found the workshop in a state of tizzy, with a stream of uninvited visitors coming in and out. Vishnuveera looked a little hassled and the gold workers, especially Suddhodhana and Kumaragiri, positively annoyed. When Shaunaka entered the working area, looking for his father, he definitely set many tongues wagging. Most of them were surprised to see Shaunaka at home – so certain were they of his rumoured wayward ways! Were they then false? What of reports of having seen him at odd hours of the day and night around the city centre?

Vishnuveera had just then gone out of the main door to see an esteemed colleague off. When Shaunaka could not see his father, he went up to where Kumaragiri was sitting and concentrating hard to work, amidst all the prying, idle visitors.

"*Pranam*, *bhraata!* What is all this?" whispered Shaunaka.

"Namaste, Shaunak, sit, sit. This is a mess. The palace has postponed the royal wedding. And everyone here is curious about how we are managing. They are here to commiserate with your father for his bad luck. Two stalled marriages or two cancelled commissions, so they think."

"What?! They have postponed the marriage of Prince Divakarasena? Why? What did the royal proclamation say?" asked a stunned Shaunaka.

"Arre, Shaunak, when does the royal proclamation give out all details? It was obviously worded in a way that is open to all kinds of speculation — most people think that the Prince is not happy about the choice of bride. You remember there had been some gossip about his dalliance with some dancer or was it a courtesan? Well, whoever she was, the talk of the town is that the Prince is still besotted and wishes to marry her only!"

"Is that so? That is very interesting. I had not heard about this dalliance that you mention. But, I thought the Prince was rather young."

"Aho, not so young, my lad. Younger than you perhaps. But just because you happen to baulk at the word 'marriage' doesn't mean everyone is averse. We were all looking forward to this happy event in Nandivardhana. God only knows what intrigues and tussles are being played out in the palace as we speak. While on the topic of weddings, it is indeed high time that you get married. I had not spoken to you about it before but that's what Somnath and I have been advising your father," concluded Kumaragiri in a paternal, affectionate tone.

"I know, I know. I do get to listen to this particular advice. Will take your leave now, *bhraata*. I had come down as I had not seen you all in many days. I will come back for a chat once this gets sorted out. *Pranam*!"

Shaunaka's mind was in a complete turmoil after he heard about the postponement of the wedding of the Prince. Was the Prince okay? Or had he taken very ill? He wished to go and find out more immediately. Just when he was about to set out, he remembered the *uttariya* that he had brought back home so that his wise Pitamahi could help decipher the script.

Sending mental prayers to Lord Vishnu, Shiva and Dhanvantri for the health of the Prince, Shaunaka headed to his Pitamahi's room to show her the *uttariya* and then decided to go to meet the *Mahakavi*, armed with whatever additional information he could gather.

"Om Namo Bhagavate Vasudevaya, Om Namo Bhagavate Vasudevaya…" the incessant, repeated chant greeted him when Shaunaka came by the door of his grandmother's room. It was the time for her afternoon prayers. As Ahalya Devi was aging, her designated time slots for prayers seemed to go up. Now what was he to do? Should he even enter? Ahalya Devi was particular about not being disturbed and was known for her fierce temper. Hoping that her innate curiosity (especially regarding this uttariya) would supersede her annoyance at being disturbed, Shaunaka knocked on the door twice, firmly and waited for her to reply. "Who is it? Come inside," chimed an irritated voice from inside, after a while.

"Shaunaka, what is so important for you to disrupt my prayers? It'd better be something worthwhile," said Ahalya upon seeing her grandson at the door. She was seated on a mat in a corner of the room designated as the pooja room. A couple of small decorated *moortis* of Lord Krishna and Lord Rama were placed there in front of whom there was a plate of some fruits offered to the Gods.

"Pitamahi, I apologise for disturbing you but I wanted to show this to you before I left for the watch. Oh did you hear about the Prince's wedding getting postponed?"

"Yes. That's not important enough. What is it that you want to show me? Oh, is this not the *uttariya* on which something is written in Brahmi? Give it to me," Pitamahi's innate curiosity won the battle over her piety and devotion, and Ahalya devi started looking at the *uttariya*.

Right then, someone knocked on the door. Ahalya Devi frowned and invited the new visitor. It was Ashwini. "*Pranam*, *Pitamahi*, namaste Shaunaka. *Maate* mentioned that Shaunaka was here, which is why I am disturbing you, Pitamahi."

The old woman certainly did not look displeased at all as it had been many days since both her grandsons had joined her for a chat. "Come on in and sit by me. It is good to see both of you. Now, Shaunaka, let me look at this piece of cloth."

As Ahalya devi inspected the cloth and deciphered the script, the brothers spoke, in a low voice, about the recent happenings at the palace. The postponement of Prince Divakarasena's marriage was indeed the talk of the town. Ashwini updated Shaunaka with the theories doing the rounds in the actors circle as to why the marriage had to be postponed.

"Well, boys, both the *uttariyas* — this one and that other one Ashwini gave me some days back — have the same thing written on them. Most definitely a code."

"I gave you a stole, Pitamahi? When was this? How come I do not remember?"

"Ashwini, remember your actor friend? The one you got drunk with some days back?"

"Aho that one! Strange man. Many secrets up his sleeve. Did I tell you? I saw him with some official from the palace the other day. Imagine, those flowers he bought that evening were not for some cheap courtesan; instead he handed them to that royal chap."

"What?!? Some royal official, you say? Were you able to take a close look at him? If you were to see him again, would you be able to identify and recognise him? Why on earth did you not tell me earlier?" exclaimed an agitated Shaunaka as the import of Ashwini's words sunk fully.

"Arre, aho, calm down, *Bhraata*! So much excitement? How is it of any importance? These actors are such wastrels, seriously. They meet all kinds of people—thugs, pimps, officials, merchants, writers, musicians, all of them!"

"Ashwini, you duffer! Use your brains for once. Shaunaka does not have to spell everything out," chided an irritated Ahalya Devi. At her age, the one thing she could not tolerate was stupidity and not using one's brains and her younger grandson's refusal to do so bugged her.

Somewhat shamefaced, Ashwini said, "Pitamahi, Shaunaka, I seriously do not understand all this. I am just a jeweller, a gold worker, and now they have forced me into this wastrel being, an actor, and I hate every minute of it. These men, they seem to be operating at another level with their own agendas! I wonder how long I would have to tour with these people under the guise of being an actor, a jester! Oh yes, our manager thinks we should take the *Mahakavi's* play to another city. I may be forced to accompany them on a *saartha* to Mathura, Vrindavan and Pataliputra," mused an unhappy Ashwini.

"Arre, why do you worry so much? I am sure the *Mahakavi* will exempt you from this unnecessary journey soon. He recruited you as he fears that there may be trouble in Nandivardhana and this *saartha*. He has a suspicion that the actors' troupe is harbouring some local miscreants. Pray to Lord Vasudeva that the troubles our city is facing get thwarted soon and that you become free," advised Shaunaka as their grandmother clucked, without an ounce of sympathy.

"Now, now, Ashwini, nothing is the matter. Stop whining. You do not want to play this role – just inform whoever it was who got you into this. No point complaining about it – especially because I pointed out that you didn't think and connect some obvious dots. Now you both listen. This is what is written in Brahmi script on both the *uttariyas*. I have an inkling of what it could mean. But see if you can make anything of it. It says - "What does the King of Vidarbha say in reply?"

Shaunaka shut his eyes in frustration. The sentence made no sense whatsoever to him. Was Vidarbha not the name of Nandivardhana and its surrounding areas in the olden days? What does this even mean? For a few minutes, there was complete silence in the room as both men tried to let the line sink in. "If you both do not have anything else to discuss with me, please now leave and let me continue my prayers," Ahalya Devi requested her grandsons and just as Shaunaka was getting up to leave, there was a squeal. It was Ashwini. "Aho, aho, I know this line. Of course how on earth could I not connect this?"

"And… what is it?"

"*Bhraata*, this line is from the *Mahakavi*'s play *Malavikagnimitra* — the very same play we have been rehearsing day in and day out. The one we were to perform as a part of the marriage festivities at the palace."

"What? Is that so? But what is it supposed to mean?" wondered Shaunaka, now back in a seated position.

Ahalya Devi's attention had been caught by this sudden, unexpected discovery. "Ok, Ashwini. Do you remember who says this line in the play and what is the scene?"

"Ganadhara says it, Pitamahi. That's a good man there. He has helped me be comfortable."

"Oh Lord Krishna. Were you sleeping when Lord Brahma was distributing brains, Ashwini? I do not want to know the actor's name. What is the name of the character this man plays? Can you recall the context of the dialogue in the play? Think a bit more."

"Ah, *Pitamahi*, of course. Ganadhara is playing the role of King Agnimitra. Agnimitra asks his minister Vahatva about the contents of the letter sent to him by the King of Vidarbha, who is a sworn enemy in the play."

"Aho, and what does the King of Vidarbha say in reply?" asked Shaunaka trying to draw a connect between the sentence and the current context.

"Oh, the King of Vidarbha in reply agrees to the release of Madhavasena, Agnimitra's brother only upon the release of his brother-in-law Mauryasachiva, whom Agnimitra had captured and imprisoned."

"Hmm, now what could this mean for us here in Nandivardhana? How is this even a code?" wondered Shaunaka.

"Give it some time, let it sink in your mind. Think about it for a day. The answer will come to you, " advised Ahalya Devi, continuing to think. "Ashwini, you think harder. What comes next?"

"Oh there is a whole discussion between the King and the minister, in which the king decides to move his troops to attack the king of Vidarbha. The minister also advises the king about the wisdom of this action, citing the treatises on policy where it is mentioned that an enemy that has lately entered the kingdom is like an unsteady, recently-planted tree that can be uprooted quickly."

"Wait, what was this comparison of enemies to trees? Can you repeat the entire dialogue verbatim," asked Shaunaka, intrigued by the overall scene. Especially the analogy between enemies and trees found some resonance in his mind and he wanted to think further on those lines. Ashwini repeated those lines, now verbatim, as the poet had written.

"This is something you both should inform the *Mahakavi*. Lines from his plays are being used as codes by people who definitely do not wish well for our city," opined Ahalya Devi. Her grandsons agreed and it was decided that Shaunaka would go and inform Kalidasa and Bharavi of these new developments as soon as he could.

Just when these plans were being made on the first floor room of Vishnuveera's house, at the workshop, a brawl suddenly broke out. Screaming and yelling voices disturbed the silence of the afternoon and the two men ran down to see what had transpired.

The sight that greeted Shaunaka and Ashwini when they ran down to the main and public part of the workshop was terrifying. Suddhodhana, the gentle, frightened soul, was standing, terrified and with a dagger in his hand! In front of him, the contents of his bag lay strewn on the ground. Crowds had gathered and the local police officials had also descended upon the place and were making enquiries. Even before Shaunaka and Ashwini could get a grip on what may have happened, the terrified and shocked Suddhodhana was whisked away by the police. An eerie disbelieving quiet descended upon the workshop. Somnath herded the shocked, disbelieving workers back into the work area and locked the door, forcing the gossiping crowds to disperse temporarily. Vishnuveera, who had stepped out for a quick meeting with a trader, was on his way back when he heard murmurs about the murderer of Vinayashura being found at his workshop. He hurried back in time to see the workers being herded inside. Locking the gate and the door, he took stock of the situation inside. Worried, sad, disbelieving faces greeted him. Why, his sons were there too. But questions writ on their faces made it clear that they were as much in the dark as he was. "Will someone tell me what is going on?"

Kumaragiri and Somnath, the senior-most artisans in the workshop looked at one another – each prompting the other to speak. Clearing his throat, Kumaragiri began slowly – with a nod to Somnath, indicating that he should step in, wherever he felt it was needed. "Arya, let me begin from the start. As you know, we have been having unwanted visitors since morning, asking pesky, irritating questions in a bid to elicit as much gossip as they can. As a consequence, tempers were running high. We were trying to work and complete the order given to us irrespective of whether the wedding takes place tomorrow or by the end of this evil Kali Yuga. Our patience was sorely tested when Haradatta's men came here earlier this afternoon. It seemed to us that these men had completely left their own work behind and were seated here just to find out more and while away their time. Their intentions were not good at all; we could not understand what they wanted from us. Were they here to copy and steal our designs? Were they here to provoke and heckle us purposely because Haradatta sent them here? While their true intention was not known, their presence soon was like thorns in a rose bush. Somnath and I requested them, many times, to leave and let us work in peace.

There was no new gossip we could provide. Why or how the Prince's marriage got postponed is not known to us; neither is the inside circumstances of the late Vinayashura's house. One of them in particular was being especially troublesome. Taranatha, I think was his name. He started making the poor Suddhodhana the target of all his questions. He purposely provoked the poor man, who was sadly unable to ignore this heckling. Suddhodhana's patience snapped when the vile Taranatha made some lewd accusations about our young Shaunaka here. His vile gossip accused our young master of not only the murder of Vinayashura but also of outraging the modesty of Vinayashura's to-be-wed daughter, due to which he claimed her marriage had been stalled."

Kumaragiri looked down shamefacedly as he paused. He had tried to give a faithful account of what happened, even if it meant causing his masters much pain. Both Vishnuveera and Shaunaka looked positively astonished. They did not know what to comment about such a ludicrous accusation. Requesting their permission, Somnath now continued with the narration.

"Arya, we were truly appalled at this despicable nonsense that the evil Taranatha was spouting, but before we could react to this, a brawl had started. Suddhodhana had lost his patience and despite his frail frame and meek nature, started punching that dreadful man with all his might. We tried to put an end to it but the yelling and screaming had attracted much attention. People were already forming a large crowd in front of the gate. Haradatta and a few of his other men also came on to the scene and added fuel to the fire. Blaming Suddhodhana for inciting trouble, they called the police authorities. By this time, Taranatha had started picking up things lying around him and throwing them. One of the objects he threw was Suddhodhana's bag. As the bag flew to the ground, all its contents were strewn on the ground. Among them was a dagger – an unusually sharp one, with a large elephant head made of precious silver. It even had some dried blood stains on it. Upon seeing that, Haradatta started shouting, accusing Suddhodhana of wishing to murder his man! The idiotic onlookers, with no minds of their own joined in too. Suddhodhana stood transfixed. It was evident to us that this was the first time he was seeing the dagger too. Muttering that it was not his, he bent down and picked it up. Unfortunately when the police officials showed up, this was how they found him and whisked him away. I have sent Ganadasa with him for some moral support. But Arya, this is what happened before you got back."

"Dhanyavadah, Somnath, Kumaragiri. Bad luck indeed seems to have befallen us here at the workshop. How else can we explain these events of the past weeks? I pray to Lord Krishna to bear whatever troubles are assigned to us in this life. I think you should all go home and rest now. No point in sitting here and feeling sad for the ill-fated Suddhodhana. I will go and meet Arya Yakshavatsa later in the evening and request him to help us free Suddhodhana. This seems like a planned conspiracy. I request all of you to be patient and also keep these matters to yourselves. We will find a solution to these problems. Shubharatri."

The workers dispersed in absolute silence. It had been an eventful day and all this was too much for them to assimilate in such a short time. Vishnuveera was left alone with Shaunaka and Ashwini. Disturbed and worried, he sat down at his usual place, a low seat near the window that opened into the inner sections of the house. Gautami and Ahalya Devi, who had also come out upon hearing the ruckus and had been listening to the entire exchange from the inner courtyard, now entered the room and sat beside him. After a few minutes of silence, Vishnuveera spoke, "Shaunaka, speak to Bharavi. Find out more about this Haradatta and that Taranatha. This sounds like a conspiracy for sure."

"Yes, Pitashri. While the provoking and heckling is understandable, what I do not understand is the dagger in Suddhodhana's bag."

"What is there to understand? It must have been planted to prove that Suddhodhana is a dangerous man and has murderous intentions."

"But why Suddhodhana? And who would do such a thing?"

"That is for Bharavi and his men — which includes you, my boy — to find out. Now get going both of you and leave my son alone." Said Ahalya Devi caustically, snubbing Shaunaka.

"Vishnu, stop worrying. Truth always wins. You know that Suddhodhana is innocent – he will be set free. Certainly do not worry about your reputation. Your work and integrity have been proven all these years. Malicious games, such as these will not taint it. It will come to naught, mark my word. And if two weddings got stalled or postponed, that is their misfortune not yours. Why do you look as if it was all your doing? " Ahalya Devi tried to comfort her anxious son, who was slowly coming to terms with the sudden reversal of his fortunes.

"You are right, *Maate*. It will all be well."

Ashwini nudged Shaunaka and they both quietly took their leave, as the family dealt with this unexpected crisis-like situation, which affected them and yet did not.

CHAPTER 10

The walk towards the city centre and the palatial estate was much longer that day. Both the sons of Vishnuveera were in a dazed state. They were also coming to terms with what had happened. Shaunaka requested Ashwini to accompany him first to Bharavi's headquarters and then to look for the *Mahakavi* somewhere on the palace grounds.

"You want me to come with you? But why?" asked Ashwini who was in general slightly scared of authority figures. Despite the recent massive changes in his life since Vinayashura's murder that had him spying upon a group of actors, his overall discomfort continued. In his current role, his daily report was just to the manager of the troupe, Avadhuta, who usually passed off as a lazy, rotund gentleman fond of his food and drink. He certainly did not look forward to meeting the Dandaposika to apprise him of his debauched existence. Truth be told, he was getting tired of playing a degenerate actor whose two-bit role was of no significance to the play.

"Just come. My mind is a mess. You can corroborate what I say."

"OK. I doubt whether I would be of any help. Since you are insisting, I will accompany you."

"*Bhraata, Pranam.*" Someone coming out of an adjacent lane to the Chitrashala called out to them. It was Ganadasa a young gold worker, their colleague from the workshop, who had accompanied Suddhodhana to the police headquarters.

"Aho Ganadasa, what news do you have of our brother Suddhodhana?"

"Oh, not good at all. They will be keeping him in prison for the night."

"What? In prison for a provoked fight? That does not sound right. We actors get drunk and punch each other's faces every night. We don't get locked up," exclaimed Ashwini.

"Oho *Bhraata*, this is not for that. It is because of the dagger found among his belongings. It is said to be the weapon used to kill Vinayashura."

This disclosure by Ganadasa had Shaunaka and Ashwini both in shock. They could not believe their ears.

"What absolute rubbish! We were also there. Of course Bhraata Suddhodhana did not kill that man," exclaimed Shaunaka feeling awfully helpless and more confused than before.

"I know. I tried to tell them that it really could not be possible. But the silver dagger with its bloodstains cannot be refuted. *Bhraata* was in a complete state of despair and was not able to speak a single coherent word. I fear for his mental sanity and peace of mind. Is there nothing you can do?" pleaded Ganadasa.

"You go home now, Ganadasa. Get a night's rest. Do not be too anxious; Truth shall indeed prevail. *Pitashri* has sent us to pay our respects to the Dandaposika and seek his help in securing the release of Suddhodhana. Ashwini and I were there, on the day of the murder of Vinayashura; and of course we know and can testify that this cannot be the case. Let us hurry, Ashwini."

Shaunaka and Ashwini remained silent through the rest of the walk to Arya Bharavi's chambers at the administrative headquarters. Shaunaka's mind was in a state of utter turmoil — too many questions were floating around. Ashwini too seemed a little dejected — he started reliving the day of Vinayashura's murder ever since this latest development.

There was a long waiting queue in front of the Dandaposika's chamber at that time of the day. This came as a surprise to Shaunaka as his previous interactions were just shortly after dawn when the city was peaceful and quiet. In sharp contrast to that, the administrative headquarters was crowded and noisy.

"Lord Vasudeva! This is Kaliyuga, indeed. How else can one explain the number of people waiting to meet the Dandaposika," exclaimed Ashwini as he started talking to an old, frail man who was obviously waiting for his turn.

Shaunaka did not reply but looked around instead for a few minutes to memorise his surroundings. Once that was done, he thought harder upon the various puzzling threads they had uncovered. A considerable sense of unease pervaded his mind as he tried to reach a logical conclusion. One thing was clearly certain – a sly conspiracy of mammoth proportions was underway.

They would have waited for more than a quarter of an hour, when a security guard came up to them." Namaste, are you Shaunaka, the son of Vishnuveera?"

"Aho, *Pranam*, that I am."

"Could you please come with me then? You are being summoned."

"Summoned by whom? Oh, this is my brother Ashwini. We were both here to meet the Dandaposika."

"I will not be able to disclose who has summoned. You will know shortly. Yes, he may accompany you; but may enter the chambers only upon permission."

Shaunaka and Ashwini looked at each other in surprise but decided to quietly follow this man. Walking through the long corridor that led to the inner parts of the building, they took a fleet of stairs and went up to the third floor. By the time one reached the third floor, one could easily forget that they were in a public office – an office of the establishment. The silence was indeed surprising. The security guard stopped in front of a room and asked them to wait while he went inside for the necessary approvals. A few minutes later, they were asked to go inside.

Inside the plush chamber decorated tastefully and appointed comfortably were seated the

Mahadandanayaka, Arya Yakshavatsa, *Mahakavi* Kalidasa and a regal-looking older man whom both Shaunaka and Ashwini could not recognise. Shaunaka and Ashwini greeted them respectfully with folded hands and bowed heads.

"Ah, there you are Shaunaka. Welcome Ashwini. While we have not met earlier, you would have heard of me," said Kalidasa. "You must be wondering why you have been called here. I was informed that you were in the queue seeking an audience with the Dandaposika. I presume that you have some information to share. Since I was here to seek an audience with the Kulaputra and Mahadandanayaka, I thought it would be better if you could also apprise all of us. Do not worry, Bharavi will be joining us in a minute."

Right then, the door opened and Arya Bharavi walked in. "Pranam Arya, I apologise for having kept you waiting. The number of people who have grouses and complaints that need to be solved has gone up substantially. Please let me know how I can be of any help. Ah, I see Shaunaka and his brother are also with us."

The older man, the Kulaputra, spoke, "We have a crisis in the palace. The Prince is seriously indisposed. While the Rajvaidya is using all his knowledge of plants and herbs, a cure is yet to be found. Our Yuvaraj is being poisoned – that is for sure. But who and why? Who are these enemies? I thought you have been looking into this. It is our duty towards our motherland to find the conspirators and expose the plot. With the postponement of the marriage, rumours are flying thick and fast – people are anguished – they had waited for this auspicious event for so long; this is certainly not the situation I want my country to be in. There is too much unrest and discontent and suspicion. I am worried."

"Arya, please do not be anguished. We are aware of the critical nature of the situation and are doing our best. I am confident that we will be able to unearth the plot and expose the evil minds before it is too late," said Yakshavatsa, the Mahadandanayaka.

"*Pranam*, Arya Agniswamin, please allow me to intervene. We have made substantial progress the past weeks – from the time when we foolishly assumed that the Prince was ailing because of his nervous temperament to now when we know for certain that his life is in danger. I have every reason to believe that the Kshatrapas are behind this."

"The Kshatrapas? Have they already forgotten the mighty defeat they suffered at the hands of the great Chandragupta? Why, has it not been only some six–seven years since that comprehensive defeat?", asked Arya Agniswamin.

"Indeed, Arya, it has been only seven years since that magnificent win of my great King. We had received reports of Kshatrapa nobles plotting revenge for the loss and death of their King, Rudrasimha. What their plans were, we had not known then. But their intent was malefide and we had heard that some of them had already sent their men into Nandivardhana and that some Nandivardhana locals were also helping them. Maharajadhiraja sent me here, on the pretext of helping with arrangements, to see if we could find out more. A plot to kill Maharajadhiraja himself was being made, according to information. But that may have been to distract us – the actual plot may have been to kill Yuvaraja Divakara. I believe the two young men here who have been useful in our investigations have more to tell you, " concluded Kalidasa, ending his long monologue.

As Shaunaka listened to the conversation, something clicked. The different pieces of the puzzle that were in his mind suddenly fit together – as he listened to the background provided by the *Mahakavi.* Mustering much courage and careful not to come across as either brash or disrespectful, Shaunaka said, "Arya, my name is Shaunaka, a goldsmith's son. With the blessings of my elders and Lord Krishna I am here today amidst all you distinguished people. Ashwini and I had come seeking some time with Arya Bharavi with whom I have been corresponding for a while. With your permission, I would like to show you what we have found."

"Yes, Shaunaka, continue please. I sent the guard to summon both of you up here when I was informed by the *Mahakavi* that you had been spotted in front of Bharavi's. You have information, I suppose," said Yakshavatsa, after discussing something with the Kulaputra in a low whisper.

"Arya, *Dhanyavadah.* These are apparently three separate, unconnected bits of information. The more I think about it, especially in relation to the background that the *Mahakavi* had outlined, I am convinced that these bits are not as incongruous as they appear."

Taking the *uttariya* out from his kamarbandh, he spread it out in front of the seated officials and continued, "Arya, I managed to snatch this *uttariya* from an intruder at the corner house where Vinayashura had been murdered. While I do not know who this man is, I will be able to recognise him anywhere. It is my suspicion that he is related to the palace – as that was where I lost track of him. The same uttariya has been seen with a Roman trader and an actor in Budhasresthi's *saartha*, again of foreign antecedents. What struck me as suspicious was that I once witnessed the trader, who has a stall in the main market, refuse to sell a piece similar to this to a lady who wished to buy it. If you look closely at this pattern on the *uttariya*, as Arya Bharavi will ascertain, these are letters from the Brahmi script. Is that not the script used by the Kshatrapas? The letters on the *uttariya* make this sentence - "And what does the King of Vidarbha say in reply?" Shaunaka paused to let the reference sink in. However, barring the *Mahakavi* who baulked at this reference to his play, the others did not react.

"Is this line supposed to mean anything?" interjected Bharavi.

"Arya, while the allusion was lost on me, my brother Ashwini informed me that this is a line from the *Mahakavi*'s play – the one that Budhasresthi's troupe of actors were planning to stage as a part of celebrations on the wedding day. Now, after listening to *Mahakavi*, it seems to me that this has been used as a code or an indicator to identify people who are here on their side. Does this line not refer to revenge from the Kshatrapas – to remind them of their plan?"

"You do have a point here – but it still does not lead to who these people are," opined Kalidasa, as he scratched his head and started pacing up and down the room.

"No, Arya, by itself, it does not. But this definitely confirms what you suspected. As you said, the Prince's murder is being plotted and there are a group of people – foreign traders, merchants, Nandivardhana locals who are involved in procuring the poisons and ensuring they get past all security and reach the Prince's quarters. The question is, how? However, there is another bit of information that Ashwini shared with me some time back that lends more credence to my theory. May I continue, Ashwini? Or would you like to speak?"

Ashwini shook his head and indicated that Shaunaka continue. He was uncomfortable in front of these dignitaries and was not sure what he would say.

"Arya, I mentioned to you that a similar *uttariya* was with an actor-friend of Ashwini's and that we flicked it from him a few evenings back. Earlier that day, I had seen him at the local market. He was buying some flowers, for his latest paramour or so I thought. Among the flowers, a foreign-looking orange flower with a particularly cloying sweet fragrance caught my attention. It was the same flower I had seen in the Prince's waiting chamber. The fragrance was overpowering, which is why I remembered it. While I would have not paid any attention to this and would have forgotten about the flower, Ashwini told me today that this actor did not give this flower to his paramour."

As Shaunaka paused, partly for effect, and to catch his breath, Ashwini intervened— "Arya, sorry for interjecting. This actor whom I have tried to befriend is a rambunctious man – loud of speech and dress. He is very fond of wine and women, with no morals whatsoever! Going all over town – talking lewdly, about his latest catch, Chatura, some courtesan. Oh, his plans of winning her over with flowers and ornaments and then bedding her were known to the entire *saartha* and its animals. But you know what this rascal did? When we were leaving the tavern that night – he onward for his nightly assignation, and me back to my modest dwelling, he took out just three or four stalks of this flower and handed it to me to keep it aside in our room. Lord Vasudeva knows I could not sleep the whole night – the smell was annoyingly sweet and I woke up with a headache the next morning.

I was so certain that this rascal had another conquest planned, with yet another unsuspecting damsel. To unmask his villainy, I followed him the next day. I was curious to see who got this flower. To my surprise, he hid these flowers under a large shawl he was wearing and handed this to someone just outside the East Gate of the palace complex. Arya, Lord Shiva may burn me to ashes, if I am proved wrong; but that someone he handed the flower too is definitely someone at the palace – an official maybe. "

Ashwini stopped, suddenly realising that he had managed to speak, and that too a lot, in front of these people. As the elderly wise men assimilated what had been revealed to them, Bharavi mentioned softly, "So this is why you wanted to meet me today."

Shaunaka nodded and said, "Yes Arya, it is clear to me that this is a follow-up to the conspiracy being hatched and many people are involved. While we may not yet have found out who the traitor in the palace is, we now know his accomplices – the actor and the two traders for sure. It is possible that various types of poisons are being used at the same time, which makes it harder for the Rajvaidya to find a cure, and hence, our Prince is ailing.

And then there is also the Vinayashura angle. Clearly, Vinayashura has some connection with those traders. While I sat on my watch the other night in front of the corner house, these two traders came to meet the lady of the house who paid them some money. When I discreetly checked with the Devi the next day, she mentioned that her late husband owed them some money and she cleared his dues. Was the late Vinayashura a merchant? Why else would he owe them money? Or was he being blackmailed? I am sorry that I am prying into a dead man's affairs but these are questions for which I have not got any answers."

As Shaunaka stood sheepishly after his monologue, Kalidasa smiled and said – "you are a smart young man, Shaunaka. You are definitely asking the right questions. These traders have disappeared again without a trace; my men are unable to find them. For a while, I suspected that they killed Vinayashura, but that may not be the case," replied Kalidasa.

Bharavi then intervened, "The line of thought being pursued by this young man sounds good to me. For now, Ashwini, I want you to tail this actor – be with him as much as you can and find out more."

Shaunaka said, "If I may be permitted, I would like to make a suggestion."

"Yes, go ahead."

"Arya, with the announcement of the wedding being postponed, speculation is rife about the Prince. It is possible that these men, the actor and his friend at the palace—if they are colluding to poison the Prince— may think that their plan has succeeded. They may stop meeting each other. Now if there is another announcement about a new wedding date, the conspirators would probably be jolted out of their complacency and would put together another plan — maybe something more heinous? It is then possible that the actor may again meet that man at the palace and it would be possible for Ashwini and others to catch them red-handed."

"That sounds plausible. Let us try it out. As of now, at the palace, the access to the Prince is highly restricted and even the officials working on the estate are not privy to Yuvaraja's health and condition. We can come out with the announcement at the auspicious Abhijeet hour two days from now. Ashwini, your job from now is to be with this suspicious foreign actor — accompany him, follow him. Do whatever it takes."

The discussion then veered towards the security arrangements and rearrangements in the palace. Sensing that their presence was not required any more, Shaunaka and Ashwini requested the elders' permission to grant them leave. They did so not before reassigning Shaunaka's duties. They collectively felt that he had much to offer than be restricted on the watch in front of the corner house through the night. He was asked to figure out what the connection between the Roman traders and Vinayashura was. Happy to not be stuck on a tree the entire night and waiting for things to happen, Shaunaka thanked the elders and the brothers left the building in a state of excitement.

They never expected to be in the nick of such action, such important events affecting the entire kingdom, and had much to discuss on the way out. When they walked out of the gates of the administrative quarters, Shaunaka remembered their helpless, ill-starred colleague Suddhodhana, locked up in a prison, for a crime he certainly had not committed.

"Oho we are so idiotic, Ashwini! Look what have we done. In our excitement, we forgot all about poor Suddhodhana and his accursed fate."

"Vasudeva! Now what? Should we go back and secure another audience with those esteemed gentlemen?"

"Hmm, no, that would seem rather impetuous. Tell you what. You head towards your local haunt –

where you are likely to meet that actor. I will follow you there, going first to the market across as a detour. Maybe we will stumble upon some lead, information that we can then take to Bharavi tomorrow morning and also submit our supplication regarding the innocence of Suddhodhana."

Thus decided, the brothers parted ways, temporarily, and set off on their respective paths, careful not to be seen with each other.

The walk from the administrative buildings in the city centre to the markets and taverns was a short but lively one. The time of the day, just past twilight, meant that the streets were busy. The stalls in the market had been set up and jewellers, tailors, weavers and garland makers were enthusiastically calling out to passers-by and exhibiting their crafts and wares. It was at this busy hour that Shaunaka left his home and walked towards the city centre. Amidst the throngs of young *nagarakas* and well-heeled gentlemen out to savour night life in the busy city, Shaunaka walked on, looking out for anything that may catch his eye. A group of young Buddhist monks, clad in their garnet--red robes walked past him hurriedly with downcast eyes. They were being chased by a couple of playful courtesans. Singling them out as targets, the courtesans, dressed in colourful silks, fluttered around these poor monks, like colourful butterflies. Seeing a curious Shaunaka observe them, the ladies changed track and started heckling him instead. Shaunaka tried his best to ignore them and continued walking towards the market. It was just outside the magnificent Chitrashala building that he stumbled and stubbed his foot against a stone, which resulted in him losing balance. Shaunaka fell forward and held on to the shoulder of a man standing there to stop the fall. To his extreme surprise, the man was none other than Madhavasena, the would-be son-in-law of the late Vinayashura. Madhavasena, dressed as a single wealthy nagaraka about to meet his beloved, in fine silks and bejewelled attire was standing in front of a young man, neat and clean but simple and poor in comparison. The young man whom Shaunaka had not seen before had a bottle of perfumed wine in his hand and a money pouch. Taken aback at someone lunging at him, he barked, "Eeeeee, who are you? What are you doing? Look out!" The young man yelped and held on to his things and extended a hand to Madhavasena, just in case he needed any help. "Please forgive me, Arya. I stubbed my big toe against this stone and lost balance. My intention was not to cause you any physical harm. *Dhanyavadah*, Arya. You saved me from a massive fall today."

"Young man, look where you are headed. Luckily nothing untoward happened now. You could have spoilt my expensive clothes. Now go on!" said Madhavasena, smoothing his clothes and turning towards the young man.

Shaunaka nodded but took his time to continue walking. Pretending to adjust his clothes and inspect his stubbed toe, he stood there to eavesdrop on Madhavasena's conversation. Not that he expected to gather anything — the late Vinayashura's son-in-law was more a pompous, intolerable braggart rather than a crook.

"Do you remember the instructions, *Nirbuddhi* (brainless man)? The bottle and the note need to reach the lovely Chandrakanta in the next quarter of an hour. Tell her to expect me in the third *prahar* of the night. Go on and I pray to Lord Krishna that you relay this message to my lovely lady despite your thick head. Leave now, *Murkha* (fool)!"

The young man who had been addressed by different appellations in less than two minutes by Madhavasena left and Shaunaka also started walking towards the market. At the corner of the market street, to Shaunaka's surprise, one of the garland makers recognised the young man and called out to him. He stopped and started a conversation. "Namaste, Deva. How is business today?" "Sharanga, good to see you. It has been so many days since you came this side. Are you here to pick up one of my fresh garlands for Madhavasena's fiancée?

"Oh no, no! I am doing his bidding, but not picking up fresh garlands. Instead, I am on my way to deliver these to his latest beloved."

"Beloved? Was he not about to get married to the late Vinayashura's daughter?"

"He was. I don't think the marriage is on now. My master was marrying that unfortunate widow because of her father's wealth. But he got himself killed and the family jewels were stolen. The widow lost her shine. My master must have called off the wedding. I have not visited her or the corner house in a while.

Why, previously he would send me there with notes, garlands and gifts; now he tears up her notes and gives away her gifts – she has been sending many. Well, what can one do when one's fate is so cursed?"

"Aho that is not right."

"Who are we to judge what is right or wrong? Chitragupta, up above, is keeping a track. Let him decide. I will do what I am told. I need to hurry. *Shubhratri.*"

Sharanga left the market and walked hurriedly on the footpath. Shaunaka, who had been listening to this conversation, now started walking past the various stalls, admiring the articles on display. As he eavesdropped and tried listening to conversations, especially as he passed by the stalls set up by several foreign traders, he did not gain any new information nor did he come across anything that elicited his attention. When he was confident that enough time had passed, he walked across to the tavern to spy on Ashwini and the troupe of actors.

The city of Nandivardhana was going through tumultuous times – if the murder of a well-known nobleman like Vinayashura and the eventual postponement of the marriage of the Prince was not enough to talk about; the next morning brought with it another shocking development that had the police establishment extremely worried and people talking!

Angulimala and his dreaded gang of bandits had been wreaking havoc on Nandivardhana for the past six months. To begin with, they used to attack every other fortnight, and in the Buddhist quarter of the city, every other home had been robbed. This was why the watch had been initiated. The police suspected the hand of the Angulimala gang even in the corner house murder case. But then the dreaded gang had gone silent for a while. The residents and police had heaved a sigh of relief, thanking the various *devatas* for this unexpected silence. But the peace was too ephemeral to last.

The night before, a daring robbery had been attempted — and that too in the official residential quarters. Angulimala and his men had broken into a palatial house in the official residential areas. Amatya (Administrative official in a city) Nagarjuna and his family members had gone to the temple in the palace estate to watch a theatrical performance. When they came back, they found their home ransacked and precious jewels missing.

For the people of Nandivardhana, this attempt replaced the postponement of the Prince's wedding and the death of Vinayashura as the most discussed topic the next morning. People in the city likened this robbery to the daring one in the corner house. Amatya Nagarjuna was considered luckier than the poor deceased Vinayashura. He, at any rate, lived to see another day.

It was a pleasant afternoon in Nandivardhana. The rocky, dry terrain was slowly preparing for the upcoming spring, after having gotten through a mild winter. From the time the market opened for its second shift, crowds of people seemed to throng the shops. It was definitely busier than usual; though not surprising since the news broke out earlier in the day. Lovers, *ganikas, nagarakas, sadhus*, monks and housewives were all out and kept the shopkeepers busy. The *malakaras* were busier than usual, stringing the various winter blossoms, be it *parijaat, atasi*, or *patal* into bright, colourful garlands. Dharasena and Kadamba were discussing the break-in animatedly. Business had become a bit dull, especially since two weddings got stalled.

A petite lady dressed in a rust *choluka* and a black *antariya* stopped at their stall. Dharasena thought that the lady looked familiar but couldn't place her. But Kadamba recognised her and said, "*Namaste*, Suvarna, this is a surprise. What brings you here to us? Pray that Lord Vasudeva Krishna has kept Devi Tanirika and the rest of you fine. How is Devi Tanirika? And the unfortunate Devi Tarika? Hope she is coping well too. How can we help you?

"*Arya*, by the grace of Lord Vasudeva Krishna, we are coping as best as we can. Whoever has committed this foul deed has taken away the joy from our abode. My kind mistress is slowly trying to recover from the dual blow – her husband being killed and the loss of her family jewels. In a moment, the household was completely ruined."

"Jewels? Oh was there a robbery? We did not get to hear of that," Kadamba exclaimed.

"Aho, the cupboard next to where the poor Arya lay dead was ransacked. All the objects kept inside were strewn on the floor. The thugs laid their hands on the family jewels and took it with them. But then the crime was so gruesome that obviously the robbery had paled in insignificance. Devi Tanirika has been unwell and in a thoughtful mood. Then there is the unfortunate Tarika – we haven't seen her fiancé since the customary period of mourning began. Devi worries that he may not be interested in marrying her."

"That is rather sad. Madhavasena seemed like such a good man. He has been seen here the past few days – we were also wondering why."

"Sad and difficult times. As Devi says, we must always bear the consequences of our own karma. She has been silent and contemplative the past months. But today she spoke to me. The Rajapurohita has advised a *pooja* tomorrow at the break of dawn to propitiate the blessings of the *kula* and *grama devatas*. I am here to select flowers for that." Saying this, Suvarna started picking out flowers, selecting fresh ones among the piles of various blossoms stacked in front of her.

"Angulimala has been captured. Angulimala has been captured," a royal sentry announced, loud and clear, as he walked around the main portions of the city. The market came first to a standstill and then as the news sunk in, burst into a state of excitement and chatter. As the visitors and shopkeepers started speaking about this latest development, brave acts of daredevilry were conjured in no time. The dreaded bandit had finally been caught.

"Aho this is big news. I should head home. Who knows Devi Tanirika may get her stolen jewels back," said Suvarna as she took her flowers and started walking back towards the Buddhist quarter.

Meanwhile, at Vishnuveera's workshop, Angulimala striking again had been the topic of the day. While Shaunaka and Ashwini may have forgotten to speak about Suddhodhana to the higher-ups, Vishnuveera had not. Late in the evening, he paid his *guru-bhai*, the Mahadandanayaka Yakshavatsa, a visit and explained the predicament Suddhodhana found himself in. While Yakshavatsa believed him and was sympathetic to the ill-fated man's cause, he also made it clear that he cannot let him go, especially because such strong evidence was found among his belongings. Vishnuveera understood and didn't press the matter further, for the time being.

It was Ganadasa who first heard about Angulimala being captured. He was out delivering an order placed by a rich nobleman for his mistress when he heard the royal guard's announcement. He ran back immediately to the workshop to convey this to Vishnuveera. The dreaded gang of robbers being caught, there was a renewed hope that maybe now their colleague would be set free. Leaving Somnath in charge of the workshop, Vishnuveera, accompanied by Shaunaka and Kumaragiri, immediately set forth to the police headquarters to find out more.

Kumaragiri had been in a state of absolute shock since the arrest of Suddhodhana. He believed that it was only due to the blessings of his ancestors that he escaped Suddhodhana's fate. Why, he was also there at that accursed house that morning. His bag was lying just next to Suddhodhana's. Whoever planted the dagger in Suddhodhana's bag could have done so in his too. Thanking his stars, Gods and the *pitrus*, Kumaragiri resolved to help the poor man in whatever way possible. When Vishnuveera decided to come to headquarters, Kumaragiri requested that he be allowed to accompany him too.

At the police headquarters, as elsewhere in the city, commotion and chaos ruled. The capture had resulted in the guards busting the gang's hideout on the outskirts of the city and seizing a sizeable loot — gold, diamonds, rubies, jewels, coins, and other precious materials stolen from different affluent households over the past few months. The royal guards had managed to recover most of the jewels pillaged by Angulimala. The dreaded bandits had been garlanded with red flowers, and dragged through the city. The guards flogged them repeatedly as excited crowds followed and watched them.

At the headquarters, several guards were painstakingly sorting the loot out and identifying what belonged to whom based on the complaints registered at the time of the robbery. Even though it had been an hour since the news had been circulated, a mob of aggrieved citizens had lined up at the gate, impatiently waiting to reclaim their stolen wealth. There was also the usual rush of curious bystanders, who having nothing better to occupy their time, had chosen to witness the unfolding drama. Several burly guards had been stationed at the gate to stop the impatient mob from forcing their way in.

"Arre! So much rush. How many homes did the wicked Angulimala rob!" exclaimed Kumaragiri, as they approached the police headquarters.

"Quite a few, I suppose. They have been active the past six months and I had heard that all the homes in that affluent Buddhist quarter, including the huge *vihara* set up by Mahendrasena had been robbed," replied Shaunaka.

"Yet, we do not see any monks here," observed Vishnuveera. "Shaunaka, do you know any of these guards? See if you can get us in. I refuse to stand here idly, doing nothing. If we cannot gain the Dandaposika's audience now, we can come back later."

Following his father's command, Shaunaka walked up to seek entrance. Luckily for him, one of the guards was the same man who had escorted him and Ashwini to the Mahadandanayaka's chamber. He immediately recognised Shaunaka and whispered something into his supervisor's ear. Vishnuveera and his men were, therefore, let in without much of a wait. Shaunaka, who knew his way around the building, led the way to the Dandaposika's chamber. Arya Bharavi was not in his room and the guards did not know how long he would be. Seated on a low stool in front of the office, a sort of waiting area for the supplicants, the three men waited for the Dandaposika to make an appearance.

"Shaunaka, do you come here every day?," asked a curious Kumaragiri, amazed at the confidence Shaunaka exhibited. Such a large office, so many important people and here is this young lad walking so assuredly. He knew that Shaunaka was collaborating with the police but was not aware of the exact details of the engagement.

"Ha ha, no, *bhraata*. Not every day, but I have been here a few times. We may have to wait a while, *Pitashri*," replied Shaunaka as he saw his father fidget impatiently.

After a while, Arya Bharavi walked in, flanked by two officious looking gentlemen, whom Shaunaka had not seen before.

"Aho, Shaunaka, here? *Pranam*, Arya Vishnuveera. *Pranam*, Arya Kumaragiri. What brings you all here?" asked Bharavi, surprised to see them in front of his chamber.

"*Pranam*, Arya. We are here to seek some time with you and bring to your notice a matter that means a lot to us," replied Vishnuveera politely.

"Ah, sure. Please be seated here. I have certain important issues to attend to, but I will be at your service shortly," saying which Bharavi entered his room with his men.

Eventually, they were granted audience with the busy Dandaposika, who was known to work day and night to ensure peace in the city. He was seated in front of his low desk. Bidding them to sit down, Bharavi apologised for making them wait. Before Vishnuveera could apprise him of the reason as to why they were here, Bharavi informed them, voluntarily, of Angulimala's arrest and the breakthrough they had made in the corner house murder mystery.

"I understand you are here for an important matter. Kindly bear with me for a minute. I have news of some importance to you — you would have heard, it is all over the city. Angulimala, the feared bandit and two of his men were captured today."

"Yes, Arya. We did hear. That is what has brought us here," said Vishnuveera in reply.

"Ah, the audacious rascals were trying to rob the jewels from the old Vaijayanta Temple near the palace. But the priest saw these rascals and alerted our guards. And by the grace of Lord Vaijayanta, they were captured. We have recovered most of the jewels stolen by them."

Picking up a heavy and filled pouch that was kept on the desk, Bharavi said, "Shaunaka, this pouch contains jewels that we think belong to Devi Tanirika. Could you kindly take it to her as soon as possible and ask her to check whether they are hers? If they are, please hand it to her."

Surprised and humbled to have been entrusted with a task, Shaunaka bowed and tucked the pouch into his *kamarbandh*. He stopped for a minute and then asked," Arya, could you please send two guards with me?"

"Sure, I can but I do not understand why you would like to be accompanied."

"Umm, actually Arya, Devi Tanirika knows me as the son of Vishnuveera. If I go there with her stolen jewels, she will have many questions as to how I ended up with the loot. It is more believable to say that you have sent me to return the jewels, and that will justify the presence of the two guards with me."

"Ok, so be it. Now please tell me how I can be of any help to you all."

Vishnuveera, who was looking for such an opening, now spoke at length about Suddhodhana's arrest and how he was certain that the man was innocent and would not have killed Vinayashura. He wondered whether now with Angulimala and two of his men being arrested, had there been any further breakthrough.

"Actually, while we still do not know who killed Vinayashura, we are sure that it was not the man in whose bag the elephant-headed dagger was found!"

"Oh that is wonderful. Will he be set free?" asked a delighted Vishnuveera.

Shaunaka, who was at the door, ready to leave, stopped and asked,"How did you find out, Arya?"

"Suddhodhana had never been a suspect. However, we could not let him go because the dagger was found among his belongings. During our interrogation, we focussed on the murder as well.

The bandits admitted that they had robbed all the houses but simply denied killing the old man. However, they repeatedly insisted that they had nothing to do with it. No amount of coercion or torture could get the truth out of them.

One of Angulimala's men, Nakula, confessed that they were at the corner house for nearly an hour and waited to rob the house. As they waited behind one of the annexes, or was it the temple on the right of the main building, they had seen a young wiry, neatly dressed man with no distinguishable features, jump out of the window from the first floor. Their plan had changed that moment. Usually all three of them would rob the place. However, that day, Angulimala asked Nakula to follow and keep an eye on this man and not to assist him in the main robbery. So Nakula followed this man, who had slipped away towards the annexes on the right side and was waiting in the store-room. When the body was finally found and there was a lot of commotion and the gold workers had stepped out of the annexe to find out more, this man had planted the dagger in one of the bags in the annexe and run away. Now we have proof that Suddhodhana is innocent, so do not worry he will be released or probably has already been by now," smiled Bharavi.

"*Dhanyavadah*, Arya. This is a relief; but what about the man that Nakula saw? Did he observe anything at all? Would he be able to recognise him again?" asked a curious Shaunaka.

"Nakula says he would be able to recognise him; but the man was bad at describing him. The only thing he says he remembers about him is his wiry frame. Ah yes, and that as he was leaving, he was stopped at the back gate by another gentleman – very neatly dressed again, a *nagaraka* perhaps. Nakula could not see that gentleman at all— just a hazy figure. That information was hardly useful, though it tells us that the murder was a planned one with two people definitely involved and not a hasty accident that occurred as Vinayashura tried to stop the robbery.

Shaunaka then took their leave and left with the guards to the corner house, while Vishnuveera and Kumaragiri, after thanking the Dandaposika, went on to Suddhodhana's house to see if he was back.

CHAPTER 11

When Shaunaka reached the corner house along with the royal guards, he was astonished at the extent to which the house had changed over the past few months. Gone was the glittering, lavish new dwelling, built on a grand scale that stirred awe and envy. In its place stood a jaded, towering structure, unkempt and unmaintained, radiating desolation. That evening, however, some amount of life had crept back in, mainly because of the hectic preparations for the next morning's pooja.

One of the maids who recognised Shaunaka, greeted him warmly and requested him and the accompanying guards to wait in the central courtyard. Devi Tanirika was busy in the store room checking whether all the *samagri* (ingredients) for the *pooja* and the *homa* were indeed in place and would be out with them shortly.

"Arre, Namaste, what brings you here today, Shaunaka? And that too with these guards? Did

Sudarshana not hand over the payment to your father?," asked a surprised Devi Tanirika upon seeing him.

"Namaste, Devi. I am sure he has handed the money to my father, please do not worry. Arya Bharavi sent me here with these men to hand this over to you. Could you please see these jewels and confirm whether they are the ones that had been stolen? replied Shaunaka as he took out the pouch from his *kamarbandh*.

Spreading his *uttariya* on the stone bench, next to which they were standing, Shaunaka laid out the jewels. Devi Tanirika bent down to take a closer look. To her great joy, they indeed were her stolen jewels; a major portion of what had been stolen at any rate. Suddenly overwhelmed with feelings of gratitude and relief, Devi Tanirika was silent for a minute, thankful to Lord Kartikeya for returning her family heirlooms to her. And then she replied, with folded hands, "Yes, Shaunaka, these are very much mine. I cannot thank you enough for all the help you have offered. *Dhanyavadah*."

Shaunaka folded his hands and asked her permission then to take leave. As they started walking towards the gate, Devi Tanirika said, "One minute please. I have a few more questions. Do you know more about these robbers? Were these men responsible for my husband's death? I know it does not matter any more, but I cannot help wondering whether my husband died such a gruesome death trying to ward off these robbers," said the lady with a plaintive expression writ large on her face.

Halting in his tracks, Shaunaka took some time to inform her about the weapon found among Suddhodhana's belongings, his subsequent arrest and release post bandits' capture. He carefully left out the description of the man that Nakula claimed to have seen the day of the murder.

Devi Tanirika was shocked and sympathetic when she heard about Suddhodhana's plight. "Oh ho, that poor man! Framed and charged for a crime he certainly did not commit. That would have been traumatic, not to mention grossly unfair. Why did Arya Bharavi lock him up when there was no past history or case for enmity with my husband? I wish you had informed me of this earlier. I would have spoken to Arya Bharavi to let Suddhodhana out."

Shaunaka was surprised at Devi Tanirika's reply. Something about it struck him as being odd. Did she know more than she was letting on? Her confidence that Suddhodhana could not have committed the crime, and her reference to some past enmity made Shaunaka wonder. Was it just a natural reaction? Careful not to reveal his budding suspicion, he tried to prolong the conversation by referring to the frailties of human nature and how one can never judge merely by appearance as to whether one is indeed capable of such heinous crimes. "I have known Suddhodhana for a long while; but do I or for that matter, does any one know him that well enough to say for certain that he would not have committed the crime in a weak moment? Besides, the bloodstained dagger was found among his belongings. My father and I did not try for his release until now when Angulimala and his men were captured."

"Dagger? Was that what was used to kill my late husband? Do you happen to know how it looked?"

"Devi, I cannot claim to have seen it, as I was not in the workshop when it was discovered among his possessions. But I have heard that it is big, about half of an *aratni,* 1 *vitasta*, perhaps and is made of silver. Oh yes, its most distinguishing characteristic is that it has a huge elephant head at the top."

The description of the dagger did make an impression on the lady. In a flash of a second, she turned pale and looked washed out. "Aho, sounds like they even stole the dagger from my house and killed my husband with it," she said ruefully.

"Oh, the dagger belongs to you?"

"Hmm, it was a family heirloom. My grandfather was a respected gentleman in Pataliputra. Maharaja Samudragupta, the great King that he was, honoured my grandfather by handing him the silver dagger. Who would have thought his own grand-daughter's husband would be killed with it? Maybe that was its ultimate purpose. Pardon my ramblings. I am an old lady and this has been too much of a shock. I need to go and rest. I would request you, Shaunaka, to keep me informed about these matters if and when you find out more." Saying this, Devi Tanirika walked away and into the main building and Shaunaka and the guards let themselves out and went separate ways!

Shaunaka's mind was now in an absolute turmoil. He had a strong feeling, an instinct, that Devi Tanirika definitely knew more. What was that she said? They stole the dagger? How did she know that there had been two men (if not more) who had been involved, as per Nakula's account? He had clearly refrained from mentioning who or what Nakula had seen. He could not shake away the Devi's reference to past enmities. Did her past have such a close connection with the present? Was the murder related to her or Vinayashura's doings or past actions? Was he reading too much into the matter? It was highly possible that Arya Vinayashura would have made some enemies during the course of his life. He had come across as particularly abominable and obnoxious to him and his colleagues — and they were not even directly connected! But was that reason enough to kill him? If indeed, the past had a huge role to play here, in connection with thc killing, what had happened way back and what prompted the murder now?

Such questions and thoughts took centre stage in his mind. The more he thought about it, the more strongly he felt it was the line of inquiry he needed to follow. It was pitch dark and quiet in the metal workers' quarter by the time he got back. The silence in the deserted neighbourhood was pierced only by the chirping of the night insects and the hooting of the owls. His mother had the door of the house open by the time he got to it — an occurrence that managed to surprise him each and every day. She had an uncanny ability to sense his appearance from a distance. As he greeted her and walked inside, he saw the light still on in his grandmother's room. "*Ma*, *Pitamahi* is still awake? Does she feel well?"

"Aho, she is fine. She must be meditating or saying her night prayers. Now you do not go and disturb her. It is rather late. Go sleep. *Shubhratri.*"

As he retired for the day, it occurred to him that the one person who might be able to help him in his line of inquiry was very much at home. Despite not stepping out of the house, except once in a while to a temple on special occasions, his *Pitamahi* was keyed into every little news about town. He decided to speak to her the next day and check whether she knew more about Devi Tanirika's antecedents.

When Shaunaka planned to meet his *Pitamahi* the next morning, he did not know that the next day would bring with it an entirely new set of excitements, and that his line of inquiry into Vinayashura and his family's past, whether glorious or not, would have to be put on hold for a while.

It was an interesting time for the residents of Nandivardhana There seemed to be a new topic for discussion, speculation and gossip each day. Barely had the news of Angulimala's capture and Suddhodhana's release sunk in that the next morning, as had been previously planned, there was another royal announcement. The Prince's wedding would happen, and that too, within the next fortnight. With Lord Vasudeva Krishna's blessings, the hindering circumstances which had led to the postponement of the wedding in the first place had been resolved. This announcement just before mid-day meant that Shaunaka's plan of a quiet afternoon with his grandmother had to be postponed to another day.

Kalidasa had instructed Shaunaka to be on a watch near the markets and taverns, once the wedding of the Prince was announced again. Shaunaka was to observe and bring to notice anything untoward or strange, whether or not it meant something. The markets and taverns were chosen as the location, for actors were generally seen there once their rehearsals were over. Ashwini had informed Shaunaka that following the previous announcement regarding the postponement of the royal wedding, the troupe had temporarily dismantled. They had been rehearsing *Malkavikagnimitra* for the great wedding. Since a doubt had been cast on the wedding taking place, the serious actors in the troupe had gone around town looking for temporary work. Of course, Budhasresthi had been informed and he released the other members of the troupe with a clause that they would all reassemble once the later wedding date was decided. Ashwini had also found out that the foreign actor-friend, who called himself Amaruka had left town, on the pretext of some personal work. It had been their calculated guess that he would once again make an appearance, especially if he was colluding in some conspiracy with a palace official.

Wait and watch was to Shaunaka's action plan for the next few days. Or so he thought, as he strolled into the busy marketplace and pretended to be idly occupied. He was aware that it could be an entirely futile exercise. By the time he had taken one round of the market, inspecting wares in each and every shop, it was late in the evening and the taverns were acquiring a life of their own. Seeing more crowds throng the taverns, he decided to tour them one after the other to see if he could discern anything unusual. Shaunaka's natural impatience was resurfacing and he began to doubt the efficacy of this plan and his hunch that Amaruka and that palace official, unnamed and unknown, could be a part of a conspiracy of such large national ramifications.

The row opposite the markets was littered with many taverns — what distinguished them was their size and their patronage. The establishment set up by Gangadharasena, a cunning wily merchant from Pratisthana, usually conducted maximum business and was patronised by people of varied strata – palace officials, *nagaraka*s, actors, merchants, members of guilds, and even workers. Since it was also the same tavern where Shaunaka had seen Ashwini and Amaruka the previous time, they had fixed this as their meeting point. Choosing a table towards the far end, from where he could observe each and every person entering this place, Shaunaka sat down trying to see whether Ashwini had already gotten there. He had. Seated in a table closer to the door, Ashwini was pretending to be sozzled as he looked here and there with a wild drunk expression. Shaunaka was amazed at how his brother's latent acting skills had come to the fore. Had anyone, a fortuneteller or an astrologer, told them a few months back that Ashwini had what it takes to become a great actor, they would have scoffed at him. But now, it was a wonder to see how effortlessly he had slipped into the role. Ashwini suddenly jerked and pretended to fall on the table, covering his head. Revellers seated next to him let him be, thinking that he was completely drunk. Initially concerned, Shaunaka realised it was an act when he saw Amaruka stride in, purposefully and keep his belongings, a big bag, next to him as he sat on one of the low stools a few feet away from him. He stretched himself and then motioned to the person serving wine to serve him.

This was interesting. Barely had the announcement been made than the actor was back in circulation in Nandivardhana. From the number of things he was carrying with him, it seemed that he had just arrived, directly choosing to come here rather than go to his dwellings. Also, his wrinkled clothes – *kanchuka* and *antariya*, and his dusty *paduka* attested to this. A while had barely passed, when to Shaunaka's extreme surprise, a familiar-looking person walked into the tavern. Exuding authority and grandeur, this man, thin and small, was dressed in silks and wore enough jewels to put some courtesans to shame! Attracting enough attention to his regal entry, this man walked up towards the counter, while Amaruka stood up and bowed to him. It was clear who the benefactor in this relationship was. Trying hard not to keep staring, Shaunaka concentrated on figuring out who this man was. Suddenly the answer flashed in his mind. When Shaunaka had come upon this man the previous time, he was not clad in such expensive clothes. Dressed as a , this man was none other than the intruder at the corner house, whom Shaunaka had almost nabbed after a long chase. Shaunaka looked to see whether he could catch Ashwini's eye across the room. Ashwini, pretending to be drunk, was also riveted on the scene unfolding in front of him.

As he was bellowing certain orders to the tavern owner, Amaruka picked up his belongings and walked out of the tavern. Ashwini also staged a small drama in front of him and slid out to follow Amaruka. The man from the palace was putting up a painful show of self-importance and pomp and making himself unbearable. That this was all a staged act was quite clear when he eventually walked out after a while. Shaunka had then just also stepped out for a breath of fresh air. The smells of the tavern were getting to him. To his surprise, the man from the palace brushed past him. Gone was his proclaimed self-importance or pomposity. He now adopted a furtive, smooth cat-like quick walk, and headed in the direction of the palace. What then was the purpose of this unnecessary show, Shaunaka wondered. He decided to tail this man without making it too obvious, lest someone was watching. He looked around and after making sure it was reasonably safe, he set about in the same direction.

It was when he turned into the corner lane in the administrative quarter that Shaunaka saw something shaped like an arrow or a dagger whiz past his head, nearly missing it. Too shocked to look around, and following his gut feeling, Shaunaka ducked immediately, crouching into a corner and praying that the shooter misses his target. He felt a piercing, stinging pain in his left arm as he saw that an arrow had struck him there. Fearing that this may have been poisoned, Shaunaka pulled it quickly out of his arm, and looked around to see who had attempted to kill him. Suspecting that it was someone from across the busy road who had been taking a shot, Shaunaka hastily opened the gate of the nearest building and hid behind it waiting for his assassin to come looking for him. As expected, a few minutes later, a tall, thin acrobat of wheatish complexion walked stealthily into the lane, looking around to see if he could find his target. He was carrying two daggers in open sight and the heavy bag he slung across his shoulder indicated that there may be many more. Shaunaka crouched behind the gate, with his right hand gripping the injured left arm tightly so as to not let the trickling blood create a trail that could be traced.

Taking a calculated guess, the acrobat had also decided to station himself in a nook on the other side. He had figured that Shaunaka would not have had the time to run towards the palace and was indeed hiding somewhere nearby. As the waiting game was being played out, a group of noisy revellers chose that lane to continue with their revelry. Amidst their hooting, loud singing and dancing, Shaunaka slowly opened the gate and slipped into the crowd – the alert acrobat saw him coming out of the building and took a quick shot at him. Unfortunately for the acrobat, the hasty aim missed his target and instead hit one of the inebriated revellers on his foot. The scream of the injured man stunned the noisy crowd into pin-drop silence. Before the surprised acrobat could make his way out of that nook and escape, Shaunaka used the situation to his advantage and pointed the acrobat to the furious crowd. Egged on by Shaunaka, the crowd turned its fury on to the acrobat and pounced on him, hitting and punching him. This noise caused quite a few bystanders to come out onto this usually deserted street and one of them had the presence of mind to alert the local law-enforcing officials. The acrobat, a potential assassin, was quickly taken into custody and into the main jail that was housed within the vicinity of the administrative quarters. After quickly tending to his bleeding arm, by bandaging it with a piece of cloth torn from his own *uttariya*, Shaunaka also followed them into the jail. The crowd tried to take him also to the local *vaidya*, fearing that the dagger or arrow may have been poisoned. However, Shaunaka felt that had that been the case, he would have lost consciousness long back. He was alive, saved twice, by the blessings of Lord Vasudeva and a very poor aim by this acrobat! Moreover, he was now too curious to find out the identity of the person who wished to see him dead!

The police station housed within the administrative quarters, where Arya Bharavi had his offices, was in a state of frenetic activity that night. There had been several incidents of petty crime reported in the city — mainly thieves and robbers who tried to make merry as the city lapsed once again into a celebratory mode following the re-announcement of the wedding. The rumours about strife and ill-health were obviously false. The nabbing of the acrobat who had made two unsuccessful murder attempts was but one of the few cases registered in the busy police station.

"Shaunaka, there you are. Where were you? I thought you would follow me. Oh oh, you are bleeding, what happened? Are you okay?" Ashwini, who was entering the premises exclaimed upon seeing his injured brother. Shaunaka gave him a quick update as to what had transpired after he left the tavern. He was more curious to know whether Ashwini found out anything about Amaruka's accomplice. Ashwini nodded and smilingly informed him that there indeed had been a breakthrough and that he was here not to waste any further time and apprise Arya Bharavi and the *Mahakavi* directly.

Arya Bharavi was not in his chambers when the two brothers reached. They requested one of the junior officials to pass on word to Arya Bharavi requesting audience with him as they waited in front of his chambers.

"Good that you came here directly. What you saw is crucial and will go a long way in saving Nandivardhana from her enemies. Ashwini, we should also check with Arya Bharavi whether we should go and inform the *Mahakavi* and other senior officials at the palace directly."

"Yes, we should. There, Arya Bharavi is here."

"Ah Shaunaka, Ashwini, I hope what you have come here for is urgent. It is a busy evening for us here. Come on in and be quick," Bharavi made his way into the room, indicating impatience in his tone and manner. There seemed to be too many matters to resolve that night.

Once the initial greetings were over, requesting permission to proceed, Ashwini started with his tale – "Arya, I was pretending to be drunk as per the previously arranged plan. I had prior information from some actor friends that Amaruka would be back at the tavern. If you may kindly recall, once the news of the Prince's wedding getting postponed had circulated earlier, Amaruka had cited some personal work and gone home, to Pratisthana Or that is what he had said. Yesterday afternoon, I overheard some actors talking about how Amaruka had sent word that he would soon be back. I took my place at the tavern and waited for him. He did arrive — with all his belongings — straight from where the *saartha* had halted, I think. Shortly after his arrival, the royal official I had seen him with also made an appearance. Shaunaka was there when this happened. Strangely, at the tavern, this royal official, who announced his presence rather pompously, did not even speak to Amaruka…."

As Ashwini paused, Shaunaka intervened, and added, "I apologise for this intervention. Arya, I observed this scene as well. It was indeed strange. This man from the palace walked in as if he were the Prince himself. He threw his weight around, acted obnoxiously and left rather quickly. Amaruka stood up and greeted him upon seeing him but barring that there was no interaction."

Ashwini continued, "Shortly after this gentleman's arrival into the tavern, Amaruka left, quietly. As had been decided, I followed him discreetly. To my surprise, he entered the palace estate and reached one of the public halls near the Chitrashala. Being rather late in the evening, the entire public area of the palace estate had started wearing a desolate look. Not many people were there. It was clear that Amaruka was there to meet someone as he put his belongings down, spread a mat and sat rather relaxedly. There was this big tree just behind the hall. I climbed on to that and sat quietly on a branch – from there, I could get a clear view of the hall.

The wait was long but fruitful in the end. Two Romakas, traders perhaps, also came into the hall. Shaunaka, I think these are the same ones you have seen many a time. Amaruka was geniuinely delighted to meet them and conversed heartily in a language I could not understand. What was clear to me was that this was a secret meeting and they were waiting for someone. That someone turned out to be the same man, the palace official who had been making a fool of himself at the tavern. But you know what was surprising, Arya? Gone was his pompous behaviour. There was a focus and purpose in his attitude as he entered the hall smoothly – like a vigilant cat. I could hear snatches of their conversation, from which I gathered his name. They called him Arya Mahendra. Do you know who this Mahendra is in the palace? I saw Amaruka take out several herbs and plants and give them to Mahendra, who was careful not to touch these at all and picked them up in a cloth instead. In return, Mahendra took out a pouch, presumably full of gold coins and handed it over to Amaruka.

Once this give-and-take was completed, the group parted ways — after a short exchange of words, again in that unfamiliar language. I waited for a while, got off the tree and came directly to you, Arya."

Arya Bharavi, who had been listening to this account with much interest, had a grave look on his face. "Good that you came here directly, Ashwini. This is big – just what we had suspected though. Thanks to your work, we now know some of the people involved in this heinous plot – Mahendragupta, the actor Amaruka and the two traders, at the very minimum. What this Mahendragupta does at the palace, I do not know — some junior official, but such a knave. Helping the enemy poison one's Prince. What a traitor! Let me find out more … Wait a minute…"

After instructing some of his men to arrest Amaruka at once, Bharavi then sent word to the *Mahakavi*, requesting his presence immediately. Once these instructions had been given, he came back and asked Ashwini some pointed questions about anything else he may have noticed. Ashwini told him all that he could remember.

"Shaunaka, now your turn. What happened to your arm? Do you have anything to tell us also?"

"Arya, there was another attempt on my life. Once again, it was the same acrobat. By the blessings of Lord Vasudeva, we were able to capture him. He is now locked up in jail. I came by to find out why he is trying to kill me."

"Aho, another attempt – this is indeed interesting. Who is trying to kill you, Shaunaka? Yes, we must find that out. Where has he been locked?"

The conversation was interrupted by the arrival of Kalidasa into the room. "Aha, *Pranam* Arya, Shaunaka and Ashwini. Now I understand the nature of the urgent summons. Should I happily assume that our plan was successful and that we know the name of Amaruka's accomplice at the palace?"

Arya Bharavi replied, "Yes, *Mahakavi*. We requested your presence urgently for the same. Is there a Mahendra at the palace? Some junior official? That seems to be the name of the person Amaruka is in contact with. Oh yes, our Roman traders also were present at this meeting, where Amaruka gave some plants and herbs to this Mahendra."

The name Mahendra definitely evoked some reaction. The usually impassive expression on *Mahakavi*'s face turned into one of complete shock and surprise. "Mahendra? I cannot believe it! He is the traitor? Of course, I know this boy. He is from my home, Pataliputra. I helped him get employed here. Why, he was introduced to me by Krishnadasa, who is an important personage back home. This bloody ungrateful traitor, Mahendra, assists the *Khadyatapakita* (the Superintendent of the Royal Kitchen), and is responsible for tasting the food before it is served to the Prince. Wonder how he is sneaking in the poison – for two other people are employed for tasting the food made for the Prince."

As Kalidasa paused to take a breath and come to terms with what he saw as a personal betrayal, Shaunaka interjected, "Arya, I remembered something else about this Mahendra. He was the intruder, the stranger whom I had seen at the corner house. He is the same man from whom I had snatched that *uttariya*. If I think harder, I am intrigued. Surely, there must have been some connection between him and the late Vinayashura. Even the traders seemed to know Vinayashura!"

"You are right, Shaunaka. Vinayashura must have been involved too — may be not in this plot but he did know them and or something. Why else would a junior *khadyatapakita* from the palace be found lurking in a dead nobleman's house? Oh wait! if I remember correctly, Vinayashura had also been a *khadyatapakita* at the court of Maharajadhiraja Chandragupta. This definitely needs some delving into."

"Arya, maybe I am being presumptuous but the last time when I went to the corner house to return those jewels Angulimala had stolen, something strange happened. During my conversation I got the feeling, uncomfortable, yes, that Devi Tanirika definitely knows more about who killed her husband. More than what she has told the police," added Shaunaka using this opportunity to openly air his suspicions, as there was a knock on the door of the chamber.

Bharavi's men had arrested Amaruka and the actor was now available for an extended interrogation. "*Mahakavi* and I will go now and talk to this Amaruka fellow. Ashwini, good work! Shaunaka, you should go home and treat your injured arm and rest," said Bharavi, as he put on his headgear and his most intimidating look to scare Amaruka into a confession.

"Arya, is it okay if Ashwini and I go and speak to that acrobat? I do not understand why he wishes to kill me. I cannot imagine how I may have wronged him. Or is he doing this at someone's behest?" asked Shaunaka, respectfully, not too keen to go home and rest when so much activity was going on.

"If you aren't that badly hurt and are feeling fine, please go ahead and speak to that man. Maybe you shall be able to ferret some useful information," replied Bharavi, as he walked out of the chamber, accompanied by Kalidasa, and let Ashwini and Shaunaka out.

The bells of the Buddhist *vihara* rang, loud and clear, that morning — dulling the sound of the loud *ghatika* that indicated the *prahara.* By mid-morning, when the incessant tolling of the bells did not stop, Devi Tanirika came out into the main courtyard, looking rather irritated as she surveyed her surroundings.

"Why are these bells ringing constantly? Sudarshana, Hemvati, one of you, go and find out what the matter is!"

"Must be some festival for those Buddhist monks. I will go check, " called out Sudarshana, as he walked towards the gate after belting out some instructions to an old hapless gardener. Tarika had taken him to task earlier in the day for neglecting the garden for the past months, ever since the death of her father. A not-so-happy Sudarshana had, hence, been supervising the pruning and paring down of the plants that had grown completely wild. "This mother and daughter duo need a break. A death and a stalled wedding are driving them up the hill. The bells ring every other day, and that too continuously. And yet, Devi seems to notice them just this morning. Jumpy, anxious women! Wonder what the matter is," he thought, rather uncharitably.

As he reached out towards the gate, it opened causing Sudarshana to start.

The Dandaposika Arya Bharavi, accompanied by a couple of guards and that jeweller's son entered the house. Greeting them at the gate and welcoming them inside, Sudarshana turned back to look at his mistress, expecting further instructions — conveyed through her flashing eyes. Was he to still proceed to the monastery and complain about the ringing bells or was he to simply wait?

Seated on one of the benches, Devi Tanirika, however, was lost in her own thoughts and was completely oblivious to the entering party. Seeing the visitors, Hemvati, one of her reliable maids quickly walked up to the stone bench and alerted her. Coming out of her reverie, Devi Tanirika, once more the imposing figure, stood up and welcomed the visitors. Having observed this scene from a distance, Sudarshana proceeded to the monastery anyway – he certainly was not expected there and besides, if the vistors were harbingers of bad news, he would be the target of her ire, for not finding out about the tolling bells!

"Pranam Arya Bharavi, Shaunaka, *Namaste.* Please be seated. Or would you like to go inside? "

"Namaste. It is fine here. With the blessings of Lord Krishna, I hope you are in good health and are coping with your recent loss," said Arya Bharavi offering his commiserations, as he sat down on one of the benches facing her slowly and consciously. Shaunaka and the guards respectfully stood behind, with their arms crossed and heads bent.

Devi Tanirika motioned to Hemvati to provide for refreshments after which she seated herself on the bench.

"If I may ask, what brings both of you here today? Something tells me that it certainly is not good news. Whatever it is, I pray that you tell me soon — directly and plainly — so that I have time to come to terms with it."

Tarika had, by now, joined her mother on the bench and was also listening eagerly to Arya Bharavi's response.

"Devi, indeed. This is not an easy task for me. But it is my duty to report whatever my men here have found out."

"Shaunaka? Your man? Is he not the jeweller's son?" asked Tarika, taking Shaunaka by surprise. That she knew who he was, surprised him.

"Yes. He is the jeweller's son, but I had enlisted his help after Arya Vinayashura's murder and he has been invaluable in the investigations that followed. Please allow me to continue and convey what I am here to," said Bharavi, authoritatively as both Tarika and her mother nodded.

"Devi, do you remember the intruder who was seen by Shaunaka in one of the annexes the other day? We finally found out who he was. He was Mahendra, one of the assistants to the *khadyapakita* at the palace. Does that name sound familiar to you? Do you by any chance know him?"

"Mahendra? I have heard his name – probably have seen him too. If I were to meet him, yes then I would be able to confirm, Arya. Why was he then snooping around in my house like a petty thief?"

"But that was exactly what he had come to do. He was here to steal something — not because he is a thief but your husband was killed before he could hand that over to him!"

"Arya, that is rather stupid of him. My husband died abruptly leaving behind several unfinished business deals. It would have made more sense had he come to me directly and explained what it was that he was to have gotten from my husband. Why, just the other day, there were these two strange, no, foreign traders who came and told me that my husband owed them a big amount of money. I knew nothing about what was promised to them – I still gave it to them. I do not wish for my husband to have any debts to take to his next life. Whichever ones I can repay, I will,"said Tanirika, rather wearily.

After letting her speak, Bharavi continued, "Devi, that was the problem. There was no way Mahendra could have come to you and asked for the thing that was promised to him by your late husband. The only way he could obtain it was by stealth and that was what he tried to do. I am sorry but what I am about to tell you will cause you and your family much distress. I apologise. Your husband and Mahendra, along with the foreign traders, and possibly many more people were involved in a treacherous plot to kill the Prince. Your husband's role, from what we have gathered, was to help procure and stock the various poisons that they planned to use. The item Mahendra was looking for was a mandrake plant — a rare, effective poison — and I believe, Shaunaka mentioned here, that there have been two accidental deaths of dogs in this house! The mandrake plant would have resulted in those deaths."

Tarika started and added, "That horrible scream. Suvarna mentioned it. Both the poor dogs died instantly and yes, both times there was a root or something in the dogs' mouths! We simply burnt the root with the dogs."

"Which is why Mahendra was unable to find it. Good that you burnt the roots; else they would have found their way into the Prince's food."

"Arya, but why would my father be involved in such a plot? Are you telling me that he was a traitor?" asked Tarika, turning pale as she finally understood the implication.

"I am afraid so. Under the garb of trade, which anyway he was carrying out, your father was definitely helping these people in their devious plot. Whether he did it for money or for some other motive, I do not know. Mahendra, along with some of his accomplices, was arrested last night and one of the names he took was Vinayashura. The others belonged to the Kshatrapa areas and we have not been able to get to them. Vinayashura and Mahendra were effectively carrying out the conspiracy from here — which is why his death put some spokes into their plan. The traders had already gone back after delivering several poisons to Vinayashura; it was in lieu of that that they demanded payment from you. Devi, I know this will pain you further but the traders informed us that when they had earlier contacted Vinayashura for payment, he had refused to do so. He had backtracked as he certainly did not want to spend such good money on just a few plants! Once Mahendra could not find the poisons in your house, he once again contacted the traders who had to come back from the west to deliver fresh poisons. They decided to take a chance and see whether you would pay them what they were owed. "

Arya Bharavi paused to let the news sink in. Shaunaka was intrigued by the way both the grieving women reacted. It was evident from the daughter's expression that she was heartbroken at the thought of her father being a traitor; that Vinayashura, however vile and despicable otherwise, must have loved his daughter for her to grieve so much. It was the wife's reaction that was interesting – she did not look shocked or surprised. Had she known something? Was she also a part of this conspiracy? Shaunaka continued to observe closely — there was definitely something fishy here.

"Thank you, Arya for taking the trouble to come here and inform us first. Mere words cannot convey my apology at what my husband has done. However, for whatever little they are worth, please accept my sincere regrets. If need be, please take me to the

Prince and Maharani Prabhavatigupta. I would like to convey my regrets to them. Nandivardhana may not have been my *janmabhoomi*; but it certainly has been my *karmabhoomi* – we have lived here for so long. Treason is unacceptable. No, I shall not ask for forgiveness on behalf of my husband. If you wish to make this news public, please do so. I will pray to Lord Kartikeya to protect the Prince always and bless him with good health and a long life. How is he? I hope and pray that he is fully recovered," said Devi Tanirika, as she stood up to go inside, implying that she would like to be left alone.

"Devi, this is not all. Please sit down. Bhagini, could you also sit down please?" Bharavi addressed both Tarika and Devi Tanirika. They looked at each other, surprised, and sat down holding each other's hands, preparing for the worst – though it was clear from the gutted expression on Tarika's face that there couldn't be anything worse than what they had already been told.

"Now what do you want to tell us, Arya? What else was my late husband up to? I wonder whether I knew the man I was married to for all these years at all," said Devi Tanirika ruefully.

"Devi, nothing else. We have found out who killed Arya Vinayashura. Madhavasena was arrested last night for planning your husband's murder. His young brother, Sharangadeva was also taken into custody. Both of them have confessed since. I know that this information is likely to cause you more grief than cheer. Please forgive us. We are just doing our duty."

"Madhava? What? No, no Sharangadeva is not his brother, he is his servant, Arya," exclaimed Tarika who looked completely shocked as she burst into tears.

Devi Tanirika put an arm around her daughter's shoulder and said, "Stop crying, Tarika. So you people figured it out. I was wondering how long you would take!"

Tarika gasped. She was as surprised as Bharavi and the others. "What are you saying, *Matashri*? You knew? Why did you keep quiet for so long?....Madhava is a murderer? I thought he was just a lout - who broke my heart. However can that be? He was not even in the house that morning. He entered the house much later. *Pitashri* was dead by then."

Bharavi continued, slowly, "Madhavasena got him killed. Sharangadeva, Sharangadeva, a cousin, brother, or some relation who was posing as his young man-servant killed your father at his behest."

"What a swine! Please hang him, have him executed. Justice should be served. Oh my poor father!" cried an anguished Tarika, now sobbing inconsolably, mourning her dead father and her broken heart at the same time.

Putting one hand on her daughter's shoulder, as if to calm her down, Devi Tanirika looked Arya Bharavi in the eye and said quietly but firmly – " Justice has been served! Arya, I have a request. Please let Madhava and his brother go. Tell them I understand...."

"*Matashri*! Do you even know what you are saying? You are asking Arya Bharavi to let your husband's killers go free. How can you even suggest such a thing?" cried Tarika, jerking up with an aghast look and shaking herself from her mother's hold.

Tarika stood up and requested Arya Bharavi tearfully, with folded, pleading hands, to do the right thing and not listen to her mother, who obviously seemed to have taken leave of her senses. This unexpected outburst, not characteristic of an otherwise stoic person, to whom destiny had not been too kind, brought every other person in the house, outside to the courtyard. This included Tarika's anguished little daughter, the other help, Suvarna and Siddheshwara who had come back from the *vihara.* Assembled at a distance, they could not understand what was going on and wondered whether they ought to do something to control Tarika and tried to catch Devi Tanirika's eye. But alas, Devi Tanirika sat, impassive and inscrutable like a statue, lost in her own thoughts and oblivious to the drama in front of her.

A few uncomfortable minutes passed before all of a sudden Devi Tanirika snapped out of her reverie, "Stop, Tarika. Please control yourself. There are many things you don't know. Arya, I stand by what I said. Those two boys must be set free. Please do not obstruct justice any longer."

For someone as experienced as Arya Bharavi also, this was a rare moment – a moment when he did not know what to do. It was not usual for a recently bereaved widow to defend her husband's killers so vehemently. As he took his time to understand the situation in front of him, and pondered on what he should do, Tarika threw a disgusted look and stormed into the house.

"Please wait here, Arya. I will be back," said Devi Tanirika as she followed her daughter into the corner house.

CHAPTER 12

There was an uneasy silence in the courtyard heightened by the continuously tolling bells in the background. The retinue of people employed at the corner house had hurriedly followed their mistress inside — whether to be of any help or gather some gossip about the ensuing family drama, was not known.

"What do you think of all this, Shaunaka?"

"Arya, we should lend a patient hearing to Devi Tanirika, who seems vehement in setting Madhava and Sharangadeva free. That is strange – I have felt now for a while, that Devi knows more than she is letting on. Why that is the case, only she can tell."

Bharavi nodded as he stood up and now started pacing the courtyard. "These bells, do they ring every day like this?"

"Not that I am aware of, Arya."

Siddheshwara walked out of the main house and walked up to them with a puzzled look on his face.

"Arya, please come in. Devi Tanirika would like to speak with you now," said Siddheshwara as he led them inside the main house.

In the main veranda, probably designated as a waiting area, stood Devi Tanirika by a window. Motioning Arya Bharavi and Shaunaka to sit down, Devi Tanirika said," I apologise for my daughter's conduct. She has taken it badly— her father's death and the broken engagement. She needs time to come to terms with her destiny. Arya, I am sure you have many questions; but before I proceed with my tale, could you please tell me about Madhava's arrest?I always thought he would leave for Pataliputra and get away."

Bharavi smiled and looked at Shaunaka. "This is this boy's doing. Shaunaka, would you like to speak? Or should I answer the Devi's query?" Shaunaka shyly indicated that he would rather not speak.

"Devi, Shaunaka has been helping us with the investigation of your husband's murder since the very next day. And he has proven to be of much help – providing details that have been useful in solving the mystery. The progress had been rather slow as the clever Madhava had covered his tracks quite well. He was under observation – but that was because he was spending too much time with some *ganika*s and this evoked much reaction. His character indeed came across as suspect – an opportunist who had rejected your daughter the moment your husband was killed and the jewels stolen.

But for one mistake he made, we may never have found out and he would have gotten away. Shaunaka's constant presence at the corner house made Madhava uneasy. Worried that he may be on the right path, he paid an acrobat to kill Shaunaka as well! Over the past few months, there had been a couple of failed attempts to kill Shaunaka. Last night the acrobat was arrested after another failed attempt."

"Krishna! Why would he do that? That is stupid. Should he not just have left for Pataliputra?," exclaimed Devi Tanirika, shaking her head ruefully.

"Well, to his credit, he elicits much loyalty from his people. The acrobat, despite being arrested, did not reveal Madhava's name. Instead, he told us many unbelievable tales – a different version each time we questioned him as to why he tried to kill Shaunaka – not once or twice. Quite a frustrating experience, but he would not tell. We may never have connected the dots but for Shaunaka's keen observation.

The acrobat is also a bit of an actor, who got carried away with the fantastic tales he was cooking up. As he enthusiastically narrated another tale, with amusement gleaming in his eyes, Shaunaka spotted something that gave it away."

"It was the lovely, unique *navaratna anguliya* he was wearing on his ring finger. I am a jeweller's son after all. I had seen and admired the same ring on Madhava's finger the day of Vinayashura's death. Last night, I saw it again and at that instant, it was clear to me – Madhava, for whatever reason, was behind this attempt on my life." Shaunaka pitched in, as Tanirika listened interestedly.

"Devi, this is how we arrested Madhava and he then confessed to his role in the failed attempts on Shaunaka's life and Vinayashura's murder."

Tanirika nodded, "I wondered whether you would ever be able to find out."

"Devi, if you knew, why did you not tell us?"

"Arya, from the moment I set my eyes on that man, I knew that my husband's end was near. Let him be, *Arya.* Let Madhavasena go back to Pataliputra. Do not arrest him."

"We would like to know why. Why did Madhava kill your husband? Why are you insistent that we should set him free? asked Bharavi voicing the one question in everyone's minds.

"It was the eighth day of the *Jyeshtha* month. This day has always been special, as it reminds me of Pataliputra. This year was no different as I looked forward to this joyous day. Everyone in Nandivardhana had been preparing for this celebration with much fervour.

Our Queen, the illustrious Prabhavatigupta, of the *Dharana Gotra*, chief queen of the glorious Rudrasena II, Maharaja of the Vakatakas, and the mother of our *Yuvaraja*, Divakarasena was gracing this year's function. Just like how her father, Maharajadhiraja Chandragupta II used to....

This festivity in Pataliputra started many years back. I was not even born then. My father told me that back in those days when our great king, *Maharajadhiraja* Samudragupta was ruling, some Buddhist monks from a faraway country, Tamraparni, came to Pataliputra. Their king requested our God-like king's permission to build a Buddhist *Vihara,* which our benevelonet king granted them. That is how a *Vihara* came up in Pataliputra – the first one. The next year, the monks at the *Vihara* celebrated this festival, which has been celebrated annually ever since. The whole city of Pataliputra used to join in - Brahmins, Vaishyas, Buddhists everyone; not like it is now, or so I have heard. How else would I know? I have not been to my birthplace in such a long time.

Arya, I know, I know I am getting stuck in my past. Do excuse my digression. My husband and I moved to the Buddhist quarter recently, not too long back, when this house got constructed. Prior to this, we used to live in the vast palace estate, in the royal quarters. My husband, Vinayashura decided not to work at the palace anymore; he had been keeping rather unwell. He did have some business and trading prospects, which he said he would like to pursue while regaining his health. The *Rajvaidya* gave him some herbs but my husband did not recover.

I do not know if you remember, a mendicant from Kamarupa, named Shapanaka visited Nandivardhana a while back. Near the Buddhist quarters, as one walks towards the guild area, there is a small hut, where he was put up. People were talking about his effective medicinal herbs. Siddheshwara heard about him and came and told Hemvati and Suvarna. Suvarna requested permission to go to this mendicant and get treated for her knee pain. To our surprise, and hers, she reported good progress. She was the one who suggested that we take my husband there. We were not sure whether we should go to him. People were not sure whether he was a Buddhist or a Brahmana or a Jaina. My husband was particular about the company he kept and this man had no antecedents. I mentioned it to the good queen when I met her and she was the one who advised us and convinced my husband to go to the mendicant. We did.

What a strange meeting that was! Shapanaka kept staring at my husband strangely for five minutes and then asked us to leave. My husband looked a bit taken aback but he did not say anything and tried to get up to leave. I was surprised because he did not say anything. I don't know if you met Arya Vinayashura, when he was alive. My husband expected to be treated in a particular way, the way he was used to, with deference and respect. Perhaps he was in pain and that's why he did not say anything.

I was rooted to the spot, I remember, not because of shock, but because of the look in Shapanaka's eyes. There was rage, pity and disgust all at the same time. My husband tapped me on my shoulder, indicating that we should leave. Just as we were leaving, the good Mahadandanayaka Yakshavatsa entered the hut and respectfully greeted us. When my husband indicated that the mendicant had refused to treat him, the good man intervened. May the Almighty bless him!

The mendicant signalled for us to leave and asked Yakshavatsa to stay back. We waited under the big banyan tree at the end of the street. It was almost noon on a pleasant day, not too sunny, not too cold. There were some old men sitting under the banyan tree and debating some issues rather heatedly. My husband and I sat down in a corner and waited for what seemed a long time. Just when we were about to go back to the palace, Yakshavatsa came out hurriedly and said "Go in. He has agreed to treat you, Vinayashura. Just do not say anything that might anger him." We went inside the sparse hut a little hesitantly. My husband used to get angry very easily and this incident had provoked him. I used all my powers of persuasion and somehow convinced him. It was after all for our own good. What is the point of having such an ego or anger when it is to our detriment? I was extremely nervous as we stepped inside. My husband was not known to observe civilities when angered; I hoped and prayed that there would be no angry outburst.

The hut was light and airy. The window was open letting in the bright, warm sun. There was a cot in one corner and next to it was a *chaityamukha* filled with water. The stern Shapanaka was sitting cross-legged on a small carpet made of tiger skin. He had a small *kamandala* next to him. The *uttarasanga* (upper garment) and the *antarvasa* (lower garment) were made of pure, expensive cotton and were red-ochre in colour. His matted hair was tied up in a *shikha* and he had a *rudraksha mala* in his hand. As I wondered whether he was a Brahmana or a Buddhist or a Jaina, I spotted some bright pictures on the wall. One was the scene from the Narasimha *Avatar* of Lord Vishnu. Next to it was a Jaina *Arhata* who was dressed like Siva. The wall opposite had a massive painting of a forest inhabited by *yakshas, yakshis and gandharvas.*

My confusion worsened but I stopped thinking about it as the mendicant beckoned us to sit in front of him. He was civil but cold. Shapanaka did not disguise the dislike he felt for my husband. Thankfully, the wise man did not let that affect the way he treated my husband.

Shapanaka asked my husband about his problems and listened to him intently. Then he closed his eyes and meditated for a little while. Once he was clear what the diagnosis was, he stood up and walked towards the window. After thinking for a while, he said gruffly, "The only reason I am helping you, wicked man, is because my dharma is to help and cure one and all. Humph! I feel sorry for your wife and children." As I stared in shock and horror, I saw my husband clench his fists and try to stand. He was furious. The mendicant continued: "Go if you will. You have but some time to live. Your karma will come back soon to haunt you, you foolish, evil man."

At this pronouncement, my husband looked crushed and gave up any further attempt to move. I still remember the chill that ran down my spine. I could not comprehend what Shapanaka meant or said. What were we supposed to do? Go back? I kept quiet and waited. If there is one thing I have learned in so many years is to be silent and wait and watch, and not react. A few moments had passed when Shapanaka turned and said in a calmer voice, "Extend your hand. I shall administer *Marma Chikitsa* now. " My husband did as he was told. Shapanaka pressed a couple of *marma sthanas* both on his hand and ankle. After fifteen minutes, he told us that our session for the day was over. My husband was asked to come every day. Since the walk from the palace quarters to Shapanaka's hut took us three-fourths of an hour, we shifted some days later to our present house, the construction of which had thankfully been completed.

Oh yes, I was telling you about the procession – the Buddhist celebrations. I remember that Tarika was looking beautiful and happy on the day of the procession. She had worn her hair in a side braid, covered with jewels. A small *mukuta* covered her centre parting, and she had worn her gold-laced green brocade, the one she had worn after her wedding, with a new yellow *angarkha* in the latest style with long sleeves. I remember wondering why she was dressed so well. What was the matter? She seemed nervous too. I did not let my surprise show, nor did I make any comments.

The lane in front of our house was filled with excited bystanders. Everyone was waiting for the procession to pass. The procession comprised two or three large chariots built like a *stupa*. The images of the Buddha and the *Bodhisattvas* were carried on these chariots. The Bhikkus from the *Vihara* led this grand procession. The chariots were laden with gems and precious stones, silk and brocade streamers. It was such a colourful sight. The queen, the rich Brahmanas and Vaishyas contributed generously to the procession. Even my husband, who was usually very particular about not spending his money, had started contributing to the procession. Ratnakara, the rich trader who lives in Pataliputra, was going to distribute medicines and gifts to the entire town of Nandivardhana this year.

Have you heard the story about how the celebrations started in Nandivardhana? Our queen, Prabhavatigupta was unhappy and lonely when she moved from Pataliputra. This was when our great king, Rudrasena, was leading the Vakataka army along with his father-in-law, Chandragupta II in a joint fight against the Kshatrapas. They had joined hands to defeat the treacherous and evil Rudrasimha III. In a bid to cheer the new bride up, her noble mother-in-law asked her what they could do in Nandivardhana to lessen her homesickness. It was the month of *Chaitra* and our queen remembered this grand two-day festivity back home and requested her kind mother-in-law for her permission to celebrate it here. And so since that year, we celebrate the eighth day of *Jyestha* just the way the Buddhists in Pataliputra do.

There, I again started digressing. Pardon me. When the yellow and red silk canopy on top of the stupa was seen in our lane, I asked Tarika to call her father.

I wanted him to watch and be part of the joyous scene. In a strange way, my husband had become both quiet and belligerent since the day we met Shapanaka. At home, with us, he would not speak much. With strangers he would be bellicose and argumentative. Something was gnawing his mind but he would not share it with anyone.

Finally, the beautifully-decorated chariot was here, with its bright golden and red canopies, and green and orange silk flags. The sight was truly breath-taking. The Buddhist *Vihara* seemed to have got more donations that year. The Buddha *vigrahas* included life-size ones of the radiant and heavenly *Amitabha*, flanked on the right by the kind *Maitreya* and on the left by *Avalokiteshwara*. I could recognise these ones. On our way from Pataliputra to Nandivardhana we had stopped for a night in Sanchi. That was when I had seen some of these images. There were images of other Bodhisattvas as well on this chariot.

As the procession passed our house, I felt at peace. My loved ones seemed happy after many years. Anagha, my granddaughter, was waving happily at the Bhikkus and the village folk walking behind the chariot. She appeared to be particularly happy when a charming young man passed us by. Who was this man, whom my grand-daughter can recognise? Just then I heard a gasp that caught my attention. My husband, who looked shell-shocked and pale, was staring at the same charming young man. I became worried that it was his ailment causing trouble again and turned to Tarika so that we could address the pain. I do not know whose reaction worried me more that moment. Tarika was looking at the man, adoration writ on her face, glowing and shy, the look of a woman passionately in love. Evidently her feelings were reciprocated for he was looking at her with an equal passion. Conscious of the people around her, Tarika broke the eye-lock and fumbled, looking down at her feet. It was then that I saw the man stare at my husband with an unfathomable look. It was the look of a victor, a look of a man in control, and a man of power. His thin lips curved into a small, vicious smile and at that moment I knew that this man was to cause my family's destruction. He was in his mid-thirties, in the prime of his youth, of a darkish complexion but with a pleasing broad, manly physique. His hair was worn shoulder length and curled with no parting. He wore a royal blue *antariya* made of silk and a cream *uttariya.* His *kanchuka* was of the latest fashion, made of rich blue brocade and had short sleeves. It was the first time I had seen Madhavasena and I knew I could not stop him. He also reminded me of someone I knew from once upon a time and from a land far away."

Tanirika paused and looked at her audience. "You must be thinking why I am telling you all this. I have been burdened with these thoughts. Please bear with me; I need to get this off my chest."

She specifically looked at Shaunaka and said, "*Arya* Bharavi and I know each other from Pataliputra. He knows about my background but you don't. I think I should start from the beginning.

Devi Tanirika's story

I was born the eldest daughter of Charudutta, of Kotivarsha Vishaya, many decades ago in Pataliputra. I have been in Nandivardhana since the time the glorious Rudrasena, the Maharaja of the Vakatakas became the king and married the brave princess of our kingdom, the majestic Prabhavatigupta. My husband and I moved to Nandivardhana as a part of the queen's entourage sometime then.

My husband was an assistant to my father, Charudatta, the royal *khadyatapakita* in the court when Maharajadhiraja Samudragupta was still alive. When Princess Prabhavatigupta, the daughter of Prince Chandragupta II, was wed, she expressed a desire that my father accompany her to Nandivardhana. Now, of course the great King did not agree to that. He was reluctant to let go of his trusted cook during such difficult times. Our kingdom was facing several challenges back then and trusted people were valued. Besides Maharajadhiraja Samudragupta was very old; he was afraid that he would not live much longer. My father was also not keen on moving out from the court of Pataliputra. He had spent his entire life in this court, first watching his own father as the head *khadyatapakita*, then training as an assistant and then becoming the head *khadyatapakita* himself. Too much of his past was connected to the palace and the King. So he did indicate his reluctance.

The matter ended there, or so I thought. The great King Samudragupta died a year later and King Ramagupta commenced his short, shameful, and cowardly reign. It sends shivers down my spine when I think of those days. Ramagupta proved to be a weak king. Queen Dhruvadevi was in love with Prince Chandragupta. The Prince's senior queen, Queen Kuberanaga, had blessed their union. And everyone knew this. You can imagine our horror when the deceitful Ramagupta forcibly married her. He was such a weak and treacherous man.

As a king, he was unable to quell the various voices of dissent. And the kingdom plunged into a state of disorder and chaos. Taking advantage of our situation, our enemies started planning attacks on our kingdom. The Kshatrapas were our biggest enemies and their ruler invaded our country. And this is when the cowardly Ramagupta showed his true colours. Instead of leading our troops into battle against the invaders, the cowardly king bought peace with the enemy. And you know how? He agreed to hand over the beautiful Queen Dhruvadevi. What a tumult it caused in our city. We just could not come to terms with it. Oh, we felt so insulted and dishonoured, all the women in Pataliputra, that is.

Luckily for Pataliputra, the younger prince, Prince Chandragupta was made of sterner, honourable stuff. He cleverly disguised himself as Dhruvadevi and entered the Kshatrapa camp, and killed the enemy king. He taught his protesting brother a lesson too by killing him. Yes, that was a bit harsh and probably unwarranted. But such were the times."

King Chandragupta II took over the reins of the kingdom and peace came to Pataliputra. Several years passed by joyfully. And then one day, when my father, husband and I were sitting in the palace kitchen for our *bhojana*, my husband requested for permission to speak. He was still an assistant to my father. He suggested that he would like to join the Princess's entourage and go to Nandivardhana. Princess Prabhavati, now the Queen of Nandivardhana, had come to Pataliputra for a visit. She was to leave in two weeks. My father was, at first, not too happy at the thought of his only daughter going so far away from him. But he thought for a day and then told my husband that he quite liked his suggestion and that he would speak to the King. So a couple of days before the Princess left, my father hesitantly approached the King with this idea. To my father's surprise, the King was very happy with this suggestion and immediately signed the decree by which my husband Vinayashura was appointed the Chief *khadyatapakita* of Princess Prabhavatigupta' s entourage.

I was nervous but excited. The thought of travelling all the way from home was interesting. It was the first time that I would be leaving Pataliputra. Since my father and his father had been *khadyatapakitas* for the great King Samudragupta, the magnificent palace in Pataliputra and its vast estate was the only world I had known. I was born in the quarters allocated for the workers in the palace. Since the Princess and her younger sister were just a few years older than me, I grew up playing and studying with them, spending time in the royal quarters. The Queen, the kind Kuberanaga, the mother of the royal princesses, was very fond of me. My mother passed away when I was a toddler. The kind Queen had told her attendant ladies to pay special attention to me. Truth be told, growing up with the princesses, and among so many ladies, I did not miss my mother. My father was relieved. I did not see him much during the day, but he would sit with me and would talk and play *Ashtapada* and *Dashapada* before we retired for the night. As I was growing up, our evening sessions became longer. We would discuss matters related to my studies and later the affairs of the palace and the kingdom. Just like the princesses, I also learnt to read, write, play the *veena*, sing, dance and compose poems. And then, when Vinayashura expressed his desire to marry me, how hesitant and fumbling my father was, when he asked me for my consent. He had been a good father and yes, the thought of leaving him all by himself in Pataliputra made me sad. I was not sure whether I would ever see him again. And as it turned out, I did not see him again. Anyway, filled with trepidation, anxiety and some excitement, I looked forward to my new life.

On an auspicious day towards the end of *Shravana* in the 61st year, the Queen and her entourage set out towards Nandivardhana. It was the rainy season and the sky was overcast as we started our journey. The distance from the palace to the main city gate took us a while longer than expected. People had lined up to bid farewell to their beloved princess. We were travelling in five beautiful, covered *shivikas* (palanquins.) Some soldiers of the army also accompanied us on their horses, taking their place in the front and at the rear. I was in the same *shivika* as the queen and her closest attendant, Nandini. I looked out excitedly as the *kaharakas* shouted to make way as our palanquins passed. As we crossed the ramparts of our town, and left through one of its sixty-five magnificent gates, I knew and rightly so that this would be the last time I was seeing my hometown. But once we crossed the ramparts of the city, and the city gates shut behind us, our progress was quicker. The countryside was lush, green as we made our way, passing through untamed lands and forests. The sights I saw on the way are etched in my memory till now. While bidding me goodbye and offering his blessings, my father said, "Keep your eyes and mind open, Tanirika. Jambudweepa is a big, beautiful country. You will learn a lot by observing." I have not forgotten that advice till now. The journey was arduous as the distance between Pataliputra and Nandivardhana is roughly 101 *yojanas*. We stopped at the *pathikashraya* in Prayaga, Sanchi and Ujjayini, where we were received very warmly and taken care of very well. In all, it took us about ten days to reach Nandivardhana.

I had heard from various people that Pataliputra is a magnificent city. It was only when we entered Nandivardhana that I understood how beautiful and great Pataliputra was. Nandivardhana is a well-planned city but nowhere as beautiful as Pataliputra. The terrain is rocky and dry in this part of Jambudweepa. The massive imposing wooden gates to Nandivardhana had the image of a *trishula* on its façade. As the gates opened, we spotted a small garden with an iron pillar in it. There was an impressive Nandi figure on the top of the pillar. Some Vakataka soldiers joined our entourage as we continued through to the palace. The small garden was at an intersection of four main streets. We took the road that was on the far right. By the road were hawkers selling food and sweetmeats. There were also some shops where grain, rice, vegetables and fruits were sold. At the end of these rows of shops, the road bifurcated and the smaller road to the right led up to the palace that was atop a hill. It was also the *Brahmana* quarter of the town. Most of the *Brahmanas* lived here and so did the employees at the royal court who preferred to live outside the palace confines.

The royal palace estate was guarded by a colourful door painted ornately in red, green and yellow. As the guards let us in, a small procession from inside the palace came towards to the gates to welcome their queen. There was a general air of festivity. A thin man wearing a bright yellow *antariya* and a red *uttariya* was playing the flute beautifully. As we got down from the palanquins, a group of beautiful dancers came towards us. Our queen was welcomed with flowers, *kumkuma* and *haridra.* The dancing girls gave way to the members of the royal family. The queen mother and the two sisters, dressed in royal finery, replete with a *nupura* and *kirita*, were there to welcome our queen.

It took us a while to get used to life in the royal palace at Nandivardhana. Things were very different over here but we managed. I did not have the same easy access to the queen's royal chambers that I had in Pataliputra. I was confined for the most part to our small housing quarter that we had been allotted in the southern wing of the palace estate. Most of the *Brahmanas* lived outside the estate and I found myself wanting to shift there too.

My days were spent painting, practising the *veena*, composing small verses and doing some embroidery. On *sukravasaras* (Fridays), I got into a routine that helped me meet the Queen. There was a small temple within the palace estate that had an idol of Goddess Lakshmi. From the first week, every *sukravasara*, the Queen went there for the Lakshmi *Pooja*. The royal family at Nandivardhana worshipped Lord Siva and I was quite sure that the Queen mother did not quite approve of the weekly Lakshmi *Pooja*. That did not deter our princess. Some of us from Pataliputra would meet at the temple for this *pooja*.

Soon, weeks passed into months and years. So here we are. I am no longer a newlywed, neither is the Queen. She is the proud mother of two sons, the powerful regent. Nandivardhana has been a kind place; the people have been good and welcoming here. But fate has not been that benevolent. No mother likes to see her children dead or unhappy. It has been my misfortune that I have had to endure both. I had a son whose name was Vasanta. Just as Vasanta is a season that showers its joys upon us for a while, so was he. He died of a snake-bite when he was merely fifteen. Oh, how that shattered both Vinayashura and me. And my daughter, Tarika, has had an unfortunate life. She fell in love with Samarthaka, a fine young man employed as a scribe at the palace. The royal *jyotisha* had advised us against this match, but Tarika was in love and did not pay any heed to the warnings. Samarthaka died barely five years after their marriage and my young girl was left a widow and a mother to baby Anagha."

Suvarna entered the room again with some refreshments, *madhuraka* on a tray and placed it in front of Arya Bharavi. Upon seeing this, Devi Tanirika stopped at this juncture and said "This was my story, my life, and my past. You know who I am, where I come from. Please partake of these refreshments. Let me then tell you the reason why Vinayashura had to die."

Devi Tanirika had a faraway look in her eyes. She sighed and continued, "When King Chandragupta II killed his elder brother and became the King there were several dissenting voices in the palace. Chief among them was the *Mahabaladhikrita* (Commander-in-Chief) of the kingdom, *Arya* Anangasena. He was said to be a close friend of Ramagupta. Oh, but do not think that he was unhappy because his friend had been killed. His intentions were suspect, we heard from people. They said that he wished to usurp the throne for himself, after having the weak and useless Ramagupta as the figurative regent. It was even said that he was the one who advised the foolish, weak king to send Queen Dhruvadevi to the Sakas as an offer for peace.

Naturally, he resented it when Maharaja Chandragupta became the King. It surprised us that King Chandragupta reposed his faith in *Arya* Anangasena and he continued as the *Mahabaladhikrita*.

Seeing the faith reposed in Arya Anangasena, I was convinced that the rumours about *Arya* Anangasena resenting King Chandragupta were just that – sheer malicious, baseless rumours. How naïve I was! If at all, they were anything but that. What I did not know till much later was that my husband was also among those who resented King Chandragupta.

A couple of years had passed, when tragedy struck our kingdom. On a stormy dark *amavasya* night in the month of *Chaitra*, the Queen Ratnavali was found dead in the royal inner bedchamber. Next to her was a handsome young man also dead. Near the bed on the floor were two half-empty glasses of the *prapaanaka*, which His Majesty usually preferred to drink every morning.

This discovery caused ripples throughout the kingdom. Further investigations revealed that the dead man was Sagara, a spy from the powerful Kushana kingdom. You will of course remember that Queen Ratnavali was the Kushana princess, whose hand our mighty King had won when he subjugated her kingdom. Sagara and Ratnavali were old lovers, who apparently had continued their illicit rendezvous whenever possible. It was clear to most that Sagara and Ratnavali were just unfortunate. The (as it turned out) poisoned *prapaanaka* was actually meant for the King, who was saved only because one of his trusted spies came from Pataliputra with some new information which compelled His Majesty to summon his council of ministers urgently. So he was spared an untimely death!

The King was livid at his wife's infidelity and even more at the blatant failure of intelligence that permitted a poisoner to get so close to success. The officials tried to find the culprits but the network was so strong that they just could not. Dreading the King's fury, the officials, in order to cover up their ineffectiveness and incompetence, decided to find a scapegoat. It was better to lay the blame upon some man, any man rather than admit to the King that they have not been able to make any headway in the investigation. "

Shaunaka looked shocked. In a moment, his youthful idealism about how kingdoms function seemed to have taken a beating. "Please pardon my interjection. Devi, are you telling me, that the officials of the great kingdom of Pataliputra, about whose wisdom we have heard so much, and who are much respected, were in reality, so callous as to convict an innocent man and ruin his entire family? All for their reputation?"

"That is indeed the sad truth. For the officials, their reputations and jobs were at stake. The King was furious – his life was under threat and for securing that, he was ready to send these ineffectual officials to prison or even to the gallows.

They found a scapegoat – a new gatekeeper who was on duty that fateful night. His name was Sridharasena, a young man in his thirties, who belonged to Anuganga, a small village near Pataliputra. A newcomer to the

King's guards, his only mistake, if it could be called one, that day was to let Sagara into the palace – alas, he did that on Her Majesty's instructions. Who was he to disobey Queen Ratnavali? Besides, he had left for his village soon after, as his wife gave birth to their second child.

Sridharasena was accused of plotting the King's death upon Sagara's behest. The accusation sent shockwaves through the palace and the city. On one level, it did not make any sense whatsoever; but on the other, we thought that if the officials were saying so, there would be a grain of truth to the matter. How wrong we were.

The poor accursed man was arrested from his village, and dragged all the way to Pataliputra. Sridharasena protested his innocence and claimed vehemently that he did not know Sagara from before and that he had no part to play in this whole sinister plot. But his protestations of innocence were ignored. He went to the gallows, shouting his innocence and cursing all those because of whom, he had been wrongly accused of this grave crime."

Devi Tanirika was visibly exhausted. Revisiting her painful past seemed to have taken its toll and she now looked years older and much weaker. She looked up at Suvarna and requested her to bring her a glass of water. It was then that Shaunaka, who had till then been so engrossed in the tale, noticed Tarika standing in the corner, equally rivetted by the past that had so much bearing on her present.

Arya Bharavi looked weary too, "I remember Sridharasena's execution, Devi. People still remember his heartrending cries and anguished curses as he accepted his sad fate. It was known that he was made a scapegoat. But by whom? That was not known at all."

Devi Tanirika smiled, a sad smile and said, "Arya, I found out the truth, barely a fortnight after Sridharasena's execution. The people behind both the diabolical scheme to kill the King and then implicate an innocent man were none other than *Arya* Anangasena and my husband! Vinayashura had poisoned the *prapaanaka* meant for King Chandragupta that night. I had known that Vinayashura had been sympathetic to King Ramagupta's cause. But I did not and could not imagine that his sympathies would extend to murder. How foolish I was! Believing my husband to be a kind and good man!

The sinister plan was to poison the King that night but it was foiled owing to that sudden meeting. *Arya* Anangasena tried to stop Vinayashura from sending the poisoned *prapaanaka* to the inner bedchamber once he was invited to the council, but by then it was too late. It was *Arya* Anangasena who advised King Chandragupta to hush the matter up by sentencing Sridharasena to death. King Chandragupta was not convinced about Sridharasena's involvement but did what his commander-in-chief suggested. *Arya* Anangasena hoped, rightly, as it turned out, that once a man was executed for this plot, the news would die down.

Over the next year, *Arya* Anangasena and Vinayashura tried three more times to kill King Chandragupta. But they were unsuccessful each time.

Two years after the execution of Sridharasena, *Arya* Anangasena was killed while leading an expedition against the invading Kshatrapas. Shortly after that, Vinayashura and I moved to Nandivardhana.

So you see, the two men responsible for this heinous plot had gotten away absolutely scot free.

An innocent man paid with his life. But none cared or even remembered, except for Madhavasena and Sharangadeva, the two sons of Sridharasena, who spent their childhood trying to wipe out the ignominy of being called a traitor's sons. Yes, Madhavasena and Sharangadeva were brothers. They stumbled upon the real culprits of this foiled conspiracy and it became their life's aim to punish the men behind their father's tragic death. They tracked down Vinayashura and killed him.

Devi Tanirika seemed peaceful as she ended the narrative. Smiling at Arya Bharavi, she said, "Now you know the reason why Vinayashura had to die. Please set Madhava and Sharanga free; tell the world that their father was truly an innocent man. Please also reveal to the world, what my respectable husband had been up to – in the past and even now before his death. I am finally at peace — the guilt of not speaking up and carrying such a serious matter as a secret had been playing up on my mind. But now, it is off my chest.

Over the past few weeks, I have understood why my son also had to die and why my daughter has seen so much sadness. After all, the curse of the gatekeeper had to be fulfilled. How can we be happy when we put him and his family through such misery?

Please do tell Madhava. I have no rancour towards him."

Turning towards the door, she smiled at her daughter, who now looked sheepish and apologetic, "So you see my dear, justice has truly been served. Do not hate him for what he has done. You were simply an instrument for the workings of fate to dole out justice. Be thankful; and remember, Madhava is a good man – he did not take advantage of you, when he could have. Forgive him and if you can, when you feel calmer, try and forgive your father; what had to happen did. Your father made poor and wrong choices and paid for it. Justice has been served after all."

It was late in the afternoon when Arya Bharavi and Shaunaka, along with their two guards left the corner house towards the administrative quarters. As they walked past the Buddhist *vihara*, they realised that the bells had finally ceased. They were no longer tolling incessantly. Shaunaka chuckled and observed, "Looks like the gatekeeper's *aatma* has finally found peace." Almost as a reply and an affirmation of his observation, a sudden breeze with a peculiarly sweet sandalwood fragrance gently wafted through the air.

EPILOGUE

"What an absolutely calm evening, *Pitamahi*. One can't hear or see a thing and it is hardly the second *prahar* of the evening." It was later that evening, much after activities had been wound up and people had started retiring to the comfort of their homes that Shaunaka stood near the window in a room on the first floor of their house and looked out.

It was his grandmother's room and he was waiting for his grandmother to finish her evening duties and for Ashwini to come back from his rehearsals. He had much to tell them, reflect about and look back upon.

"Shaunaka, the view is the same every other night. You seem to have spent too much time with the *Mahakavi*! Assigning meaning to the same sight that greets you every night from this window. It is just your perception – you are calmer now that the killer of Vinayashura has been identified. Really, my boy, at my age do not expect me to subscribe to this line of thinking. Now, are you going to speak up and tell me about what happened today? Where is this

Ashwini? He's become a wastrel ever since he took up this drama. Aho, now that your sleuthing is over, can he come back and help Vishnu in the jewellery work?" said Ahalya Devi seated on a mat in a corner of the room. She clearly looked exhausted and was impatiently waiting to retire for the night.

Ashwini entered the room, excitement largely written all over his face. "*Pranam, Pitamahi.* So Shaunaka, I heard. The news of Madhavasena killing Vinayashura and Devi Tanirika pardoning him is all over the city. I came as fast as I could. Do tell us more."

Ashwini settled into a comfortable position as Shaunaka turned towards his audience and narrated the events of the day in detail. In particular, he told them that he required some advice regarding a decision he would have to make about his future in the coming days and months. During a meeting with the *Mahakavi* that afternoon, Kalidasa had suggested that Shaunaka go to Pataliputra with him and work there for the Maharajadhiraja Chandragupta. While Shaunaka was excited about this new possibility of travel to the great city, he was not sure whether he should take such a big risk. What did they think he should do?

At this point, Ashwini interjected. He had his own dilemma to share. The *Mahakavi* was of the opinion that he should continue being an actor with Budhasresthi's *saartha* and tour the entire *desha* while gathering intelligence for Nandivardhana and Pataliputra. What should he then do?

As Shaunaka and Ashwini passionately discussed and debated the choices in front of them, pondering upon the consequences, Ahalya Devi looked at her grandsons with much love and affection. She prayed to the Gods — the village and family deities — to protect her children wherever their lives and destiny took them.

GLOSSARY

Saptami – The seventh lunar day in one of the two phases in a month
Ashtami – The eighth lunar day in one of the two phases in a month
Navami – The ninth lunar day in one of the two phases in a month
Dashami – The tenth lunar day in one of the two phases in a month
Sukravasara — Friday
Jyotisha — Astrology
Amavasya – New moon night
Shukla paksha – The waxing phase of the moon
Krishna paksha – The waning phase of the moon
Chaitra – Name of a month in the Hindu calendar, corresponding to March–April
Jyeshtha – Third month of the Hindu calendar, corresponding to May-June
Shravana – Name of the fifth month in the Hindu calendar, corresponding to July–August
Ashadha – A month in the Hindu calendar, corresponding to June–July
Bhadra – A month in the Hindu calendar, corresponding to August–September
Kartik – A month in the Hindu calendar, corresponding to October–November
Pitru Paksha – A fortnight in the month of Bhadra, when Hindus pay their respects to their ancestors
Abhijit – A special nakshatra, corresponding to the Vega star; an auspicious time in the day for any work according to Vedic astrology
Saayankaal – Dusk/ early evening
Rahukalam – Inauspicious time of the day
Parihara – An astrological remedy to get rid of the ills associated with past life karma

Ratnanguliya – A finger ring encrusted with gems
Anguliya – Finger ring
Malakaras – Garland makers
Aho, Bhuk – An exclamation of surprise
Peetha – Study desk/ escritoire
Kumbha – Pitcher filled with water, water pot
Mahaamatya — Chief Minister
Mahabaladhikrita – Commander-in-chief
Mahadandanayaka – Chief Judicial officer
Kulaputra – A nobleman
Dandaposika – Head of police
Rajapurohita – Royal priest
Rajavaidya – Royal healer and practitioner of Ayurveda
Amatya – Administrative official in the city and villages
Vaidya – Healer and practitioner of Ayurveda.
Dutaka — Spy
Deepam – A lamp
Arya A prefix used to address a person with respect
Swagatham – A welcome greeting in Sanskrit
Shubhamadhyanam – Greeting, good afternoon
Shubhratri – Greeting, good night
Acharya – A respected teacher
Kutaja — Name of a scented flower (from the connesi/tellicherry tree), mentioned in Sanskrit poetry and literature
Ganika — Courtesan
Nagaraka — A fashionable young man of the city
Kunda, Atasi, Patal — Names of flowers in ancient Sanskrit literature, corresponding to Star Jasmine, flax and paral flowers respectively
Cholaka – Short blouse with apron front
Antariya – Lower garment
Uttariya – Unstitched upper garment or scarf

or a stole (I have taken the liberty of using this interchangeably with a shawl)

Potalaka – A small bundle or bag, probably like a potli bag

Muktajala – An ornament of pearls; in this case worn as headgear, a net of pearls.

Matashri - Mother

Pitashri – Father

Pitamahi – Grandmother

Bhraata – Brother

Navaratnanguliya – A finger ring made of the navaratna (nine gems namely ruby, pearl, red coral, emerald, yellow sapphire, diamond, blue sapphire, hessonite and cat's eye)

Chaityamukha – A water pot belonging to a hermit

Kamandala – Water pot, smaller than a kumbha

Uttarasanga – Upper or outer garment

Antarvasa — Lower garment

Shikha — Topknot

Rudraksha Mala – A chain/ necklace strung together with the seeds from the rudraksha tree; said to have spiritual benefits

Avatar — Incarnation

Arhata – A saint of one of the highest ranks in Jainism

Yakshas and Yakshis – Name of a broad class of nature-spirits, largely benevolent appearing in Hindu and Buddhist literature

Gandharvas – Name used for distinct heavenly beings in Hinduism and Buddhism

Marma Vidya – A healing therapy within Ayurveda that works with 108 subtle and sensitive energy points in the body to open energy channels

Marmasthanas – The subtle energy points in the human body. There are 108

Mukuta — Crown

Angarkha – Tunic with side fastening
Kanchuka/ Kancuka — Tunic
Khadyatapakita – Superintendent of the royal kitchen
Shivika — Palanquin
Kaharaka – Palanquin bearers
Yojana – A Vedic measure of distance used in ancient India. 1 yojana = 8km approximately though this value is disputed among scholars
Pathikashraya – Rest houses
Trishula — Trident
Kumkuma — Vermillion
Haridra — Turmeric
Nupura — Anklet
Kirita – Crown
Prapaanaka – Sherbet
Ghatika – A type of clock based on water; a time measure
Prahar – The four parts into which day and night were divided into
Gurukula – Residential school where an Acharya imparted teachings in all disciplines to his students
Chaturanga — Chess
Sanghas – Buddhist monasteries
Bhikshus – Buddhist monks
Ramtek – Name of an ancient town in the Vidarbha region (modern day Maharashtra
Mandhal – name of an ancient town (modern day Mandal, Maharashtra)
Pratisthana – Name of an ancient town (now known as Paithan in Maharashtra)
Anuganga – Name of a fictitious village near Pataliputra in this story; in the Gupta period the east/ middle Ganga basin region was called Anuganga
Yavana – Of Greek origin

Romaka — Roman
Chitrashala – Art gallery
Aatma – Soul
Desha – Country
Grahagati – Planetary movement
Soma — Wine
Kamarbandh – Waist belt
Saartha – Travelling company of pilgrims or traders
Mleccha – Of foreign origin
Paenula – A cloak, similar to the poncho, worn by ancient Romans
Vatsanabha – Aconite
Kashmirajanman – Saffron
Nadi – energy channels in the body

References

Majumdar R.C., Altekar A.S.: *The Vakataka-Gupta Age*, Motilal Banarsidass Publishers Private Limited, 1967, reprint 1986, 2007.

Mookerji, Radha Kumud: *The Gupta Empire*, Motilal Banarsidass Publishers Private Limited, 1973, reprint 1989

Hinds, Kathryn: *India's Gupta Dynasty*, Marshall Cavendish Corporation, 1996

Auboyer, Jeanine: *Daily Life in Ancient India: from 200 B.C to 700 A.D.*, Phoenix Press, 2002

Ramulu, A., Ramalu, A.: The Times of Kalidasa — An Epigraphical Approach, Bulletin of the Deccan College Research Institute, Vol. 51/52, Professor S.M. Katre Felicitation Volume (1991-92), pp. 655-658

ACKNOWLEDGEMENTS

This story originated as a short story more than five years ago – a part of a group writing activity – triggered by a Facebook group to which Madhulika Liddle kindly added me. It stayed in an unpublished short story form all these years and would have continued in that state had it not been for Vineet Bajpai, who believed in this idea and signed me on for this novel – only after reading the synopsis! Thank you, Vineet! I would also like to thank the extended team at TreeShade Books that worked in bringing this to shape. Some names in particular need to be mentioned here. My thanks to Ruchika Khanna for keeping me up-to-date through the entire publishing process. My special thanks to Pritsikha Anil for copyediting the book in no time at all. I am also thankful to Munisha Nanda, Creative Director, for her creative inputs for the overall book design.

While writing as a process is largely an individual/ solo activity; it needs a group of people who act as sounding boards – to lend an ear, just listen and tell the writer that the story doesn't or does make sense. I have been thankful to have a group of dear friends who have acted as sounding boards through this writing journey. I am thankful to my friends and family, who at some point of time, have checked on the status of the book. However, some special mentions are definitely in order.

Hemanshu Kaul had read this story when it was written and his first reaction was – this is a novel. Expand it. Of course I never got to it… till now. Through the writing process, the past few months, he has been checking on the book, supporting, suggesting and thrashing ideas, reading material and listening to me patiently — his inputs have been invaluable. The entire Prince subplot was devised during one such long distance phone call – night time in Chicago and morning in New Delhi. Thank you very much, Hemanshu!

Priyanka Sondur, Manisha Kalaver, Kanchan Gupta and Sonali Mahajan – thank you so very much. You listened to me, checked on my writing progress, read my beta drafts, provided me honest feedback despite your own hectic schedules and more importantly, have kept me motivated!

Angel Sivan – a special thank you, my dear girl. I am so glad that we were together when the first draft of the novel was completed.

Liji Narayan – I do not have any words for the support you have been – through the years! Thank you – for being my go-to-person for those panic calls. My thanks to you for volunteering to and editing my book in no time at all. You have managed to trim my ramblings and give this a good shape and title! Lots of love and hugs to you.

Last, but certainly not the least – my thanks to my patient family – my husband, Vinod, for not complaining about the clinking of the keys every morning at some wee hour in the bedroom every day;

and for those long discussions – wherein I got inputs and direction; my son, Nigamanth, for checking daily whether I am going to meet my deadline and for wondering what would happen if I did not; Malini and Srirangan, for all questions and encouragement; and Amma & Appa for their blessings and unstinted support – in any and every imaginable way.

COMING SOON

THE PATALIPUTRA MURDERS

BY HARINI SRINIVASAN

About the Author

An aficionado of literature, history and dance, Harini Srinivasan has found innovative ways of bringing her passions to her work. Among her achievements is her contribution as an editor of several prestigious publications published by the Publications Division, Ministry of Information and Broadcasting, Government of India, such as *Selected Speeches of the President: Pranab Mukherjee; The Republican Ethic: Selected Speeches of Shri Ram Nath Kovind; Indian Dance – Through a Critic's Eye; Abode Under the Dome; Legends of Indian Silver Screen; and Selected Speeches of the Vice President: M. Venkaiah Naidu.* She also has to her credit a children's book "The Wizard Tales - Adventures of Bun-Bun" (now into its second print) and a blog on classic Hindi films and books (www.bagsbooksandmore.wordpress.com)

Along the way, she undertook different roles (Civil Servant, Project Manager, Communications Professional and Editor) across countries (India, Germany and the Netherlands). A doting mother of a 10 year old son, Harini Srinivasan lives with her family in Gurgaon.